Also by Emma Lathen

MURDER TO GO
COME TO DUST
A STITCH IN TIME
MURDER AGAINST THE GRAIN
DEATH SHALL OVERCOME
MURDER MAKES THE WHEELS GO ROUND
ACCOUNTING FOR MURDER
A PLACE FOR MURDER
BANKING ON DEATH

PICK UP STICKS

AN
INNER SANCTUM
MYSTERY
BY
Emma Lathen

SIMON AND SCHUSTER · NEW YORK

Contents

AH, WILDERNESS . . .

WALL STREET, the great money market of the world, accomodates buyers and sellers from the four corners of the earth. Turbaned industrialists from Karachi and Tanzanian bankers do occasionally descend on Trinity Place, but most financial transactions are consummated over long distances. To make this possible, Wall Street has perfected a communications network that is a far cry from the homing pigeons that carried news of Waterloo to anxious investors in London.

As befits one of Wall Street's most august institutions, the Sloan Guaranty Trust, third largest bank in the world, maintains a mighty array of news-gathering and news-transmitting devices. There are thousands of telephones to put trust officers on the sixth floor minutes away from any inhabited area. There are direct lines to London, to Washington, to Zurich, to Beirut. There are chattering ticker tapes, flashing the latest quotations not only from the New York Stock Exchange, but from the Board of Trade in Chicago, as well as the bullion market in Johannesburg and the sterling houses in Bombay. The Sloan even has its own closed circuit television system, to give each part of its far-flung empire immediate access to every other.

Red lines and hot lines apart, there are few communications systems so comprehensive and responsive as that serving the Sloan Guaranty Trust, at home and abroad.

All of this added muscle to Charlie Trinkam's grievance.

"What do you mean, I can't get in touch with John?" he demanded.

Miss Corsa, secretary to John Putnam Thatcher, senior vice

president of the Sloan, looked up from her desk with her usual calm.

"Mr. Thatcher circularized the memo that he was going to be away from the office for three weeks, Mr. Trinkam," she said. "I'm sure you were on the list."

Since Charlie Trinkam was currently acting director of the Trust Department precisely because Mr. Thatcher was away, he glared at her. His retort, however, was forestalled.

Everett Gabler, the oldest, and certainly the most meticulous member of Thatcher's staff, ripped off his glasses, gave them a heated swipe, and carefully avoided glancing at Trinkam. At all times, Charlie's expansive bonhomie and slapdash life style pained him; when Trinkam was his nominal superior, pain yielded to pugnacity.

"Of course, we know that John is taking a holiday, Miss Corsa," he said. "What we want to learn from you is how to reach him. After all, he left you his itinerary, didn't he?"

It was not so much a question as an accusation. When important Wall Street bankers leave the financial district, they do not go to ground. Their secretaries know where they are, or at least where they can be reached during most of the relevant hours of the day.

There lies the rub. Those same secretaries have strict orders not to divulge telephone numbers except in cases of emergency. And not everybody agrees on what is a real emergency. At the moment, for example, both Trinkam and Gabler were divided over the Sloan's response to some ominous queries from the State Banking Commission. They were, however, united in suspecting Miss Corsa of savoring this moment of power.

But Miss Corsa, an extremely competent young woman, was above pettiness.

"Yes, I know where Mr. Thatcher is," she explained precisely. "But I don't know how you can get in touch with him."

Charlie fairly gnashed his teeth, but Gabler raised a pacifying hand.

"Why not?" he asked, imagining the worst.

Miss Corsa silently produced a typed card from which she

read aloud: "From September fourth through September fifteenth, important mail for Mr. Thatcher may be forwarded to the Long Trail Lodge, Sherburne Pass, North Sherburne, Vermont, marked: *Hold for Appalachian Trail Hiker.*"

There was a pause. Then, sadly, Charlie said, "Not again?"

Miss Corsa was in some sympathy with the sentiment.

"I'm afraid so," she said.

Even Everett Gabler was moved to recall common hardship long shared.

"Do you remember the year we tried to send Ingersoll to get in touch with him?" he reminded his audience. "That was the time we needed his signature on the revised Bannister contract."

"How could I ever forget?" Charlie replied rhetorically. "That was somewhere down in the Smokies. You remember what Ingersoll said when he finally got back?"

They all did.

Charlie rose and studied Miss Corsa's card.

"Hold for Appalachian Trail Hiker," he repeated. "Well, one man's meat . . . Now listen, Everett, this puts the lid on it. We don't have time to play games. We have to work out some sort of compromise between ourselves. If you want to bring Lancer into it . . ."

"What do you mean by compromise?" Gabler replied stubbornly.

They were again deep in dispute when they left Miss Corsa to the solitary possession of John Thatcher's corner suite on the Sloan's sixth floor.

She returned to her sorting of the mail. She was not surprised by this conflict between Trinkam and Gabler. If past performance meant anything, it was the first of many. Furthermore, she confidently expected Mr. Bowman, from Research, to try wheedling some extra meetings of the Investment Committee.

All because Mr. Thatcher had this strange predilection for long walks.

Things were always difficult when Mr. Thatcher was away. Not that difficulty troubled Miss Corsa. She was fortified by explicit instructions covering most foreseeable contingencies. As well as a strong inner conviction that things were even worse at the Sloan when she was away.

Still, in the privacy of her own thoughts, Miss Corsa agreed with Charlie Trinkam. She accepted most of her employer's foibles even if she did not understand them. But, incurious as she was, Queens-bred Miss Corsa did wonder why an important man like Mr. Thatcher should be so attached to marching through the countryside between Maine and Georgia. A stroll around Kissena Park was one thing—

The telephone put an end to these thoughts.

"No," she said. "Mr. Thatcher is not available. No, I'm afraid not. . . ."

John Putnam Thatcher, methodically placing one foot before the other, three hundred miles north of Wall Street, was removed in fact and in spirit from New York State's menace to its banks. He was trudging along America's longest foot trail. It unrolled endlessly before him over each successive horizon.

The Appalachian Trail, extending from Maine to Georgia, is over two thousand miles long. A crest path, it follows the summits of one range after another, the White Mountains, the Green Mountains, the Blue Ridge and the Great Smokies. On federally owned lands, a mile-wide swath on either side is preserved as natural wilderness. On state owned lands, the swath diminishes to a half mile on either side. Happily, over half the trail passes through public lands. On private property, hikers are urged to keep to their right of way, in order to avoid charges of trespassing. Scattered along the Trail, a day's easy march from each other, are sleeping shelters.

Thatcher had not seen the Trail for a year. He was reminded of how much he forgot between each annual retreat to the perfect antidote for Wall Street. There were the white blazes systematically marking the way. And, here in New England, of course, there was the surprisingly sporadic nature of the views. To the uninitiated it might appear that a crest trail would provide one vista after another. And so it did, in the northernmost reaches of New Hampshire and in the Blue Ridge in Virginia. But Thatcher and his companion, Henry Morland, were cutting southward across New Hampshire into Vermont. So they were below the timberline and inevitably hemmed in by forest on either side. Only an occasional clearing or a fold in the hillside revealed the valleys and lakes scattered far below. In its own way, this was more satisfying than a continuing panorama. It provided more than beauty: it provided anticipation and suspense.

"We'll get there in good time," Henry Morland spoke over his pack frame.

"Good," said Thatcher.

"How do your boots feel?"

"Fine."

Moving forward with the easy, slow pace of the experienced walker, Thatcher contemplated his boots with approval. Then, since he was not one of those who take to the hills to leave the world behind, he considered also a commercial establishment, L. L. Bean, of Freeport, Maine.

The boots currently performing so satisfactorily had come from L. L. Bean—in parts, to be sure. They had recently been refitted with new lug soles; earlier they had had tongues removed, uppers restitched, bindings replaced. Each transaction, whether by mail or by personal visit, had convinced Thatcher that these boots remained as technically interesting to L. L. Bean as they did to him. On this, the second day of a prolonged trek, he had reason to be grateful. L. L. Bean, he recalled, was open twenty-four hours a day, 365 days a year, ready to serve hunters bound for the Maine woods, climbers setting forth to scale Mount Washington, and backyard barbecuers renting places in Boothbay Harbor, with any conceivable gear they might desire. Thatcher reminded himself, stepping meantime over a fallen branch, to talk to Henry about this.

For Henry, a small spare figure topped by a nut-brown pate,

was the owner of The Pepper Mill, a mail-order business in Pepperton, New Hampshire. In that guise, Henry dispatched maple syrup, sconces, early American TV carts and deacon's benches from Pepperton to most of the fifty states. The Pepper Mill was basically a warehouse. But, with an eye to tourists, Henry had appended a picturesque country store, complete with apothecary jars filled with penny candies. Anyone who made as good a living as Henry did exporting Yankee handicrafts (frequently imported from Hong Kong) must know how businesses were run in northern New England.

This was another noteworthy aspect of modern America, Thatcher thought, registering at the same time that the trail had begun climbing again. He himself had been born and reared in Sunapee, New Hampshire. But he had left small-town New England for Harvard many years ago, and after that for Wall Street. Consequently, for specialized insights into modern ways to play the Down East game, he would have to consult Henry Morland. Henry, born in Cedar Rapids, Iowa, had carved a respectable business career in New York before deciding, years ago, to strike out with his own firm in rural New Hampshire.

They plodded on in companionable silence. September was a good time to be on the trail. Peak foliage color still lay weeks ahead, but here on the heights there were already brilliant crimson touches. The long light of the westering sun painted the valley below, sometimes visible through clearings, with dramatic shadows. Filtered by greenery, a golden warmth mellowed the austere New England light.

"Good God!"

Henry had halted abruptly. A step brought Thatcher to his side. Henry was peering into the distance, down the trail.

"Do you see what I see?" he demanded.

Thatcher, whose vision was excellent, replied that he did.

A turn on the trail had brought them to a long, straight alley. At its end, perhaps thirty yards ahead, two young people sat slumped against a huge boulder.

"What are they doing here?" Henry asked.

"Well, after all, Henry," Thatcher pointed out reasonably, "the Appalachian Trail is open to the public. Think of how many people you would have met up here before Labor Day."

Henry shook this observation aside with a vigorous to-and-fro of his bald head. "That's not what I mean at all, John. Just look at those getups, will you?"

Thatcher did, and conceded that Henry had a point. The young woman was wearing a complex garment of bold black-and-white stripes which flowed from neck to ankle. Her escort, a young man, sported a striped French sailor's shirt over saffron yellow slacks.

Anything less appropriate for movement anywhere in rural New England, let alone the Appalachian Trail, would have been hard to find.

"I tell you—" muttered Henry, setting forward on the trot.

But Thatcher was not the hard-core purist that Henry was. The world, he knew, abounds with people who want to climb Mount McKinley in opera pumps, to cross the Atlantic in a canoe, to bicycle through Afghanistan.

Possibly Henry had retreated from the big city too early to appreciate this. However, any comments Thatcher might have been contemplating along these lines were not destined to be uttered. For, as they approached, it became painfully evident that the young couple was not only singularly ill equipped for a September evening 3,000 feet above sea level on the Appalachian Trail. They already knew it.

The young woman was a picture of misery. Long black hair hung in disarray around a small, dejected face. The young man clambered painfully to his feet as Henry fetched up before him smartly. Thatcher brought up the rear at a more leisurely pace.

"Hello," said the young man.

Henry, who enjoyed throwing himself into roles, immediately became a kindly but stern schoolmaster, of the old school. "What's the trouble?"

The young man, who had rather long black hair himself, was past taking offense.

"We're lost," he confessed unhappily. He looked back at his companion. "Don't worry, Sukey. They'll help us."

Henry, like most enthusiasts, could be obtuse in some ways.

"Lost?" he said with high good humor. "Now, you can't get lost up here. The whole trail is marked. Where do you folks want to be?"

He was now doing the Yankee handyman to perfection.

The young couple, however, did not recognize dramatic performances. "We left our car on Route 27," they reported.

"North or south?" Henry asked artlessly.

Two blank stares were his only response.

"Well, where were you coming from?"

This evoked a spate of tumbled explanations which Henry finally quelled with an upraised palm. "Now, let's get this straight. You'd been to some construction site and you were heading back south to the White Mountains Motel. About three miles short of the motel, you decided to take a walk?"

"And we got lost so that there was nothing but trees, trees, trees, until we found this place," they chanted in unison. "Then we stopped—"

But Henry was interested in geography, not suffering.

"Then as near as I can make out," he broke in firmly, "it's simple enough to get you back to your car. You go back north along the trail until you get to the place that's got a white blaze and a blue blaze, then you head off the trail, going due southeast, until you hit the riverbed, and follow that east by southeast to Route 27. Then, head south for your car. Should be about three miles, all told."

The young man stared at Henry with a hopelessness that Thatcher had rarely seen equaled.

"Three miles?" he repeated dully, following Henry's gesture toward the tree-lined trail. *"Three miles?"*

Then, as Thatcher had feared she would, Sukey burst into tears.

2 LITTLE ACORNS

APPALLED, HENRY MORLAND stared at the results of his cheerful directions. As the sobbing continued, his bewilderment became tinged with resentment.

"What's she crying about?" he muttered to Thatcher.

The young man had moved behind the girl and placed his hands on her shoulders. Now he straightened and glared across her bowed head.

"Sukey," he said defiantly, "is upset."

"What's she got to be upset about?" Henry demanded. "All I did was tell you how to get back to the road."

Thatcher thought he saw light. "Maybe they didn't understand your explanation," he suggested. It was useless, of course, to expect Henry to realize his instructions might just as well have been phrased in Mongolian.

"Oh, is that all? Well, I'll show you on the map. Get it out for me, will you, John?"

Obligingly Thatcher unstrapped the outer pocket of Henry's pack and extracted the mapcase. While Henry found the proper U.S. Geological Survey section, the young man relayed the good news.

"Sukey! Did you hear? They've got a map. Everything's all right." He accompanied these tidings with several hearty thumps on her back.

Under this bracing treatment, Sukey revived. She lowered her hands and smiled at him. "Oh, Alan, go and find out how to get out of this awful place!"

Alan beamed happily. "By the way," he said, advancing to Henry's side, "we're Sukey and Alan Davidson."

The jubilation was short-lived. While Thatcher completed the self-introductions, Alan bent forward to look at the survey section. The next instant, he gave an involuntary yelp of protest.

"But it isn't a *real* map," he stammered. "It doesn't have any roads on it."

"It's a topographic map," Henry explained. "See, this is where we are now, on the Appalachian Trail. It's a crest trail, so it's at the highest point on the map."

Steadily, Henry droned on. The shortest route to the road where they had left their car was south by southeast. Unfortunately that route involved the steepest grandient. Perhaps it would be wiser, on the whole, if they went southeast until they hit the road and then turned south. It was really quite simple. There were any number of points on which to take bearings. All they had to do was . . .

Henry's voice, eliciting no response, was steadily growing less confident. Even Sukey became anxious.

"What is it?" she asked. "Is something wrong, Alan?"

"No, no," her husband lied gallantly. "Everything's fine, Sukey. But I think maybe I'd better look at this a little longer."

A hideous suspicion began to dawn on Henry.

"You do have a compass, don't you?"

"Well, actually, we don't." Alan lowered his head studiously.

To keep Henry from comment, Thatcher intervened. "Tell me," he asked kindly, "what exactly are you doing on the Appalachian Trail?"

As an exercise in drawing fire, this was not successful since Sukey unguardedly exclaimed, "Oh, is that where we are?"

"Control yourself, Henry," Thatcher murmured.

The Davidsons proceeded to a somewhat disjointed account of their plight. They were weekending in New Hampshire, with a view to buying a vacation home. They had inspected a large construction site. They had studied model summer cottages and ski chalets. They had, Alan Davidson said, decided to go for a walk.

"I mean," he said, "the one thing we hadn't seen much of was New Hampshire."

Well, that was another question answered. Not only did the Davidsons not have a compass. They had probably never seen a compass.

Wordlessly, Thatcher caught Henry's eye. Their duty was clear. Simple humanity demanded that these innocents be personally escorted to the nearest road.

"We'll go with you," he announced.

Alan and Sukey overflowed with gratitude.

"It's terribly nice of you," Sukey said warmly. "We're sorry to take you out of your way. I mean, I suppose you're going somewhere." She ended with a dubious glance at their surroundings and at the older men's packsacks. Clearly she regarded their proceedings as some form of madness.

Thatcher made no attempt to enlighten her. "That's all right," he said. "It's not far. It won't take us more than forty-five minutes."

At first he did not realize his error. Alan and Sukey were so relieved to acquire an escort that they set off in Henry's wake with an initial burst of energy. Thatcher brought up the rear, content with his mild act of charity.

But, with the best will in the world, they could not achieve a smooth rate of progress. As they stopped for the fifteenth time in ten minutes to untangle Sukey from the embrace of a tendril of briars, Thatcher permitted himself a comment.

"These slacks of yours," he said, sucking a thumb, "aren't very practical."

Sukey looked down. "But they're my country clothes. I don't see why I have so much more trouble than the rest of you."

Henry had followed her gaze. The slacks started off trimly enough at the waist but, somewhere around the knees, they blossomed out into an abundance of material and became miniature Zouave skirts.

"What kind of country did you have in mind?" he asked, genuinely interested.

Sukey flushed. "I've been wearing them all summer without any trouble. Everywhere. All over Europe."

"We were on our honeymoon," Alan amplified. "Spain and the South of France and Greece."

"Oh," said Henry without enthusiasm. "Beaches."

Sukey shifted from defense to offense, "I'll tell you what. The country in Europe isn't like this at all. There are always people around and there isn't all this stuff growing everywhere." She scowled resentfully at the trees and the underbrush.

Henry Morland was nothing if not a gentleman. He wasn't going to hit Sukey when she was down, even though his gorge rose at this comparison between resort *plages* and the Appalachians.

"I can see how it would be different," he replied evasively. "Are you ready now?"

But Thatcher and Morland had failed to appreciate just how far down Sukey was. The rejuvenating effect of companionship had worn off now. Henry, loping effortlessly ahead and sliding neatly through branches that became stinging whips when the Davidsons approached, knew only that Thatcher called to him three times to slacken the pace. Thatcher, who had fallen back to protect himself against the effects of the Davidsons' tumultuous passage, could see only that Sukey was limping. Finally they came to a grove of tall pines, where the mulch of pine needles had kept the underbrush at bay. Thatcher pulled abreast, took one look, and called a halt.

Sukey's face was white, her lower lip was gripped tightly under her teeth and she swayed as she stood. Thatcher frowned, recalling what the Davidson boy had said. If the girl had only been in the woods for an hour, or an hour and a half, she couldn't possibly be as exhausted as she looked.

"What's up?" asked Henry, cantering to their side.

Thatcher shook his head irately. He was silently conning a list of alarming possibilities. Convalescence, pregnancy, debilitating disease . . .

Sukey released her lip and spoke tremulously. "It's my feet," she gasped. Then she hitched up her slacks and the mystery was clarified.

Simultaneously Henry and Thatcher breathed sighs of relief. Sukey was not suffering from exhaustion and shock. Sukey was in pain. The voluminous folds breaking over her instep had concealed the fact that she was shod in sandals secured by a thong passing between her toes.

Thatcher directed a look at his old friend. Now was no time for Henry to ask why Sukey went mountain climbing in sandals.

"They have very thick soles," said Sukey, answering the unspoken accusation.

Thatcher went down on one knee. "I don't think that's the problem. Here, let me take a look."

As he had expected, grit and fine splinters had lodged under the toes. In addition, the thong had rubbed a broad raw patch wherever it passed.

"You're going to have a fine crop of blisters," he remarked, restoring her foot to ground. "The less walking you do, the better."

Henry was already deep in his map. "It's simple enough. There's an old logging trail near here. We'll get Sukey that far, and I'll go ahead to send a car for you."

"You could get our car," Alan suggested. "I've got the keys here."

Henry repressed his impatience. "I will if I have to. But this construction site you mentioned must be nearer. And we probably ought to have a jeep or something for that trail. Do you know when they stop work at the site?"

Neither Davidson had the slightest idea.

"It's five-thirty now," Henry pointed out. "What about a phone? Is there one there?"

Again Alan began to shake his head, but Sukey stopped him. "Yes, there is. Remember, Alan, Mr. Quinlan used it while we were there."

Thatcher and Henry made their plans as they moved at a cripple's pace to the logging trail, Alan supporting Sukey behind them. Henry would go ahead to the site and phone the motel for a vehicle. Thatcher would remain with the Davidsons until succor arrived. With luck this good deed would be completed within the hour; they could still regain the trail and reach the shelter where they proposed to spend the night. With a last cheerful grin, Henry bounded athletically into the brush.

A short exploration led Thatcher to a bubbling brook not thirty yards from their rendezvous point. Carefully stacking the two packs so they were visible to an approaching car, he shifted the Davidsons to brookside and directed Sukey to soak her feet.

"It will be cold," he warned, "but it will save you a good deal of discomfort tomorrow."

Sukey obeyed and, after a period of acclimation, agreed that it was heavenly. "In fact," she said, "it's the first time I've felt comfortable this whole weekend."

"But I thought you said you were staying in a motel," Thatcher remarked. "That you'd come up here to inspect a summer place."

"That's what we thought," Alan said bitterly. "They said it would be a weekend when you could see New England at its best. But it hasn't turned out that way at all. It's been a rat race from beginning to end."

"They think just because it's free, we have to do everything they say. You'd think we'd sold them our souls or something!" Sukey's spirits were recovering something of their natural fire.

Alan became very grave. "Of course, we realize that we live in a materialistic society where everything is directed to a profit goal, but we'd never seen anything like this!"

Even on vacation, a banker is interested in profit goals. And Thatcher thought he recognized the situation underlying these plaints. "Do you mean that you were offered a free weekend here by one of these development colonies so they could try to sell you a lot?" he asked.

Alan and Sukey flowered under this interest. They had received a brochure in the mail, they explained. It was all about a colony of vacation homes to be built in New Hampshire, called Fiord Haven.

"Fiord?" Thatcher exclaimed in spite of himself. "But this is nowhere near the sea."

"They have a lake. And there's going to be a ski tow and tennis courts and a golf course. And once you buy the lot, you can use that as a down payment against a house."

"But the main thing is the private tow." Alan's eyes sparkled with enthusiasm. "Then you wouldn't have to wait in line for hours the way you do at Cannon Ball and Black Mountain. And they are going to have really good ski trails."

"Naturally we have no intention of committing ourselves to any kind of property now. We believe in human values, not property rights." Sukey seemed to feel that Alan was not as alert as he might be to this aspect of the situation. "But they offered us a free weekend at this motel to come up and inspect the development. And we'd never been to New Hampshire, so we thought—why not? We thought it would be fun."

Alan barked a short laugh. "Fun! Were we ever taken! The minute we got here, the hard sell started. That was last night. And it hasn't let up since."

Almost apologetically, Thatcher said, "I suppose that's why they offered you the weekend. So that they could deliver a hard sell."

Alan realized he was being accused of naïveté. "Naturally we expected something like that. We know big companies don't do things out of charity."

He expanded this theme, assisted by Sukey. The Davidsons had no illusions, they wished to make that clear. But still, they had been surprised, very surprised.

"We expected to give them an hour or two of our time. That wouldn't have been too bad. As a matter of fact, we were interested to hear how these places are arranged." Alan was again showing signs of apostasy.

Gently Thatcher explained that realty companies could get

an hour or two of prospective clients' time without any extraordinary efforts. The reason they transported a whole batch of potential purchasers to deserted country spots was in order to force them to listen for much longer periods than they would ordinarily agree to.

"But you don't understand what it's been like. It's just unbelievable." Sukey was in full swing. The tide of woe broke over Thatcher's head. They had been awakened at seven. They had listened to a two-hour lecture. Then they had been taken on a two-hour tour. After lunch, they had been split into small groups, each the object of attack by a single salesman. Then, out to the construction site again to see individual sites. Tonight there would be slides and another lecture. Tomorrow would be a repeat performance.

"And that salesman, Burt O'Neil, he tried to tell us that we weren't supposed to take tomorrow morning off to visit some friends. How do you like that?"

"That's really why we went for a walk in the woods," Alan intervened. "We knew if we went back to the motel, someone would be waiting to grab us with another sales pitch."

"That's a pretty stupid way to run a business." Sukey swept back a curtain of dark hair scornfully. "All they do is make people mad."

Thatcher forebore to point out that, however unpleasant the process, it seemed to have succeeded in waking some spark in Alan. It would be unkind and, in any event, he had other things to think about. He looked at his watch again. Henry had been gone for nearly an hour. It should not have taken him more than half an hour to get to the development site. What had happened?

As Alan and Sukey continued their antiphonal lament, Thatcher reviewed the possibilities. He was not personally worried about Henry. That is, he did not fear a fall, a sprained ankle, a wrong direction. What he did fear was Henry's excessive zeal. Suppose the phone at the site had been locked up? What would Henry do? Probably break in. Suppose it had been disconnected? Henry was not above overcoming that difficulty too.

Heedless of the chatter raining down on him, Thatcher frowned. That was the trouble. Henry was efficient and Henry was determined. However misguided his actions, they usually achieved their goal. Even if he had been forced to strew disgruntled realtors and phone companies behind, Henry should have returned by now. Or a car should have arrived.

Thatcher squinted at the lengthening shadows. Soon he would have to decide. He could wait for Henry or he could move Sukey down the logging trail while there was still light. Night closed in on the woods sooner than on open country. He would give Henry exactly one half hour.

The shadow of the tall oak which he was using as his measuring stick was just creeping toward the large boulder in the stream when he heard voices calling. Good, Henry had arrived with reinforcements. He arose from his log and let his own voice ring out.

"Henry! We're coming!"

Letting the Davidsons follow slowly, he strode rapidly back to the packsacks. At first, he could not see clearly because of the gloom after the glare of sunset on water. He could dimly make out the shape of a car and several men. Then his eyes adjusted. Oh, my God, he thought to himself, what has Henry done now?

Because Henry, looking much smaller, was flanked by two enormous state policemen.

"John," he said, sounding almost embarrassed, "I'm terribly sorry, but there's been a murder!"

3 ASHES, ASHES

WHATEVER JOHN THATCHER had expected, it was not this. Before he could demand further information, one of the troopers intervened.

"Now just a minute," he said. "Let's get a few things straight, right away. Mr. Morland said there were supposed to be three of you. Is that the other two I hear?"

Crashing thuds indicated that the Davidsons were making their usual progress through cover. A moment more, and they emerged from the trees to join the group. They seemed indifferent to Henry's official companions. Sukey had eyes only for the vehicle which now blocked the logging trail.

"A car!" she said rapturously. "How lovely!"

The trooper, after a swift inspection of her attire, nodded to himself.

"We'll drive you back in a little while," he offered. "If you'll just be patient, I have a few questions to ask first." He turned to Thatcher. "Would you mind telling us what you're doing in these parts?"

Thatcher restrained his impatience. Clearly the police were checking on Henry's story. With a view to substantiating Henry's alibi, Thatcher explained that they had left the Morland home yesterday morning after breakfast with Henry's wife. They had done eighteen miles in easy stages, arriving to spend the night at the Upper Brook Shelter. After an early start, they had proceeded southward an additional twenty miles to their encounter with the Davidsons.

"Anybody else at the shelter last night?" Captain Frewen asked.

Yes, there had been two members of the Dartmouth Outing Club on their way north.

Thatcher concluded with a careful account of the Davidsons' tribulations, culminating in Henry's decision to seek a telephone.

"That checks out," the captain said. "Now, Mr. Morland tells us he owns The Pepper Mill up in Pepperton. You from up there too?"

Thatcher shook his head. "No, I'm from New York. I'm on vacation."

"Address?"

Thatcher produced his business card. The captain inspected it and carefully inserted it in his notebook. He showed no surprise at finding a Wall Street banker on a three-week hiking trip. The Appalachian Trail, he knew, attracted all sorts.

"Fine," he said calmly. "Now, if you two don't mind waiting here, there are a few questions I want to ask the young people. But we might as well get Mrs. Davidson sitting down in the car while we're at it."

Either the Davidsons were a remarkably incurious young couple, Thatcher decided, or they had given up expecting to understand anything that happened to them in New Hampshire. Maybe they thought State Police and alibis were the natural consequence of becoming lost in the woods. Certainly they seemed to regard the activity of the police as less eccentric than that of others. As they trailed off to the car, Alan's voice came floating back.

"Thirty-eight miles, Sukey! They must be crazy."

Thatcher gave the entire party time to get out of earshot. Then he wheeled toward Henry.

"Well?" he demanded. "What happened?"

Henry sighed. "There isn't that much to tell." But obediently he unfolded his tale.

After leaving the logging trail, Henry had set himself a smart pace through the woods. His only thought was to hang the albatross of the Davidsons around someone else's neck as rapidly as possible. He had experienced no real difficulty in locating the construction site of Fiord Haven.

"Although I would have gotten there ten minutes earlier if that boy could tell the difference between north and north by northeast," he grumbled.

"He never pretended he was much of a navigator. Go on."

At the site, Henry had first located the telephone line coming into the clearing, then followed it to a builder's hut. There he encountered his first problem. The hut had been windowless, its crude batten door firmly padlocked.

"So you decided to break in," Thatcher said sadly.

Henry was inclined to cavil. "I don't know that you could call it breaking in. I was just going to open it up, use the phone, and then close it again."

"Leaving everything tidy."

"Well, naturally," said Henry, rather affronted.

To accomplish his end, Henry had examined the obstacles. The door was powerful, the padlock was huge, but the hasp and staple were affixed to the building with ordinary nails. Like Archimedes, all he wanted was a lever. Henry set off to examine the site, confident that wherever there was construction there would be at least one tool someone had neglected to stow away. At first he had been unsuccessful. To the right of the hut, individual homes were being laid out. But the work consisted chiefly of bulldozing cellar holes and pouring foundations, neither activity encouraging the use of hand tools. Then he had retraced his steps and had been more fortunate. To the left of the hut, at some distance from the rest of the compound, there was a building clearly intended as a main lodge. It was large and, more to the point, the framework had been completed.

"I didn't spot it at first because it was so low," he explained. "No gables or anything. Can you imagine a flat roof on a ski lodge?"

"That's modern architecture, Henry." Thatcher dismissed esthetics firmly. "I suppose you went in?"

Henry had. Once inside, he had been pleased to observe that even the interior framing had been erected. This raised the possibility of stray chisels and crowbars but, at the same time, made search more difficult.

"It was getting dark in there, and I had to go slow. I didn't want to miss anything on the floor. And that's where it was. The fourth room I went into, I looked down at the floor and there, in the shadow, was a body. And, right by its side, was this hammer covered with blood." Henry gulped. "I tell you I almost panicked."

"Was it very messy?" Thatcher asked delicately.

"No, that's what was so terrible." Henry did not seem aware that his answer was surprising. "You see, I couldn't tell whether he was dead or alive. Oh, there was blood all over his head, and I was pretty sure he had a fractured skull. The chances were nine out of ten that he was dead. But what if he wasn't? I didn't dare move him. Finally I decided the only thing to do was to get help as fast as possible."

"You were absolutely right."

"Then I thought I was going to have to use that hammer to get into the phone. I didn't want to touch it. I knew the police wouldn't like me messing around with it, but what the hell! The important thing was to get an ambulance right away. But I was lucky. There was a big screwdriver in there, too. I pried off the staple and phoned the police. Waiting for them was pure, undiluted hell. I suppose they didn't take as long as I thought. It's not even nighttime yet." Henry broke off to look at the twilight in mild surprise. "But they told me over the phone to make sure his nose was free, so I had to go back to the lodge. Then it didn't seem right to leave him alone, so I just stayed there, wondering if there was anything I should be doing. But it was all right. I mean about my not doing anything. When the ambulance came, the doctor said he'd been dead for over an hour, maybe longer."

Thatcher was glad that Henry was absolved in his own mind of all responsibility, but he could see shoals looming ahead.

"Tell me, Henry. You said you knew the police would be annoyed if you touched the hammer. There wasn't any question, then, that it was murder?"

Henry snorted. "He was lying on his stomach, he'd been hit on the back of the head, and the hammer was lying about ten feet from him."

"That seems conclusive. What did the police make of all this?"

"They asked me what I was doing there, naturally. I told them my story. Then I said that the three of you ought to be gotten out of the woods before nightfall." Henry gave a sudden weak grin. "I didn't think you'd enjoy hefting two packs on top of shepherding those two flower children down to the road. As a matter of fact, I didn't have to be very persuasive. The police sounded damned interested in the Davidsons."

Thatcher considered this and nodded. "I suppose that's logical. They have a man killed over an hour ago. Then we tell them we met two people connected with that construction site running around in a frenzy about an hour and a half ago. There could be a connection."

"Oh, come on, John. If Alan tried to hit someone with a hammer, he'd brain himself."

"You may be right. In any event, it really isn't our business. We've got to decide what we're going to do when the police are through with us. You don't think they have any doubts about you?"

Henry had recovered his composure. "Why should they? I don't have anything to do with this site. And, while it may seem small potatoes to big bankers like you, The Pepper Mill is a well-known and respected local enterprise. They know I'm not the sort to run around bashing people just for the fun of it."

"Then, I repeat, what do we do next? It's too dark to beat our way back to the Trail."

As usual, Henry showed that he had not studied his maps in vain. The surrounding countryside was now dark, but its main features were indelibly recorded for Henry to scan in his own mind.

"Look, the Trail crosses Route 113 about one mile south of the shelter. If Frewen would give us a lift down to the junction, we could make our way back as soon as the moon rises. The sky is clear as a bell."

Accordingly, when Captain Frewen signaled that his interrogation of the Davidsons was complete, they put their plan to him. He was inclined to cooperate.

"Sure. Stick your packs in the trunk, and we'll crowd in. We'll have to figure out some way to keep in touch. I suppose you realize that you'll probably have to come back here?"

They agreed that they would hold themselves at his service. Before they entered the car, Frewen told them that the news of the murder had been broken to Alan and Sukey. Under the circumstances, Thatcher was not surprised to find his companions less vocal during the bouncing ride down the logging trail back to the county road.

Here another police car was parked at the side of the road, its roof blinker slowly revolving.

"They'll have the latest news for me," Frewen said. "I'll be back in a minute."

They could see his bulky figure leaning into the other car and heard snatches of conversation.

"They've got an ID for you, Cap."

"All right. Let me get at the radio."

Muffled voices continued for several minutes. When the captain returned, he was carrying his open notebook. He took his place by the driver before speaking. As if by accident, he had left his door open so that the ceiling dome light shone down on the faces of his passengers. His voice was almost casual as he turned to examine the Davidsons.

"We've got an identification on the dead man," he said baldly.

"Oh?" Alan muttered when the silence threatened to become oppressive.

"Yes. I wonder if it means anything to you. His name was Stephen J. Lester."

But Frewen was looking in the wrong direction. Before the Davidsons, their faces white and strained, could evince any reaction, there was an astonished gasp from Henry Morland.

"Lester!" he exclaimed. "Do you mean to say that was Steve Lester back there?"

Everybody stared at Henry. Thatcher, who was sharing the front seat with the police, could feel Frewen go rigid. He himself stiffened, first in surprise, then in dismay.

"They found a driver's license on the body," the captain reported. "It said Stephen J. Lester of Weston, Massachusetts. Friend of yours, Mr. Morland?"

Henry had had time for second thoughts. "Well, I wouldn't say that."

"An enemy, maybe?" Frewen persisted.

"No, no!"

At last, the Davidsons spoke up.

"He was at the motel," Alan said.

"Mr. Lester was thinking of buying a lot at Fiord Haven," Sukey explained more precisely.

Frewen didn't even look at them. "I thought you said you didn't have anything to do with Fiord Haven, Mr. Morland?"

"I didn't. I don't. I never even heard the name." Henry was all too clearly wishing he could say the same for the corpse.

"But you knew Mr. Lester?"

"Look, you'd better let me explain. I belong to the Appalachian Mountain Club. That's down in Boston."

"I know all about the club." Frewen's voice was now a controlled growl.

"Well, Lester belonged to the club, too. We were both on a committee together. I've never seen him except in Boston."

"How long have the two of you been on this committee?"

"About a year or so, I'd say."

"And you stood by his body for half an hour and didn't recognize him?" Frewen did not attempt to disguise his incredulity.

"That's right." Henry's natural pugnacity was asserting itself. Thatcher could not believe that this was the ideal time for it to surface. "Our committee meets every three months. Sometimes I don't get down to Boston for a meeting. I've seen Lester maybe three or four times, that's face to face. I've seen his name on papers twenty or thirty times. Today I spent half an hour with a body lying on its stomach, its head covered with blood. It never occurred to me it was Steve Lester. Make what you want out of that."

What Frewen made out of it became speedily apparent. "All right, Mr. Morland, that's your story and you're sticking with it. But I'd give up this idea of yours about going back to the Trail tonight. I want you where I can keep an eye on you."

4 ROOM AND BOARD

AND WHERE Captain Frewen could most conveniently keep an eye on Henry was at the White Mountains Motel, the locale for Fiord Haven's ill-omened weekend.

First to feel the chill was the owner of the motel. He disliked having the police in his office. Even more, he disliked being asked to house their suspects.

Frewen, having sent the Davidsons to their room with strict injunctions to keep their mouths shut, looked at the motel manager.

"You've got some empty units." It was not a question.

"Fiord Haven has taken the whole motel for the weekend," said the owner. "They're building only four or five miles up the road."

"Then get the Fiord Haven people in here," Frewen ordered.

Glowering, the manager reached for the phone. "Mr. Valenti? I wonder if you and Mr. Quinlan could step into my office?"

During the interval, Henry smouldered in Frewen's direction, Frewen tapped stubby fingers on the counter, and the motel manager projected outrage. Thatcher wondered where the bar was.

Finally, two men entered to break the trance. They were, it developed, the Fiord Haven people.

Bluntly, Captain Frewen told them what had happened to Stephen Lester.

"My God!" said Ralph Valenti, a big man who somehow looked soft. "My God!" He sounded distraught.

His partner, Eddie Quinlan, had the politician's fluent, automatic response: "What a terrible tragedy!"

"Now," said Frewen, "I want Mr. Morland and Mr. Thatcher here for the night. Then I'm going to have some questions for you people—"

Henry started to mount another protest but Quinlan was too quick for him. "Sure, sure," he agreed instantly. "Anything we can do."

"Okay," said Frewen. "I think Mr. Morland and Mr. Thatcher can leave now."

He had reckoned without the motel owner.

"If you don't mind," he said, thrusting registration forms toward his unwanted guests.

As he was filling in the form, Thatcher was given a preview of what lay in store.

"My God," Valenti said again. "And Lester's wife! Who's going to tell her?"

Frewen refused to be excited. Almost heavily, he said: "Don't worry about that. I'll tell Mrs. Lester what happened. I'm going to want to talk to her, anyway."

Quinlan, who had jammed his hands in his pockets, roused himself. "Listen, captain," he said huskily. "Do we have to break this news to everybody we got up here for the weekend? We have an evening planned. If we could . . ."

At this point, the motel manager opened the door, and prepared to usher Thatcher and Morland to their rooms.

"You'll find," he said, trying to do his duty, "a program of the evening's activities on the bureau."

Accordingly, ten minutes later, Thatcher and Henry were attending a cocktail party. For the time being, at least, Fiord Haven's Fun Weekend was continuing.

Thatcher looked around. A pianist was playing soft, intricate variations on familiar themes. The bar dispensed cheer with prudent open-handedness. The crowd of perhaps thirty, gathered in the Pine Cone Lounge of the White Mountains Motel, was elegantly clad; the ladies wore colorful cocktail dresses, the gentlemen sported those antic ensembles advertised as stylish informality.

This was, the schedule had informed Thatcher, *an hour of sociability before dinner.* It was to be followed by *a luxurious buffet with roast beef, lobster and other delicacies.* This in turn would give place to a talk by Mr. Quinlan on *the second home as an investment in the future.* Mr. Quinlan would be succeeded by James Joel Finley, AIA, *the world-famous architect who will discuss the elements of design at Fiord Haven.*

But all of this, Thatcher knew, was not destined to be. And although no more selfish than the next man, he was relieved. Things were bad enough, without the elements of design.

Even the hour of sociability was not, to the disinterested eye, a great triumph. Conspicuously absent was the rising buzz-buzz that is the hallmark of the successful cocktail party.

". . . on top of that, you can cover almost all the costs of your second home by renting when you're not using it yourself. Fiord Haven will have a rental agency taking full-page ads in the Boston and New York papers to promote ski weekends as well as summer holidays . . ."

Thatcher sighed and sipped his Scotch and water. This torrent of words, earnestly uttered by a bearded young man—"Call me Burt"—was not directed at him but at a silent couple whom Burt had cornered.

". . . and so you see, Oscar—you don't mind if I call you Oscar, do you?—Fiord Haven is going to be a friendly community, as well as a real great place to get away from the rat race . . ."

Thatcher edged away, leaving Oscar to his fate. He looked very much as if the fight had been knocked out of him. Mrs. Oscar was dazed. Burt was reaching for a contract form and suggestively brandishing a pen.

". . . variety of plans," another persuasive voice inundated a cowed foursome. "You've seen the James Joel Finley-designed lodge. That proves it. Fiord Haven will consist of show places . . ."

Under the best of circumstances, cocktail parties were not Thatcher's favorite form of social intercourse. He had however learned to cope with them with only minor vexation of spirit. Unfortunately, the lessons learned over many years were singularly inapplicable here in the Pine Cone Lounge. It was, for example, a practice of his to discharge his obligations by speaking briefly to the guest of honor or the host, then to blend into the background and let the ebb and flow of guests camouflage discreet withdrawal. Furthermore, that withdrawal was as early as possible.

At Fiord Haven's party, his hosts were either closeted with the police or, alternatively, bent on selling him a half-acre lot. In addition, there was damned little ebb and flow; most of the guests had been nailed down by voluble salesmen. And finally, he could not delude himself that he and Henry were susceptible to camouflage. Boots, whipcord pants, flannel shirts —and in Henry's case an ancient sweater of vaguely Oyster Bay provenance—all suggested that the management had hired them to provide local color.

As for early withdrawal—well, the police had been quite firm about that.

So, instead of contentedly settling down in the Spartan surroundings of the Dunster Shelter to a meal made by adding water to a freeze-dried concentrate, he and Henry were doomed to the untimely comfort of two units at the White Mountains Motel, with inner spring mattresses, showers and other amenities. With roast beef and lobster to come. It was all highly unsatisfactory.

"Strange setup, isn't it?" Henry said. He was still indignant at both fate and the police but, being Henry, he was incapable of remaining uninterested in his surroundings. Psychologically speaking, Henry often reminded Thatcher of a beaver.

He did not have a chance to ask if Henry was referring to Fiord Haven's sales methods, or to the discovery of Steve

Lester's dead body at the main lodge which was being described as "the heart of Fiord Haven, where Havenites will enjoy an Olympic-size indoor swimming pool, a magnificent library, and a fun room for year-round socializing."

"Hi," said a young man brightly. "I'm Gerry Wahl. You gentlemen just get here?"

"We are not part of your group, Mr. Wahl," said Thatcher stoutly.

But anything that lived and breathed was a potential sale to Gerry Wahl and Fiord Haven. Ignoring a lackluster response, as well as costumes that did not suggest year-round socializing in fun rooms, he rattled on: ". . . nine hundred and seventy-two of the most beautiful acres in New Hampshire, with one of the best ski areas ever developed. And a private bathing beach . . ."

"But Mr. Thatcher isn't interested in buying a lot, are you, Mr. Thatcher?" a youthful voice interrupted. "Mr. Thatcher is only here because—"

"Sukey!" warned Alan Davidson. He then assumed an expression of extreme solemnity. Both the Davidsons had not only recovered from their misadventures, they had blossomed under them.

"Oh yes," said Sukey very guiltily.

Smiling determinedly, Gerry Wahl ignored this provocative byplay and switched targets: "I'll bet you're about ready to sign up, eh, Mr. Davidson?"

"Well now," said Mr. Davidson, metaphorically drawing on a pipe.

"Besides," said Sukey, "we haven't seen this Fiord Lake."

"That's because the access roads to the lake aren't in yet, Mrs. Davidson. Here, let me show you the photographs of the lake in our brochure."

He had hooked them neatly and just as neatly drew them away.

Thatcher was amused. "That's really quite a sales routine," he observed to Henry. "Let-me-call-you-Oscar to the elderly, and Mr.-and-Mrs. to the very young. Nice touch."

Henry, too, had certain professional responses. "Wonder how they assembled this bunch."

"I understand they're all from the Boston area."

That was not enough for a specialist in mailing lists. And now that Thatcher came to think of it, potential Havenites showed an unexpected range; there were one or two couples clearly thinking in terms of retirement, many more young parents all too obviously offspring-oriented, together with some newlyweds.

"Home owners in the wealthier suburbs?" he suggested.

"I don't think so," Henry said. "Lester lived somewhere out in Weston, didn't he? And the Davidsons seem to have an apartment in Cambridge. It's probably one of those special lists—you know, like subscribers to *Life* magazine, or owners of common stock. There's Valenti. I'll ask him."

"Looks as if he has other things on his mind," Thatcher said watching Ralph Valenti smilingly circulate through the lounge with a non-stop flow of comment.

"Hi there, Phil! . . . sure is a beautiful building, isn't it? . . . well, we want nothing but the best up here at Fiord Haven, and James Joel Finley is the best you can get. . . . evening, Mrs. Falks . . . did you and your husband like that site Burt showed you? Now listen, folks, don't let him talk your ear off. . . . We want you to ask any questions you have . . ."

This practiced patter was delivered in a warm friendly voice that seemed to deprecate the insistence of Gerry, Burt, Barry, Walter and other young men. They, in turn, grinned dutifully, then resumed their pitch the minute Valenti had passed by. It was a good performance in itself, the more so since Thatcher guessed that Valenti's partner, Eddie Quinlan, was still trying desperately to convince the police that murder should not be allowed to disrupt the Fiord Haven Fun Weekend.

Valenti had a round hopeful face and a vague air of benevolence. He dropped very easily into a confidential tone of voice with Thatcher and Henry.

"Terrible thing," he said. "They've told Mrs. Lester. Got hysterical, poor woman. Eddie's trying to calm her down . . ."

He sounded more worried than sympathetic, and Thatcher could understand why. Stephen Lester's death was not going to do Fiord Haven any good.

But officially Fiord Haven, in the forms of Valenti and Quinlan, was doggedly optimistic.

"The police will have this wrapped up within hours," Valenti assured them. "Probably some psycho who got loose . . ."

Thatcher kept a firm eye on Henry Morland. There was very little to be gained by pointing out that New Hampshire woodlands do not act as natural magnets for unbalanced personalities driven by irrational lusts to kill. If this was the line Valenti and Quinlan had decided to take, the New Hampshire State Police could be relied upon to provide a severe test of their salesmanship.

"You've got a remarkable merchandising operation here," said Thatcher, to keep Henry from pursuing the topic. Valenti took this ambiguous observation as a compliment and brightened.

"That's just what I'm saying tonight in my talk after dinner. It *is* a remarkable merchandising operation. That's because Fiord Haven really is a remarkable place."

Here was a born salesman. Every time he spoke, he convinced himself. No one, not even John Thatcher, could doubt his sincerity.

"We're not peddling anything cheap or shoddy. Eddie and I decided that we'd settle for nothing but the best. We could have gotten a lot of architects for less than James Joel Finley— but no cutting corners for us."

"Quality always pays off," Henry offered cunningly.

"That's right," Valenti said, hailing a new truth.

Thatcher would have preferred more facts and fewer homilies, but just then Eddie Quinlan joined them to sink wearily into a chair.

"Whew! I don't want to go through that again," he declared.

"Amanda?" Valenti asked.

Quinlan nodded. It was a moment before he replied to his partner. "Of course, you can't help feeling sorry for the kid. She's having hysterics. She doesn't really know what she's saying."

Valenti looked worried. "Who is she saying it to?"

"Who do you think?" Quinlan smiled tightly. "The police are getting an earful."

Valenti's confidence needed reinforcement.

"Eddie," he shook his head, "I don't like the sound of that at all. It could mean real trouble."

Quinlan shrugged. "There's nothing much we can—" He broke off, looking across the crowded room. "Oh, oh! Maybe there is something we can do, Ralph. Look! There's another one of our problems."

There was an exchange of glances and the two men were making their apologies. As they moved away, Valenti called to a trim blond woman in her thirties: "Oh, Mrs. Lester. Do you have a minute?"

This was too much for Henry.

"Did he say Mrs. Lester?" he asked.

"He did," Thatcher replied cautiously.

Henry was thinking, and that was always dangerous. "I thought he said Mrs. Lester was having hysterics in the office."

"She's not only recovered, she's stopped being a kid," Thatcher replied. "Tell me, Henry, how would you rate the likelihood of selling any of these people a lot here once they learn about the murder?"

Henry responded to the spirit of this rhetorical question. "Quinlan and Valenti are just keeping the machinery in working order. And Valenti may be right. If this gets cleared up fast— well, people do have short memories." Suddenly he narrowed his eyes at a tall man who had entered the lounge. "Who's he? And why's he wearing those things?"

Henry did not regard hiking gear as a sartorial solecism. Jabots and velvet smoking jackets, however, were something else again.

"That," said Thatcher, "can only be James Joel Finley, the eminent architect."

If James Joel Finley was not an eminent architect, he was very much a great man. He accepted admiration from the ladies who crowded around him with a regal condescension. Lean, hawk-like, white-maned, he had piercing blue eyes in a deeply tanned face. He had also a resonant voice.

". . . values. No, my dear Mrs. Carruthers, what we must do is tie each building to its site. We cannot violate the integrity of nature . . ."

He had casually raised his voice so that he was addressing the entire room.

". . . fundamentals of honest design. In this kind of situation, the first thing we have to preserve is the organic unity."

They were going to get that lecture after all, Thatcher thought irately.

He was wrong.

James Joel Finley was in full flight when he suddenly realized that he had lost the rapt attention of much of his audience. With stately displeasure, he turned to the entrance behind him.

There stood Captain Frewen. Beside him were two uniformed officers.

Joining them was Eddie Quinlan. Without apology, he interrupted James Joel Finley and said, "Ladies and gentlemen. I'm afraid that I have some bad news . . ."

"Well," said Henry in an undertone. "If this does nothing else, it will put an end to this selling."

Thatcher thought he had taken the measure of Fiord Haven.

"Temporarily, Henry. Temporarily."

5 WEEPING WILLOWS

IT WAS some hours before John Thatcher or anybody else saw that luxurious buffet with roast beef, lobster and other delicacies.

Like the hour of sociability, it was not a howling success. The delay interjected by the news of Stephen Lester's murder and the first round of police questioning had disheartened the chef: the roast beef was dry, the broiled lobsters were cold and the other delicacies were variously limp, sodden or scorched.

Then, too, the human components showed signs of distress. Stephen Lester's death may not have taken away all the appetites whetted by crisp New Hampshire air, but there was, Thatcher saw, a general feeling that hearty feeding would be in poor taste.

Even those relentless automata, Fiord Haven's salesmen, had been instructed to suspend operations for the time being. They were gathered into a group apart, far from the groaning board. At Fiord Haven, Thatcher would guess, every rib of beef, every lobster claw, every scoop of coleslaw, was expected to produce sales results. The guests saw social awkwardness; the staff saw waste.

"Try one of the watermelon pickles," Henry advised. "Not bad."

Thatcher took one. He and Henry, by virtue of their attire, were exempted from the prevailing atmosphere of genteel abstinence; they were hearty outdoorsmen and, hence, trenchermen. Insofar as he could, Thatcher proposed taking advantage of this.

He joined Henry at their table and looked around the dining room. Most of those lining up for food looked sheepish. Those already seated pecked unhappily at their plates.

He and Henry were certainly the only persons at ease in the dining room.

Thatcher was not misled into confusing this mass discomfort with guilt. For, in the preceding hour, it had become fairly apparent that none of these unfortunates knew much about Stephen Lester, or his death. Or, he amended, if they did, they were successfully concealing the fact.

"I'm beginning to feel sorry for Frewen," he remarked.

Henry was having none of that. "Frewen!" he exclaimed, eviscerating a lobster ferociously. "Of all the stubborn, stiff-necked—"

Thatcher was used to Henry's view of the universe. "Oh come on, Henry. You can't blame him for wanting to keep you here, at least until he checks you out. After all, you did discover the body. And you did know Lester. At the moment, that appears to be almost all the information poor Frewen's got."

Henry downed knife and fork and looked balefully at his old friend.

"In the first place," he said, "it is technically impossible for me to have murdered Lester—"

"Of course. And as soon as Frewen confirms it with a medical report, he will allow us to move on," Thatcher replied. "Unless, Henry, you are hiding a powerful motive for wanting Lester dead."

Henry ignored this. "Why focus upon the fact that I was acquainted—barely acquainted, mind you—with the man? Why does Frewen detain us when endless possibilities leap to mind immediately?"

This elevated strain, Thatcher knew, was Henry telling the Supreme Court that The Pepper Mill might be small, but there were those who loved her. He tried to divert the Dan'l Webster across the table.

"I wonder how soon he will let this whole Fiord Haven crowd go."

Henry was single-minded. "Of course, we don't know what he learned from the wife—or that other woman."

"Mind if I join you?" said a new voice.

Eddie Quinlan stood before them, plate in hand.

Thatcher and Henry invited him to sit down. Quinlan's streak of self mockery was to the fore. "You're the only two people in the room who don't have anything to do with Fiord Haven," he said frankly. "Right now, I can use that."

"Just the man I want to talk to," Henry said alertly. "Who's having hysterics if it isn't Mrs. Lester?"

Quinlan frowned. "Oh, there was some sort of foul-up in our mailing list. Too many of Lester's women showed up. It's the kind of mistake that shouldn't happen."

He did not sound very interested and Thatcher, if not Henry, could understand why. Quinlan was only marginally concerned with Stephen Lester. His energies were monopolized by Fiord Haven. And at the moment, Fiord Haven was in trouble.

". . . couple of sales," Quinlan was saying. "Now they aren't sure they want to buy. Of course, I've told everybody who signed a contract before this happened that we won't hold anybody against his will. But my God, does Frewen know how much damage he can do to us? And what's he got to show for it? Not a damned thing! I could have told him that."

Eddie Quinlan might want to sit with people who had nothing to do with Fiord Haven, but he could not keep from probing the sore tooth.

"I told him it must have been a tramp, something like that . . ."

"Frewen said there was no sign of robbery," Henry pointed out. "Lester's wallet had a couple of hundred dollars in it. And he was wearing an expensive watch."

Quinlan might have been seeing Henry for the first time.

"You probably scared the murderer away," he said. Again he was not much interested.

Thatcher watched a white-hatted chef back through the

swing doors from the kitchen with a tub of tossed salad. It was Quinlan who could not remain silent.

"Whatever happened," he said impatiently, "I wish we could convince Frewen that it doesn't have anything to do with Fiord Haven. Otherwise, he's going to cost us a fortune. It's bad enough that we've already lost one sale—"

Henry pounced. "Was Lester going to buy?" he asked.

"Yeah," said Quinlan with that crooked smile. "Hell, I can't complain about that—not when the guy got himself killed. But, God knows how many other sales it's going to cost us if Frewen drags this thing out . . ."

He looked around the dining room, gulped his coffee and jumped to his feet, saying something about talking to Valenti. It was more fundamental than that, Thatcher thought; Eddie Quinlan was finding it hard to sit still.

They watched him thread his way through the close-set tables, stopping here for a brief conversation, there for a word or two.

"He may be right," said Henry grudgingly. Obviously, anything as simple as a homicidal tramp held no appeal for him.

"Give him the benefit of the doubt," Thatcher urged. "For the moment at least."

Certainly it did not appear that Frewen and the police had unearthed any hard information in their questioning of Fiord Haven's guests and personnel.

Mr. and Mrs. Stephen Lester had arrived at the White Mountains Motel Friday evening. Lester was New England sales manager for a large pharmaceutical firm. He lived in a comfortable suburb outside Boston.

Had anybody noticed anything unusual about him? Captain Frewen had asked the room at large.

Nobody had.

Had anybody talked to him?

A lawyer from Haverhill cleared his throat. "I exchanged a few words with him this morning," he said, flushing as he became the focus of many eyes.

"What about?" Frewen asked.

The lawyer shrugged. "Oh, about how this was a pretty nice spot. And how the whole setup sounded pretty good. You know, just passing a few minutes until my wife got dressed. Oh, and maybe they should lay off the hard sell a little . . ."

This ingenuous disclosure broke the ice of reticence; it did not loose torrents of relevant information.

Between Friday night and Saturday evening, when the body was discovered, Lester had exchanged desultory comments with many people. To a man, they agreed that there had been nothing significant about them.

"Except," said one middle-aged matron in pink, "when it turned out that Eunice Lester—"

She broke off delicately. Thatcher should have been warned by the gleam of interest in Henry's eyes. This, it subsequently developed, was the point of no return.

"We know all about that," Frewen said curtly. "What we want from you, now, is a picture of how Lester spent his time. and how you did too."

In other words, the most interesting police interrogation was taking place elsewhere. And the account of that particular twenty-four hours, pieced together by nearly forty-five persons, was as garbled as might be expected.

According to Burt, the salesman, Stephen Lester had attended the morning talk about land values at Fiord Haven aimed at the husbands.

"He was real interested," said Burt. "He saw the possibilities all right . . ." Burt continued in this vein for several minutes, momentarily forgetting that this was no occasion for a sales effort.

Then Lester, with the rest of the party, toured the construction site, inspecting not only available lots but the skeleton of James Joel Finley's lodge.

Frewen looked inquiringly at the architect. James Joel Finley did not object to being the focus of any number of eyes. Drawing dramatic brows together, he thought deeply.

"No," he said finally. "I'm afraid that I can't place Mr. Lester particularly. Possibly I did speak to him. I did talk to several people about my design for the lodge which is a radical departure from conventional forms. But no, I do not particularly recall Lester."

Like Burt, James Joel Finley found it difficult to suspend operations.

Lunch at the White Mountains Motel had brought together the Lesters and the Davidsons who had shared the table with them.

". . . yes . . . what did we talk about? . . . Well, that's hard to say. Mr. Lester was telling us all about New Hampshire. He knew a lot, didn't he, Sukey? Then he was explaining how careful you had to be about building to stand up to the New Hampshire winter . . ."

After lunch, Lester had dropped by Eddie Quinlan's office. Then, he set forth on a long, solitary walk, successfully evading an intensive session with Burt O'Neil. He returned to his motel unit, told his wife he was skipping the second tour, then set off alone again.

And no one knew where he had gone.

"Frewen will have his work cut out for him trying to check all that out," Thatcher summarized. "After the second tour, people were either sitting in their motel rooms, or drifting aimlessly around—like the Davidsons. Most of the Fiord Haven staff, including Quinlan and Valenti were double-checking plans for the evening program. The only hard-core alibis are for guests trapped by salesmen."

Henry was up and away.

"Two women," he said significantly. "Eunice and Amanda."

"Henry," said Thatcher firmly. "No doubt the police are concentrating on any possible sexual improprieties."

"Naturally," said Henry. "It's the one strong lead there is."

"Leave it to them."

"What? Oh, of course, of course," said Henry.

With cause, Thatcher was filled with deep foreboding.

6 FAMILY TREE

WHEN THATCHER emerged from his room the next morning the lawn was deserted except for the motel owner, hovering around the sprinkler system. He surveyed Thatcher without enthusiasm.

"Your friend's around someplace," he said bitterly. "Stirring things up."

Thatcher was taken aback. Coolness he could understand. But why naked hostility?

The owner was now addressing a whirling jet of water. "They tell us tourism is the state's biggest industry. But how do they expect us to attract tourists if people won't keep their mouths shut. Nobody wants to come someplace where they have murders. Hell, that's what they're trying to get away from."

"Nonsense," said Thatcher crisply. "This is not a local secret. Since the eleven o'clock news last night, half of New Hampshire must be talking about it."

Brute facts do not sway motel owners. This one said that, here at the White Mountains Motel—where they normally attracted a good class of customer—everyone just wanted to forget about it. He would have said a good deal more, but Thatcher resolutely marched off to the dining room. At the door he encountered the Davidsons, on their way out.

"Hello, Mr. Thatcher. Mr. Morland's already had breakfast," Sukey greeted him.

"He stopped by our table. He said he doesn't see any

reason why the police should suspect us," Alan repeated faithfully. "Not now, when they know there are a lot of people here who had a real reason to kill Mr. Lester."

Henry must have been making himself popular in the dining room, Thatcher thought as he exchanged reassuring words with the young couple and passed inside. No doubt everyone within earshot had visualized Henry compiling a list of suspects.

On the threshold he paused. The tables were set up to accommodate parties of five. At each table were two couples—and a salesman. Incredibly the murder seemed to have made no difference. Blueprints, brochures and sales contracts were again in evidence everywhere. Thatcher had no intention of exposing himself to yet another spiel about Fiord Haven. As he was edging toward a deserted table in the far corner, he was hailed.

"Mr. Thatcher!" boomed a mellifluous voice. "Won't you join us?"

James Joel Finley had risen to his feet and was indicating a chair. Resignedly Thatcher strode forward and acknowledged an introduction to Burt O'Neil. Finley beckoned a waitress with lordly assurance.

Yesterday evening the distinguished architect had had no time for two strangers in dusty boots and flannel shirts. Since then his intelligence system had been at work. James Joel Finley was not the man to dissimulate.

"Mr. Morland was telling us that you are a senior vice president at the Sloan Guaranty Trust. Now I find that truly interesting."

Thatcher maintained a prudent silence and attacked his melon. The architect flowed smoothly on. "Many people might be surprised to find you in these surroundings, but not I. It is a very good example of what I was explaining to our guests only the other night. As a man rises to the pinnacle of his profession, as his responsibilities and his material rewards increase, he feels a need to return to fundamentals. Can it be that our modern urban environment cuts him off from a life-sustain-ing force? I refer, of course, to the nourishment derived from the organic union of man, habitat, and nature. This, I shall always maintain, must be the prime goal of modern architecture."

"Just so," Thatcher murmured, watching his melon rind disappear, to be replaced by a steaming platter of ham and eggs.

"Ah! You understand. I understand. But how many do not understand?" Finley grieved. "Too often, far too often, those who do not understand—one might even say those who *will* not understand—are in a position to frustrate the dreams of those who do."

Burt O'Neil was puzzled. John Thatcher was not. He was familiar with Finley's attempts to obtain financial backing for a revolutionary housing development in California. The whole colony, green belts and all, was to have been suspended on pilings over the Pacific Ocean. The reaction of the building inspector to this vision climaxed the favorite after-dinner story of many West Coast bankers. No one denied that the view would have been incomparable.

"Indeed," Thatcher said sedately, pouring himself more coffee.

"And that is why it is doubly satisfactory to meet a man in your position, who obviously values the integration of man and situs."

Thatcher was tempted and fell. "Of course, such integration does not present much of a problem in a shelter on the Appalachian Trail."

Belatedly Finley realized that the union of man and nature could be pressed too far—to the point where residential housing was dispensed with entirely. While he was regrouping his forces, Burt O'Neil made his first contribution to the conversation.

"There are the police." He gestured toward the driveway beyond the window. "They're bringing back Mrs. Lester."

James Joel Finley became avuncular. "Poor, poor child."

He shook his white mane sadly. "So young for so much sorrow. Who would have thought, seeing her full of high spirits yesterday, that fate had this blow in store for her?"

Curious, Thatcher turned to look out the window. A state trooper was helping a woman alight from the car. As she stepped into full sunlight, she was revealed as little more than a girl, tall, slim and auburn-haired.

Meanwhile, Burt took issue with Finley. "You're thinking of Friday, when she came, Mr. Finley. That was before she found out about Eunice. Yesterday, Amanda was mad as hell."

Thatcher did not normally pursue leads like this. But after all, he thought, by now Henry certainly knew about Lester's women. It might be only prudent if he did, too.

"Is that Mrs. Lester? That girl?" he asked. "Then who was the Mrs. Lester having cocktails last night?"

"It is difficult, extremely difficult,"—Finley's displeasure was Augustan—"to counsel a recreation colony whose sales force does not display elementary competence."

O'Neil was more responsive. "Amanda is the one who's married to Lester now. Or, anyway, she was until yesterday. The blond woman, that's Eunice, is his ex-wife. Didn't Mr. Morland tell you? He couldn't talk about anything else at breakfast."

All was clear now. No wonder the Davidsons had mentioned other suspects. Whom else had Henry been chatting with?

"I haven't seen Morland this morning," Thatcher remarked.

"It was a big surprise to him. Hell, it was a big surprise to us, too," O'Neil replied with conviction. "Nobody knew anything about it until dinner, Friday night. Then Eunice Lester and Steve Lester saw each other, and the fat was in the fire."

Finley folded his napkin with mathematical precision. "I should have thought that anyone compiling the list for this weekend would have noticed the presence of two Mrs. Stephen Lesters."

"I don't know about lists," said O'Neil heatedly, "but I do

know it put me in a helluva spot. The minute they cottoned on, Eunice said she wouldn't buy if the Lesters did, and Amanda said they wouldn't buy if Eunice did. And management expects me to sell prospects like that!"

Thatcher reached for his final piece of toast. "Your problem seems to have solved itself," he pointed out. "With Stephen Lester dead, there is only one candidate left in the field."

Burt O'Neil was not sidetracked. High-pressure salesmen seldom are. Instead he produced further evidence that Henry was spreading sunshine with fine impartiality.

"That's what Mr. Morland said. He thought the police might even consider it a motive for murder. But it's not true. I don't have one candidate left. I've got none!"

"How does that follow?" Thatcher asked. He did not suppose that O'Neil considered the murder of an ex-husband enough to diminish the attraction of a choice lot.

O'Neil lowered his voice before continuing. "Well, last night when the cops pulled up, you know they wanted to keep things quiet at first. They got Amanda out to the office and broke the news to her. Then they asked if anybody else was connected with Lester. So Mr. Quinlan told them about Eunice. She was in here having cocktails with the rest of us, so the troopers went over to her room. You know what they found?"

James Joel Finley was not above human curiosity. "What?" he breathed softly.

"Her things were all packed up. She'd been planning to hightail it out of here without anyone knowing. You can see how that looks."

Under the circumstances Thatcher was not surprised to find, half an hour later, two figures deep in conversation by the deserted swimming pool. One was the blond woman of yesterday evening. The other, naturally, was Henry Morland.

"John, come on over." Henry's face lighted with innocent pleasure. "We're talking about the murder. Eunice, this is John Thatcher, who's hiking with me. John, this is Mrs. . . . ."

For once, sheer gusto was not enough to take Henry over the top of social difficulty. Eunice Lester smiled ruefully.

"I'm the first Mrs. Lester, Mr. Thatcher," she said, shaking hands. "Not the Number-One widow."

"How do you do?" Thatcher seated himself on a redwood chair.

Eunice shook a cigarette out of a small gold case and accepted a light. "Henry and I have been talking about Steve."

This was exactly what Thatcher had feared. Did Eunice realize that Henry was busy compiling a list of murder suspects? Or didn't she care? Perhaps she was so distraught she was saying things she would later regret.

"I told Eunice that I'd met Steve at the club," Henry explained, "and that took her back." He at least was at ease in his double role as confidant and detective.

"Way back," Eunice said, meditatively watching cigarette smoke. "When Steve and I were married, he was a student and he was always going off to the Trail with the Outing Club. But that was over ten years ago. And now look"—she gestured hopelessly—"Steve is dead and I'm a murder suspect."

"For that matter, so am I," said Henry. "But you'll see, things will straighten themselves out. You've already explained that business about being packed up and ready to leave."

Eunice shook her head. "There's no point being foolishly optimistic. I've explained to them that, as soon as I found out Steve had bought a lot, I was through. It wasn't a surprise to Eddie Quinlan. All along I'd told him that the minute Steve bought, I was going back to Boston."

"That sounds reasonable," Thatcher said.

Eunice Lester smiled humorlessly. "Sure—until Amanda claimed I was lying. She did her best to make me look suspicious by saying that Steve hadn't bought a lot. She claims I made up an excuse on the spur of the moment."

Henry's good cheer diminished. "I didn't realize she was denying it. Then it's just your word against hers?"

Eunice laughed bitterly. "Oh no. For once luck was on my

side. The police talked to Eddie Quinlan before Amanda was
through with her hysterics. He told them Steve had agreed to buy
lot seventy-three yesterday afternoon—which is exactly what I
told them. So all Amanda's little game accomplished was to
make the police think twice about believing a word that little
bitch says."

"Now, now." Henry was pained by this reference to the
youthful widow. "After all, she was upset last night. Either she
didn't know what she was saying, or Steve hadn't told her
about the sale yet. There's no need to think she was deliber-
ately trying to get you into trouble."

"You can afford to be charitable. I can't." Eunice's jaw hardened. "When the police check back, they'll find out that you
had nothing to do with Steve, no reason to murder him. When
they check back on me, they'll find plenty. And most of it is
Amanda's fault."

Thatcher was torn between courtesy and curiosity. Happily
Henry was always more alive to the second.

"Eunice and Steve were having a custody dispute," he explained tactfully. "About their son."

"*My* son," Eunice corrected him shortly. "Steve's connection with Tommy was a biological accident."

Thatcher reviewed the various altercations which could arise
between ex-spouses. In his experience nothing approached the
viciousness of a savagely-contested custody battle. Divorces,
property settlements, claims of adultery and physical abuse
paled in comparison.

"Is the suit in progress now?" he asked.

"It started last winter. And do you know why?" Eunice was
deriving satisfaction from her recital. "Because Amanda can't
have children, that's why! Steve has been playing the gay man-
about-town since he walked out on me. Having himself a ball
in San Francisco, while I brought up Tommy. Then, a couple of
years ago, he decided it was time to settle down. So he married
Amanda and they had a great time being a swinging young
couple. Finally they decided to come back East and start

family life. They built themselves a house in a fancy suburb, and Steve got to be in charge of the New England territory for his company. Everything was going along as if they were color advertisements in a magazine. Then the blow fell. No children. So what does Steve do? After ten years, he suddenly remembers he has a son and decides to take him away from me. And poor little Amanda thinks that's a wonderful idea."

The outburst came to a sudden halt. Eunice was breathing hard and her face had gone white. She looked years older. Henry was quick with his sympathy.

"That must have been a terrible shock for you. And I can understand why you don't see much good in Amanda. But, after all, could Steve have gotten away with it? No court would give him custody, not after you'd had to bring up the boy alone."

A bleak smile of gratitude appeared on Eunice's face. Impulsively she leaned forward and squeezed Henry's hand. "You're a nice man, Henry. Too nice to realize the tricks that a Steve Lester could get up to."

Like most men, Henry did not welcome the view that he was too wholesome to comprehend the depravities which were an open book to his female companion.

"I admit that I didn't know Steve well. I didn't know anything about him, except his ideas on trail maintenance. But he didn't strike me as up to anything special. I don't mean his morals. I mean his intelligence."

Eunice took him up instantly.

"It didn't take intelligence. Just a single-minded idea of what he wanted and no compunctions about how he got it. He found out I am getting married this fall. So, he hired detectives to dig into my past. I've been divorced for over ten years. He didn't have to be a genius to figure out that there would be something he could use. In his own simple way Steve thought if he threatened a really nasty fight over my morals, I'd be scared out of court."

After a brief tribute to the depth of Eunice's feelings, Henry ventured: "He had you in a bind, didn't he?"

Eunice's eyes flamed at emotions recalled. "Not the way he thought he did. I didn't work and sweat to raise Tommy to lose him to that Neanderthal. One thing was perfectly clear to me from the start. I wasn't giving Tommy up, no matter what. I decided something else, too. I'd already let Steve Lester ruin too many years of my life. I wasn't giving up my marriage to Peter either." She looked at them challengingly. "The police will find all this out. They'll say that this murder was how I managed to keep Tommy. They're wrong. I don't know who killed Steve or why. But I know one thing."

"Now there's no reason to think they'll say that," Henry began half-heartedly.

Eunice rode right over him. "Dead or alive, Steve isn't standing in my way any more. I'm going to have Tommy and Peter both. And nothing is stopping me!"

Her voice rang clearly through the still air. But even before its throbbing became an echo, Thatcher heard something beyond defiance.

He heard fear.

7 TIMBERLINE

THE TORTURED complexities of the human spirit are, as we all know, extremely interesting. People will talk endlessly about themselves. With very little encouragement, they will talk just as much about their friends. They will even pay good money to plumb the depths of the human condition in total strangers—as witness, the Living Theater, the *cinéma vérité,* and the nonfiction novel. Such explorations are variously regarded as: palliative, recreational, liberating, or compulsory. Whatever the rationale, many people relish the process of peeling layer after layer to come to essence.

Human essence being what it is, John Putnam Thatcher was not among their number.

Normally he thoroughly enjoyed his vacations from Wall Street, but this one was proving the exception. Fiord Haven's sales mill he could take in stride, for short periods at least. But he could not enjoy witnessing Eunice Lester's unhappiness. And worse was sure to come.

Never had the Sloan Guaranty Trust looked so inviting.

Not that the trust department was unnaturally harmonious. There was, for example, the unceasing guerrilla warfare between Everett Gabler and Charlie Trinkam. Thatcher would have been mildly cheered to learn that, from the rugged north, he had been instrumental in effecting an armed truce between these ancient adversaries.

"What did they want to know?" Everett Gabler sputtered.

An ad hoc committee was in session around Miss Corsa's

desk, composed of Charlie Trinkam, Walter Bowman from Research, and Everett, himself.

Miss Corsa was on the firing line.

"They only wanted to know how long Mr. Thatcher has worked for the bank, and when he left for his vacation," she replied. "And when he is expected back."

"Good God!" said Walter.

"But Rose," Charlie expostulated, "didn't you even ask why they wanted to know?"

He broke off, defeated by her look. If, that look said, Miss Corsa were going to go around asking questions, she could start closer to home.

It was all very unfortunate. Through some sort of administrative lapse, the New York Police Department, cooperating with the New Hampshire State Police's routine inquiries, had dispatched two uniformed officers to the Sloan and to Thatcher's secretary. The officers had put their questions briefly, received precise replies, and departed. Both they and Miss Corsa had been able to remain unexcited.

Not so the rest of the trust department. Mounted Cossacks charging down the corridor could scarcely have roused greater response. Thatcher, whether physically on the premises or not, was a presence much felt in the trust department, and indeed throughout the Sloan. As a result, everybody felt proprietary interest in his comings and goings. A reference to him in *The Wall Street Journal* was comment-worthy from Brooklyn Heights to Westport. A quote in *Time* magazine kept the staff buzzing for days. A policeman left Thatcher's subordinates burning with curiosity.

Except Miss Corsa, that is.

"You don't think John is in any difficulties, do you?" Charlie asked the world at large.

"No, I do not," Miss Corsa replied coldly. There were times when Mr. Thatcher did not meet her levels of expectation, but she was not going to put up with this sort of thing.

"How could he get into difficulties on the Appalachian Trail?" Walter Bowman asked. "Unless he fell off, of course."

"You're thinking of Mount Everest, Walter," said Charlie absently. "John hasn't been hurt, has he, Rose?"

"No," she said. Clearly more was needed. "There has been some sort of accident. Mr. Thatcher and Mr. Morland were witnesses, that is all. The police just wanted—"

"An alibi!" Walter Bowman exploded. His great bulk precluded much familiarity with mountaineering, rock scrambles or cross-country hikes, but he knew all about police routine.

"Certainly not," said Miss Corsa, again affronted.

But Everett Gabler, as usual, had been thinking critically along more specific lines. He came to a sharp-witted conclusion before Charlie and Walter did.

"So, John isn't on the trail now. That means that he's somewhere we can reach him."

Miss Corsa admitted this was true.

"Aha!" It was triumph. The confrontation triggered by the State Banking Commission had not abated one whit.

But Trinkam realized that prying further information out of Miss Corsa would be no small task. Misguidedly, he appealed to her softer side.

"I don't like the sound of this police business, Rose. Walter's right. John may need us. Perhaps we should ring him up to see if we can help . . ."

He had gone too far.

"If Mr. Thatcher is in any need of us," Miss Corsa announced, "he will no doubt call us. Now, I am afraid I must finish this report."

Even this dismissal did not terminate the entente.

"That," said Everett, giving credit where credit was due, "was a good effort, Charlie."

Charlie recognized generosity. "Thanks, Ev," he replied sincerely.

To the north, no such meeting of minds obtained.

"I don't understand you, John," said Henry in a peppy voice. "Aren't you interested in all of this?"

Henry was ominously full of frisk.

Thatcher admitted mild interest in Stephen Lester's murder. This was not enough for Henry, who glared out the window of the car taking them to the State Police barracks and formal statements that would signal—Thatcher hoped—the end of their involvement with Stephen Lester and Fiord Haven. If he could keep the lid on Henry.

"Put it this way," said Henry finally. "I'm a suspect, you know. Can't blame the police for suspecting me, but you can't blame me for wanting to know who did Lester in—"

"Henry," said Thatcher wearily, "you are not a suspect, as you yourself were insisting last night. I understand you feel sorry for Eunice Lester—"

But Henry did not accept easy outs.

"Of course I'm a suspect," he said proudly. "I knew Lester, didn't I? I had plenty of time to knock him over the head . . ."

How, Thatcher wondered, had that admirable woman, Ruth Morland, managed to endure her husband these many years? More to the point, what was their police driver making of this?

"Here we are," said Henry, all anticipation.

The barracks of the New Hampshire State Police was a small, utilitarian crackerbox on Route 12. It was not set up for the rapid processing of large numbers of people. For that matter, the staff of Barracks Four, even augmented by additional personnel, was not able to handle the number of witnesses involved. Top-level efforts were being reserved for the two Mrs. Lesters. Routine interviews with thirty assorted potential Havenites were continuing at the White Mountains Motel.

Furthermore, since Stephen Lester's body had come to light at the site of James Joel Finley's lodge, it was necessary to talk to an entire construction crew.

So when Morland and Thatcher entered the barracks, they found that they would have to wait their turn. Ahead of them, in the waiting room, were a baker's dozen of construction workers. After a brief lull, the conversation resumed.

"One damned delay after another," said a middle-aged man with small eyes and sinewy arms. "Now *this*."

There was a murmur of agreement.

"You figure this killing will hold things up more, Alec?"

Alec was clearly the man in charge. He shrugged.

"This guy Finley's planning big changes after the foundation's already in. What can make for more delay than that? Even if this guy, Lester, wasn't killed down at the job, we've still got six or seven days of sitting on our hands. Big brain, our architect. I'll hand him that."

Alec, Thatcher saw, was not included among James Joel Finley's admirers.

But if Thatcher was the man to settle back and listen, Henry was not.

"Alec Prohack," he said, bounding up to shake hands vigorously. "Didn't recognize you at first."

It developed that Alec Prohack had bossed the crew that built Henry's new warehouse some years ago.

"Mr. Morland," he said enthusiastically.

Not to Thatcher's surprise, Henry Morland was absolutely at home with Alec and the rest of the boys. A vague gesture toward Thatcher was introduction enough. Predictably, Henry felt free to ask questions.

"Didn't know you were working over at Fiord Haven," he said.

There was a low, meaningful silence, the sort that leads all city people to expatiate on the subject of taciturn Yankees. Thatcher knew better. Alec and the gnarled, brown, tough men with him were sharing a joke. A monkey-faced oldster put it into words:

"We're following orders," he said slyly.

Somebody guffawed.

"That's right," said Alec Prohack gravely. "We follow orders. They got big plans up there, those fellows do."

"Smart, those fellows," said Monkey Face, no doubt the group wit.

Again, that silent, shared joke. The most youthful member of Alec Prohack's crew played straight man.

"Big businessmen," he said in mock admiration. "Come here from Boston. They do things different, in Boston."

"Yup," said an elderly man.

Now, tourists from Brooklyn may take these *yups* at face value. But Alec Prohack and his men were indulging themselves. Whatever this signified, Thatcher did not think it was deep respect for Fiord Haven.

There was, of course, the usual small-town attitude toward outsiders. There might be something else.

The door from the inner office opened. Eddie Quinlan was ushered out by a trooper.

The trooper, too, was a local man.

"Alec, you and the boys don't mind if Lieutenant Barteau takes Mr. Morland and Mr. Thatcher first, do you?"

"Go on," said Alec largely. "Besides, we've got all the time in the world."

As Henry disappeared behind closed doors to deliver his formal statement, Thatcher felt a momentary qualm. Yet even Ruth Morland had often conceded that no one could really protect Henry from himself. Fortunately, Thatcher's attention was reclaimed.

Quinlan showed no disposition to hurry back to the White Mountains Motel.

"I'm sorry you've gotten tied up by all this, Mr. Thatcher. I still maintain that some nut must have done it. The police will probably catch up with him down in Nashua . . ."

"Maybe Boston, even," said Monkey Face.

Eddie Quinlan nodded, missing the irony.

"Yeah, he could be almost anywhere," he said.

Thatcher returned a noncommittal reply, meanwhile registering that Quinlan, amidst his other preoccupations, had learned who John Putnam Thatcher was. Today there was a slight deference in his manner that was directed to the Wall Street banker, not the Appalachian Trail hiker.

Quinlan belatedly recognized Prohack and his crew.

"They interviewing you too, Alec?" he asked with a friendly grin.

Alec said that they were.

"I suppose they have to," Quinlan commented quickly. "They're being damned thorough, I'll give them that. They're interviewing every single one of the guests, too. I suppose they're checking you guys out because Lester's body was found up at the site. You never even met him."

Quinlan's husky Boston voice was encouraging.

But, Thatcher sensed, Alec and his friends did not need encouragement. There wasn't an ounce of tension in the whole crew.

Prohack, meanwhile, took his time.

"Well now," he finally drawled, "what makes you think that?"

Quinlan was surprised. "But Alec, we break our necks to keep the customers from getting under your feet. You're the one who insisted on it."

Prohack nodded. "Sure. But this Lester must have wandered off the beaten track. One or two of them always do. The rest of you were at the buildings when he turned up at our trailer, just when we were quitting for the day."

Thatcher saw Quinlan's involuntary movement.

"But, Alec, that could be important! My God, that was only an hour or so before he got killed. How did he act? What did he say?"

Alec shrugged. "He acted like everybody else who's bought a lot. All steamed up about when everything would be ready. Roads, the ski trails, the tows. How were we going to develop the beach? Hell, the longer he looked at the plans, the more questions he asked. You know, once they've bought themselves a lot, most of your buyers forget that they've still got a house to build."

What a shame, Thatcher thought, that Henry was not here for this confirmation of Eunice Lester's story.

Quinlan, however, had been reminded of another problem.

"How long is this going to put us back?" he asked, not masking his worry.

Alec crossed brawny arms. "Depends on what changes Finley's got in mind, now."

Eddie Quinlan ran a hand over his sleek hair. Alec and the crew watched stolidly.

"Well," Quinlan said, "I guess we'll just have to take things the way they come."

Not a bad philosophy, Thatcher decided, when five minutes later a crestfallen Henry reappeared.

8 BEATING AROUND THE BUSH

HENRY'S DEJECTION was explained when Thatcher succeeded him in Lieutenant Barteau's office. Together with the other luckless guests of Fiord Haven, they were requested to remain at the White Mountains Motel for at least a short time.

"My impression, Henry, was that you found this whole mess more interesting than hiking," said Thatcher, to dam a flow of complaint.

This provoked Henry into an impassioned declamation. He was unalterably devoted to the Appalachian Trail, but he retained the normal man's interest in the passing parade, particularly if it incorporated an unsolved murder.

Henry was not as contradictory as he sounded, Thatcher reflected during this spate of eloquence. His slight person camouflaged a gargantuan zest for living; a burning commitment to the great outdoors left him with plenty of energy for Stephen Lester and his affairs.

Henry had switched from volubility to portentousness. He narrowed his eyes. "Boston," he said heavily.

Oh God, thought Thatcher. Henry had another idea.

The New Hampshire State Police had had the same idea earlier. Already reports were pouring in from Boston, from Weston, Massachusetts, and for that matter from California.

Not that they were particularly informative. A preliminary survey showed that everyone was what he claimed to be. There were no criminal convictions, there were no undesirable associates, there were no official bankruptcies.

Stephen Lester, aged thirty-five, was a resident of Weston, and the owner of a home and two cars. He was employed as sales manager by North American Chemical Company. His wife, Amanda Trainor Lester, was aged twenty-six. There were no children.

James Joel Finley, aged fifty, member of the American Institute of Architects, was a partner of Finley & Ching, in Carmel, California. Finley & Ching were the designers of the Eugene Bullard Memorial Amphitheater outside Los Angeles, the Lawrence Library of Taos Community College, Taos, New Mexico, and the Pineapple Pavilion in Honolulu. Finley was currently separated from his fourth wife. Particulars would follow as available.

Arlington, Massachusetts, reported that Eunice Lester, aged thirty-four, was a divorcée with one son, employed as a personnel manager in a Boston department store.

"It's a sure thing that anything interesting about the wives isn't coming up on a police wire," said Frewen, tossing papers aside. "What's Boston got to offer?"

"Quinlan and Valenti," Barteau replied.

But Boston was not much more helpful.

Edward J. Quinlan, the teletype informed New Hampshire, was a Boston lawyer aged thirty-five, who had been active in real estate for ten years. Ralph G. Valenti, aged thirty-eight, had joined him four years ago. Together they had developed River Estates, a garden apartment complex in the Jamaica-way, before launching Fiord Haven. Both men were married. Each had two children.

Reports about the salesmen, the guests and everybody else associated with Fiord Haven were just as useless. Gerry Wahl, Burt O'Neil, the young Davidsons, all added up, as Frewen said, "To one big fat zero." He slammed his hand on the desk. "No reason, on the face of it, for any of them to kill Lester."

"You don't buy the wives, either?" Barteau asked.

"Right now they're the best bet," Frewen replied. "Especially the ex." He broke off. Eunice Lester's life, home and activities were due for more stringent examination. Her fiancé would be investigated as well. Currently, Frewen was with-holding judgment. "But I still can't figure out why the wives would come up here to kill Lester. Hell, it's a lot safer down there."

This libel on the Commonwealth of Massachusetts roused no objection from Barteau.

"So, it all boils down to nothing," Frewen continued. "Lester has lunch with the whole gang on Saturday. Then, afterwards, he hangs around for a little while, closes his deal with Quinlan, runs into the ex-wife and tells her about it. Then he goes for a walk, promising his wife he'll be back in time to tour the site with her. He *does* come back but now he tells her he's skipping the tour. And after that, the only people who see him are the construction crew, just before they quit work. From what Pro-hack says, Lester was avoiding the whole Fiord Haven crowd."

"And what does the wife say?" Barteau asked.

Frewen stubbed out his cigar, recalling the hysterics, the doctor, and the sedatives that had stood between him and Amanda Lester. But that was forty-eight hours ago.

"Let's go and find out," he said.

". . . sure, sure, use our office," said Ralph Valenti, ap-propriately solemn.

Behind him, Mrs. Lester had tucked herself into the corner of the leather sofa. On Frewen's entrance, she sat up, straighten-ing her shoulders as if an act of will could dissipate her be-wilderment. Her ordeal had left her pale and drawn but, for the first time, Frewen realized that Amanda Lester was a little beauty, graceful as a doe with the same fine bones and enormous eyes.

"Yes, of course I want to help you," she said in a voice that was low but perfectly steady. "I'd rather have Mr. Valenti and Mr. Quinlan stay with me, though. My parents haven't gotten in from California yet. They're coming tonight."

Captain Frewen was not an imaginative man but the contrast

between Stephen Lester's two wives was striking enough to capture him. Eunice Lester fought her own battles. Amanda Lester had gone from being somebody's daughter to somebody's wife; her husband's death had left her alone but she did not know it. Instinctively, she expected supporters.

It had not occurred to her that she might need defenders. The same examination being trained on Mrs. Eunice Lester, divorcée with son, was being extended to Mrs. Amanda Lester, housewife. Eunice, Frewen suspected, knew this. Amanda did not.

Quinlan cocked an inquiring eye at the policeman. "Sure, we'll stay if it makes you feel better, Mrs. Lester," he said. "That is, if it's all right with you, Captain?"

"Sure," said Frewen, grimly amused. Amanda did not think of herself as a suspect; neither did she think of Eddie Quinlan or Ralph Valenti as suspects. Frewen knew why. The hysteria of Saturday night was gone; the accusation remained.

"Has Eunice confessed?" Amanda asked in a matter-of-fact voice, before the men were seated. Quinlan and Valenti froze, but she paid no attention.

Frewen cleared his throat. "No, she hasn't confessed, Mrs. Lester. And we don't have any evidence—"

"For God's sake, what have you been doing?" Amanda exclaimed. "Everybody knows she did it."

This time Ralph Valenti got as far as a muttered protest.

"We all know what happened. She hated Steve. She had a fight with him. Then—"

Amanda was still seeing things in black and white. Eunice Lester hated Steve. Steve was dead. Therefore . . .

While Frewen concentrated on framing his first question, Eddie and Ralph avoided Amanda's eyes. She swept on:

"You can't deny that they met each other after lunch. Eunice admits it herself. Then she trumped up this story about Steve buying a lot."

Almost apologetically, Quinlan hitched himself forward. "Now, Mrs. Lester, I think that there's some sort of confusion here. When I spoke to your husband after lunch, he did make up his mind to buy. I was going to have a sales contract ready Sunday. Probably he bumped into Eunice and was just being polite—"

Indignation brought color to Amanda's cheeks. "Polite? Does that sound likely? For heaven's sake, Eunice couldn't see Steve without starting a fight. You saw what happened Saturday morning. Imagine what it would have been like if I hadn't been there."

If life was a stage for Amanda Lester, she was the star in every scene. Other people had witnessed the Lesters' meeting on Saturday. Everyone agreed that it had been unpleasant. Not everyone, however, cast Amanda as the peacemaker.

"Okay, Mrs. Lester," Frewen said soothingly. "Have it your way. Your husband fought with his ex-wife before he set out on his walk. But what did he do after that? He was gone the whole afternoon. He must have said something to you when he stopped back in your motel room."

Amanda Lester did not like being humored. Stiffly she said, "He simply said he was not coming on the tour."

"Did he say why?"

"No, he didn't."

"Didn't you ask?"

"No, I did not."

Almost imperceptibly, the atmosphere in the room changed, and not in Amanda's favor. Valenti, Quinlan, and Frewen were all married men. Not one of them believed her.

"All right," said Frewen. "He skipped out on you for the first half of the afternoon. He skipped out on you for the second half. You didn't ask him where he was going. Did you ask when he was coming back?"

"No," she cried out. But three skeptical faces made her falter for the first time. "Well, if you must know, he was . . . he was preoccupied."

Inwardly, Frewen relaxed. So Steve Lester had had something on his mind other than one of Fiord Haven's vacation homes.

"What was he preoccupied about?" he demanded.

"He didn't tell me," Amanda replied almost desperately. "He wouldn't explain anything. He just snapped at me, then he stamped out."

"Now Mrs. Lester, don't get upset," Valenti murmured uselessly.

"I am not upset," she retorted. "I'm mad. Why are you wasting time this way! Why are you hounding me when you know that Eunice had a fight with Steve? She's the one you should be going after—"

Captain Frewen's long temper had limits. "Look, Mrs. Lester. Eunice may have had a fight with your husband at two o'clock. You sure as hell had one at four. And by six, he was dead!"

First she gasped at him, then she leaped to her feet, her hands clenched.

"You can't talk to me that way and I'm not staying to hear any more! You don't see me again until I've got my father on one side and a lawyer on the other."

Head high, she marched out of the office. Frewen made no move to stop her.

Quinlan turned his crooked grin on Frewen. "Listen, Captain, I've got a complaint, too. Why the hell did you let us in for that?"

Valenti seconded the sentiment with a look of mournful reproach.

"Do you both good," Frewen said robustly. "And as long as I've got you here, I've got a couple of questions for you."

"We'll make a deal," Quinlan said easily. "We answer your questions and you call off the cops. Let these people we've got on our hands go home. We're running up a helluva motel bill."

"That doesn't bother me," said Frewen. "The owner's my nephew. Now listen, what do either of you know about this scene when the Lesters ran into Eunice for the first time?"

Quinlan shrugged as Valenti replied, "Neither of us were there, thank God. Ask James Joel Finley for a blow-by-blow account. He told me all about it."

"Most of the salesmen can do the same, Ralph," Quinlan reminded him. "Frankly I got the impression that it was the women who made most of the noise. The way I got it, Lester was more embarrassed than anything else."

That figured, everybody agreed.

"Another thing," Frewen said, rising to leave. "I know how you ride herd on the prospects you get up here. Why weren't you keeping tabs on Lester? If you'd been doing your job, mine would be a lot easier. Didn't anybody notice how he was ducking most of these sales pitches of yours?"

Neither Quinlan nor Valenti was affronted. Valenti in fact took the question seriously. "I'm the one who goofed on that. Somebody told me that Lester was missing around three o'clock. That's it, Burt O'Neil told me he had cut the talk session—"

Quinlan broke in as he, too, rose. He was more lighthearted. "I guess you and Burt didn't know that we'd already sold Lester, Ralph." He turned to Frewen. "Captain, once they've signed up, they can go visit their grandmothers if they want. We're busy trying to sell the holdouts."

"In that case, it's a shame Lester decided to buy," Frewen mused.

"The real shame," Valenti said bitterly, "was that he ever got on our list."

Frewen was speaking more to himself than to the others. "I guess there isn't much more to do here."

Quinlan picked him up. "You mean we can let everybody go?"

That was exactly what Captain Frewen meant.

"It isn't as if we have much chance to make any sales now," Valenti remarked as he retailed the scene to Thatcher and Henry. They were sitting in the lobby of the White Mountains Motel. Around them was a purposive bustle, as Fiord Haven's prospects got out while the going was good. The packsacks under Thatcher's chair contrasted strongly to the matched sets of luggage piled everywhere. Their message however was comparable; everybody was packed and eager to escape.

Henry had not been listening.

"I've never seen so many Porsches in my life," he said, returning from a reconnaissance of the driveway. "Everybody here seems to drive one."

He lost Thatcher but not Valenti. "That's right," Valenti said. "Eddie's got a nephew in the Registry of Motor Vehicles. We got a list of Porsche owners in the Greater Boston area. That gives you a pretty good list of prospects, don't you think? Real smart idea—until all this popped up. Eddie's got a million ideas like that."

The explosion of departing exhausts momentarily deflected him. But only momentarily:

"Next weekend, we've got thirty medical doctors coming up. That's even better than Porsches. If we don't sell twenty to thirty lots—well, I'll be surprised."

Thatcher felt his way. "Your sales program is . . . er . . . continuing?"

Valenti was disingenuous. "Why not? This will blow over."

Neither Thatcher nor Henry found any suitable reply. Their silence spurred Valenti on to indiscretion.

Lowering his voice, he looked around the crowded lobby. "But I'll tell you one thing," he said in a savage undertone. "I wish I'd been the one to find Lester's body."

"I do, too," said Henry, who seemed to have taken a dislike to Valenti.

Thatcher waited.

"Because if I had, I'd have rolled it down a mountainside, that's what I'd have done. Then everybody would have thought Lester had some sort of accident. And that would have been that."

"Except for a murderer on the loose," Thatcher objected.

Unheeding, Valenti continued: "It was just more lousy luck. Any other Saturday, I'd probably have been up at the site. This time I had to see about getting some blueprints changed."

A horn from the driveway brought an end to these revelations.

"Well, good luck," said Henry, smartly hoisting his pack.

It was an abrupt withdrawal from Fiord Haven. Thatcher softened it by a few conventional good wishes, then followed Henry from the motel.

As they left, Ralph G. Valenti was still thinking hard.

9 KINDLING

JOHN THATCHER had not expected to be back at the Morland home in Pepperton, New Hampshire within four days of leaving it. Nevertheless, he viewed his surroundings with approval. He had always been an admirer of this kitchen. Like most women swapping New York City for Northern New England, Ruth Morland had demanded a modern kitchen. She had resisted the temptation to encase the electric range in a stove-black exterior, to surround the freezer with knotty pine paneling and to cover the vinyl floor with braided rugs. On the contrary, the only reminder of the original kitchen—a wood and oil range prudently preserved as insurance against electric failure—was concealed in a niche behind folding doors. As a result, Ruth had a genuine farmhouse kitchen. Only city people live in a sea of cranberry scoops and scorn formica and stainless steel.

The breakfast nook, in a similar move toward comfort, had been set against a wide east window through which the morning sun was now pouring. Thatcher eased his shoulders in a shaft of warmth and contemplated his hostess. Henry, busy as a beaver, had already bustled off to his warehouse. This was a golden opportunity for a few words of warning.

Happily, Ruth had few illusions about her husband.

"I'm surprised you were able to get him back here, John," she said, putting her own interpretation on their arrival the night before.

"It wasn't easy." Thatcher had decided to be blunt. "And the problem now is to keep him here."

"Henry does get enthusiastic about things," Ruth said fondly. "It's one of his charms."

"Look here, Ruth. It may be one of his charms for you, but I doubt if the police see it that way."

Unperturbed, Ruth poured coffee and extended the sugar bowl. She was a pleasantly plump woman with gray hair that sprang vigorously from a center part.

"Henry told me that the police were suspicious of him at first. But after they checked with the Appalachian Mountain Club and found out how casual his acquaintance with Steve Lester was, he said they were inclined to forget about him."

"True enough," Thatcher conceded. "But now Henry's started being an amateur detective. He's been closeted with Eunice Lester, and I know he wanted to cross-examine everybody at Fiord Haven, if not everybody in New Hampshire."

Ruth tut-tutted. "I suppose you tried to explain how the police might misinterpret all this interest of his."

"Repeatedly."

"And he didn't understand," Ruth concluded comfortably. "That's my Henry for you."

"Seriously, Ruth, I think it would be a worthy project for you to dampen this enthusiasm. Surely there's some other hobby he can take up."

"I gave up trying to dampen him thirty years ago. It's impossible." She smiled reassuringly across the table. "But, sometimes, he can be deflected. I suppose the important thing is to keep him away from Fiord Haven."

Thatcher admired her confidence. "Certainly that's the first step."

"Let's see, maybe I could promote a crisis at The Pepper Mill. No, I don't think that would do much good. He's not likely to be very interested. Or, I could tell him that he doesn't know enough about Steve Lester's background. That, at least, would take him in another direction. What a good thing it is," she ended in a burst of parochialism, "that those wives were there for the police to suspect."

"If there hadn't been any wives, there might not have been any murder," Thatcher said, trying to introduce a semblance of logic into the conversation.

Ruth rose above logic. "See? That's exactly what I mean. I suppose it's the first wife who's the prime suspect."

Thatcher's agreement was not wholehearted. "She leads the field in motive, there's no doubt about that. But otherwise, I'm not so sure. There's no indication that she left her motel room during the critical period. And no one noticed any abnormal behavior on her part. She wasn't seen sobbing hysterically or trembling with rage that afternoon. Nor does there seem to have been a sudden deterioration in her relations with Lester, just a steady hostility that had been going on for months."

"What about when they met each other without warning on Saturday morning? Henry said there was some sort of excitement then."

"Both Lester and Eunice were upset at the sudden confrontation. All the spectators are agreed on that. They came face to face without warning at the morning lecture. But some people say that the one who did the raging was Amanda Lester."

"The second wife," Ruth mused. "I suppose the police aren't overlooking her."

"By no means. The great strength of Eunice's position is that she tells a straightforward story which is reasonable on its surface and, insofar as it can be checked, is truthful. She was disturbed to find her ex-husband in the weekend party and was determined not to buy a lot at Fiord Haven if he did. The minute he told her he was going to buy, she decided to leave."

Ruth pounced. "But she didn't leave. She was still there hours later."

"She explains that, too. She had made plans to be away for the weekend. Her son was with friends, her refrigerator was bare, and she had been swept up into the treadmill of Fiord Haven activities. Lester announced his decision that afternoon. She decided to stay for cocktails and dinner, then drive home."

"That sounds reasonable," Ruth nodded dubiously. "But Amanda doesn't go along with that, does she?"

Thatcher was warming to his story. "That is where the complications begin. I don't suppose the police are ever prepared to exonerate a resident spouse without close examination. Particularly where the murder seems to have been an unpremeditated emotional outburst. And, when the spouse starts lying, they become very interested, indeed."

"Unpremeditated?" Ruth seemed to be testing this new concept. "Yes, I'll go along with that. You said he was hit on the head with a hammer, didn't you? Then, the police are right. No woman would plan to kill her husband that way."

Thatcher was amused at her air of expert judgment. "Oh? And how would you go about murdering Henry?" he inquired.

"Strangling," she said cheerfully. "Sometimes when he goes burbling on for hours, I plan it out in great detail."

Behind the curtain of fifteen years as a widower, Thatcher's memories of the marital state stirred into life. "Well, never mind about that," he said hastily, "the important thing is that Amanda denied Lester had decided to buy a lot. But the police had already questioned Quinlan, the owner of Fiord Haven, and he corroborated Eunice's story."

"I don't think that's so suspicious. This all happened on the day of the murder. Maybe Lester didn't have a chance to tell his wife."

"No, that won't hold up. The police have gone into Lester's movements that day very thoroughly. If everybody is telling the truth, this is what happened. Directly after lunch, Quinlan made an impromptu sales effort which was successful. Lester agreed to buy lot number seventy-three, and Quinlan was to have the contract ready for him the next day. Lester then left for his walk and met Eunice in the parking lot. Their encounter was seen but not overheard. He told Eunice he had bought a lot and went on into the woods. Eunice remained in the parking lot in full view until she was joined by the rest of her group. Two hours later Amanda and Lester were together for fifteen minutes during which time, so Amanda claims, Lester said nothing about buying a lot. Then Lester stormed out of their motel room, returned to the site and was murdered."

Ruth was thoughtful. "If he stormed out, they were probably quarreling. Maybe that's why he forgot to tell her."

"It's more likely they were quarreling just because he did tell her." Thatcher paused to organize his arguments.

"After all, the whole question of a vacation house had become entwined with the custody fight. If the Lesters won custody of Eunice's son, then the worst thing in the world that could happen would be to find themselves cheek by jowl with Eunice and her new husband in a private housing colony."

Ruth's maternal instincts were roused. "It wouldn't be so much fun for the little boy, either. He'd turn into a football."

"Precisely. Under the circumstances it seems incredible that Lester would have forgotten to mention the purchase to Amanda."

"And what does she say to all this?"

"I gather she doesn't say much," said Thatcher, recalling Valenti's account. "She simply insists that Lester never would have chatted casually with Eunice. Hence, Eunice is simply trying to conceal the real reason for their encounter in the parking lot."

"And what does Eunice say?"

Thatcher sighed. "What do you expect? Eunice says Amanda seized what looked like a glorious opportunity to be spiteful and throw suspicion."

For a moment Ruth was silent, pouring more coffee and wordlessly offering a plate of hot rolls. At last, she spoke.

"You know what strikes me as odd?" she asked. "It's Eunice. Oh, I don't mean her story of what happened on the day of the murder. I mean her general attitude. For instance, why is she so hostile to Amanda? Why does she assume that

Amanda is being spiteful? After all, when Amanda first told her story, she must have been in shock and she's only a young thing."

Thatcher stared across the table with frank disbelief. "What do you mean, why is she hostile? You've seen plenty of divorces, Ruth. It's not uncommon for the first wife to be antagonistic to the second."

Ruth shook her head gently. "But there's usually a reason. Very often the second wife is the 'woman who stole my husband.' That doesn't apply here. Or, there's just plain jealousy. If the first wife is reduced to loneliness, she's likely to see red at the sight of the second wife enjoying the comforts of marriage. But Henry said that the Lesters first approached Eunice when she was already engaged. Now that's usually a time when a woman is feeling very pleased with herself. She's not likely to be jealous of an ex-husband. If she has grounds for detesting him, she's far more likely to pity his second wife. You know, the thank-God-he's-her-problem attitude."

"I may have been overhasty," Thatcher acknowledged. "I simply accepted Eunice's dislike as natural. Of course, there's always that custody battle. The Lesters, after all, were threatening Eunice's coming marriage and trying to steal her child. That's enough to promote dislike."

"Perhaps. But I bet Eunice blamed most of that on Steve. Amanda wouldn't be much more than his follower in all this. But there's another thing that bothers me about Eunice. That's this marriage of hers."

"What's wrong with it?" Thatcher demanded impatiently.

"Well, they're not exactly rushing to the altar, are they?" Ruth asked reasonably. "Eighteen months ago Eunice was getting engaged. It's not as if they were youngsters waiting to finish college. Not that they do, these days," she reflected.

Thatcher tried to remember what Henry had told him. "There's no question of divorce," he reflected aloud. "The man's a widower with grown-up children. The wedding is planned for next month, I believe. This vacation house is to be a wedding present for Eunice."

"And he drives a Porsche," Ruth said significantly.

"What makes you think that?" Thatcher was confused.

"It was Eunice's fiancé who was originally on the list for Fiord Haven's weekend. Because of his car." Ruth suddenly metamorphized into a shrewd retailer. "That's not a bad way of narrowing down a field for a mailing list. People with money and sports car instincts."

Henry had been busy to some purpose, Thatcher thought grimly. How many police suspicions had he stirred while getting this information?

"I suppose you're trying to tell me that the man in Eunice's life has money," he remarked.

"Well, he's a catch for a divorcée working to support a child. And she seems to be having trouble landing him."

Not for the first time Thatcher had cause to reflect on the ruthless realism of women. How much of this quality did Amanda's candy-box fragility conceal? His ruminations were interrupted by Henry's return. The man of the house plumped himself down, accepted coffee and plunged into his news without preliminaries.

"I was talking to Calvin. Our local state trooper," he explained for Thatcher's benefit. "He doesn't seem to know much that we don't. The police have crossed off all the prospects at the motel except the wives. It seems that everybody was in their room dressing or showering and they cancel each other out. The only ones who were alone, besides the Fiord Haven management running around setting things up, were the wives. The salesmen were in a huddle. So that narrows it down to Eunice, Amanda, Quinlan, Valenti, and that architect. That's if you forget the Davidsons."

"And if you forget passersby like Thatcher and Morland," his guest contributed.

Henry regally waved this aside. "Why should I rush up to somebody I barely know and bash his head in?"

Absently, Thatcher reached for a turnover. "Is that just one of your flights of fancy? Or do the police assume this was a crime of impulse, no matter who the murderer?"

"That's the official version," Henry replied, quaffing his coffee with gusto. "I'm not so sure I go along with that theory myself. I may have to look into it more."

For once Thatcher disregarded the need to suppress Henry. "I think they're right. That would explain the location of the body, which has always puzzled me."

"What's wrong with the location of the body? A nice secluded spot, no workmen due until Monday, ease of egress. If I hadn't happened to stumble across Lester when I did, the police probably couldn't even have pinpointed the time of death. A first-class choice, if you ask me," Henry concluded.

"You could do better," Thatcher said. "What about Valenti's idea?"

Henry disliked having his expertise questioned. "That bag of wind?" he said. Here was something Ruth had not heard about. "What was Valenti's idea?" she asked.

Thatcher told her. "Valenti thought suspicion of murder could have been avoided entirely. Why not tumble the body down a hillside? With a little stage management, say a rock in the right place, Lester would just be another unfortunate mountain fatality."

Henry did his best to spot flaws.

"It would have to be a clever stage set to fool a real investigation."

"And what chance would there have been of a serious investigation? Lester wouldn't have appeared for dinner. People would remember he had gone off on his own, but it would already be too dark to mount a search. The next morning he would be found in a natural setting. I doubt if the police would have cordoned off the area, searched it rigorously, demanded a postmortem. No, the murderer just wasn't thinking. There was probably an argument, a sudden fight, and then a panic-stricken flight. The murderer is probably having second thoughts just about now." Thatcher could see the whole scene.

"Possibly." Henry was becoming more professorial by the minute. "But remember, the group only had one free hour between tour and cocktail party. Maybe the murderer had to rush back to the motel to be on time."

"Aren't you boys forgetting something?" Rush asked blandly.

"I doubt it," said her husband.

"The murderer may not have been strong enough to cart bodies around the countryside." Ruth leaned back, an enigmatic smile on her lips.

She didn't have to say anything else and she knew it, Thatcher realized. All three of them were suddenly visualizing Stephen Lester's wives.

10 MIXED HARDWOODS

HENRY WAS not the man to sit enthralled by someone else's imaginings. Pushing aside his cup and saucer, he announced that he couldn't sit here wasting the day. He had things to do.

"By the way, Ruth," he said, elaborately casual, "if you've got a list, I could do the marketing for you. I've got to go to the lumberyard anyway."

His wife did not point out that the shopping center was ten miles from the lumberyard. Instead she produced her list and eyed her husband thoughtfully.

"With that schedule, I don't suppose you and John will be home for lunch," she offered.

Henry was much struck with this observation. "Now that you mention it, I guess we won't. But, then, you weren't expecting us to be here today so, really, it's a help to you."

All wives are familiar with husbands hell-bent on doing what they want and, at the same time, determined to be regarded as benefactors. Sensible women do not fight nature.

"That will be a great help," said Ruth kindly. She did not speak again until the two men were in the car, ready to leave.

"Oh, Henry!" she called from the back door. "If I were you, I'd start at the bank. That's where the real gossip will be."

An hour and a half later John Thatcher realized what she meant. They had driven into Gridleigh, the county seat. On the sidewalk in front of the bank, they had met the State Conservation Agent. Henry's opening question was forestalled.

"I hear you got mixed up with that bunch of developers at Fiord Haven, Henry. Finding bodies for them, or something," the agent said disapprovingly. "What are they like?"

"I was going to ask you," Henry replied promptly. "We didn't see much of them. Haven't they been around your office?"

"Like hell! Big operators like them don't use local talent. They brought up some experts of their own to test that lake of theirs. Probably cost them a fortune."

Henry and the conservation agent grinned pleasantly at each other. The same tests would have been performed free of charge by the State of New Hampshire. The agent then admitted he was looking forward to Fiord Haven's approach to the fish problem.

"Their advertising is big on hunting and fishing being available. How do you think they'll find out what streams are stocked with trout? They could get a list just by calling my office. So I suppose they'll hire a big shot who'll spend days checking every drop of water for miles."

Henry, with every evidence of satisfaction, agreed that this was likely. The agent, who seemed to be keeping abreast of each action and each publication by Fiord Haven in his jurisdiction, then took his leave, saying he was sorry that he couldn't help Henry.

"But you might try Guy Villars. They might have contacted him and I just saw him in the bank."

Within seconds, John Thatcher was towed indoors and Henry was bearing down on a rumpled, middle-aged man stuffing bills into his wallet.

"Guy!" called Henry, who opened his interrogations with an artless lack of pretense. "Do you know anything about this Fiord Haven crowd?"

Except for differences in wording, Guy's reply was the same as the conservation agent's. The management of Fiord Haven had not condescended to utilize the services of a local lawyer. Nonetheless, the local lawyer was surprisingly abreast of their movements.

"This Quinlan is a lawyer, himself. Guess he and Valenti figure if they're sharp enough to take on the opposition in Boston, they can take care of themselves up here." Villars permitted himself an earthy chuckle. "You think it ever occurs to these sharpies that New Hampshire has had to make a living out of them for the past eighty years?"

The conservation agent, Thatcher had noticed, was indistinguishable from any young man on Wall Street. Guy Villars, on the other hand, flaunted a slow drawl, rural colloquialisms, and laborious frowns. Thatcher was willing to bet that he had been to Harvard.

Henry said briskly that sharpies had to learn from experience, just like everybody else, and had Quinlan done all the preliminary legal work himself?

"Yup," Villars nodded. "Not that there was much work to it. He waited until the plans for the new highway were finished, then he just scouted around for a big parcel of land that would be convenient for Boston commuting. Didn't need much except a pond and some hills for skiing. God knows, if there's anything New Hampshire's got, it's ponds and hills. Then he bought a couple of farms and got down to work. Did all the paperwork from his city office. He and that Valenti set up a corporation." Villars paused to smile blandly. "And good luck to 'em, I say. We could use some big spenders around here."

"It might change the character of the place," Henry warned.

"Not as long as they're not registered voters, it won't." Villars gave a valedictory grin and moved off.

"One of your politicians?" Thatcher asked curiously.

"He's our state legislator now," Henry confirmed. "But he's got his eye on the Congressional seat. Look, it's one o'clock. Let's see if we can get hold of Don Cavers for lunch."

Don Cavers turned out to be the president of the Gridleigh National Bank. While Henry was rooting him out of his office, Thatcher had leisure to examine his surroundings. It was a long time since he had seen a bank like this. There was dark oak wainscoting halfway up the walls, the single plate-glass window bore the bank's title in gold script, and behind the elaborately carved grilles, an ancient and gigantic safe stood in the tellers' quarters.

The man in charge of this period piece was all of thirty years old.

"Glad to meet you," he said warmly. "I guess this doesn't seem in the same league as the Sloan."

Thatcher agreed that there were surface differences.

"But we're doing well, very well," said Cavers, leading the way across the street. "Of course, all this second-home building helps. And the ski resort business is booming. You wouldn't believe how much we've grown in the last five years. We'll be putting in an electronic data processing system this winter. High time we modernized our systems!"

Thatcher seated himself in the tavern booth and applauded these signs of prosperity. "I suppose you'll be modernizing your premises at the same time?"

Cavers hooted. "Not on your life! You can't believe what an attraction that turn-of-the-century look is. When people come in to see about a mortgage to buy a vacation place, the bank's appearance does half the selling job. They think they're really getting away from it all. Back to small-town America and old-time virtues."

Thatcher readjusted his ideas. "That safe I saw in a corner?" he probed experimentally.

"Great, isn't it?" Cavers beamed. "I picked it up last year. Of course, we've got steel-lined vaults in the basement. But the summer people don't know that."

Henry felt he had allowed decent time for shop talk. "John and I were down at Fiord Haven for their murder," he said. "Interesting bunch, I'd say."

"Really?" Cavers didn't look as if he believed it. "They didn't do any of their financing through us, you know."

Fiord Haven, it seemed, had not tapped the local conservation agent, the local lawyer, or the local banker.

"Did they get stung?" Thatcher asked frankly.

Cavers considered the question. "About average, I'd say," he concluded. "Of course, in the long run, they'll do all right. Any developer up here does, if he can sell off his lots. I don't know about their financial position, but they bought four farms, all abandoned, or semi-abandoned, including Miller's Pond. And they've done their good deed for every other farm in the area. Land that had been a drug on the market started to skyrocket the minute the first bulldozer rolled in. I hear Courtney Blair is selling off his south field in half-acre building lots for A-frames."

Henry said there were no flies on Courtney Blair.

"In the long run, you'll do well out of it, too," Thatcher observed.

"And how!" Cavers agreed enthusiastically. "Sooner or later, Fiord Haven's customers will be coming to us for mortgage money to build. I can wait. I'd just as soon some outfit in Boston took the high risks on the land development and the communal building. Not that Alec Prohack has had any complaints about slow payments. I'll stick with the individual mortgages. Do you know that we haven't had more than ten foreclosures during the last fifteen years in the whole state? Funny thing, people seem to hang on to country places even harder than to their regular homes."

A discussion of this point carried them through beer and knockwurst. It was agreed that people might overextend themselves financially for a first home because they had to have one. But a vacation place was genuinely optional.

"By that time, people have picked up a lot of luxuries like second cars and boats that can be sacrificed if the pressure goes on. There's some slack in their financial position," Cavers argued cogently. "And they're the kind we need in New Hampshire. God bless them all."

When Thatcher and Henry left him, he was audibly planning the introduction of a Franklin stove into the main area of the bank.

"A bright young man," Thatcher observed. "I wonder when he'll get to wooden Indians."

"Don? I do all my business with him. He did his training at some New York bank, then came back here to take over from his father. Old Cavers is the one who financed The Pepper Mill." Henry sighed nostalgically. "Those were the days."

Long experience had taught Thatcher that everybody looked back longingly on the days when payments to the bank constituted a monthly crisis. Nothing could convince Henry he had everything now that he did then, except the suspense.

"Where to next?"

Henry looked shamefaced. "Now, I suppose, we've got to go to that damned shopping center."

At the supermarket Henry seized a shopping cart with one hand, clutched Ruth's list in the other, and cantered down the aisles. A rain of staples flowed into his basket, from onions to canned soup. This orderly program collapsed at the delicatessen counter. Here he abandoned lists and took the bit between his teeth.

As Thatcher watched smoked salmon, fried rice and Greek olives succeed each other, he found himself wondering what kind of menu Henry had in mind. It was, he saw, providential that weight restrictions on the Appalachian Trail confined them to unimaginative freeze-dried foods.

Henry noticed his companion's look. "Women," he said largely, "don't understand delicatessen food."

"Don't you think you have enough?" asked Thatcher. Henry had just ordered some cheesecake as a last-minute inspiration.

"That's right. We still have to get to the lumberyard."

But fate was cooperating with Henry that day. At the checkout counter they took up their positions behind a familiar plaid shirt.

"Alec!" said Henry happily.

Alec Prohack, chief of the construction crew at Fiord Haven, turned to greet them over a basket filled with six-packs of beer and pretzels.

"Having a few of the boys over to watch the game," he explained with a wave of the hand.

"Not working at the site?" Henry inquired.

"The cops aren't letting us start until tomorrow."

"Too bad," Thatcher sympathized.

"Doesn't make any difference," Prohack said heavily. "You can't get on with the job unless the guys you're building for make up their minds what they want."

"Don't they know what they want?" Thatcher was surprised. Indecision had not seemed characteristic of Fiord Haven.

"It's not them. It's the professor. You know, with the long hair and the lapels. I told Finley at the beginning, he'd need closer roof joists. *Now* he agrees. But he's in a huddle with the cops. And, with Quinlan screaming about the extra cost and Valenti worried about the time schedule, nobody's willing to give us the go-ahead."

Henry brushed aside irrelevancies. "What's Finley doing with the cops?"

"They found out about some argument between him and that guy, Lester. Naturally if you have a bust-up with a guy who's murdered, you have to explain to the cops." Prohack shrugged. "Hell, the cops just want to be able to file it away. No one thinks Finley hammered Lester."

"Why not?" Henry asked baldly.

"Never picked up a hammer in his life," Prohack said simply.

Protests from the rear of the line and beckonings from the cash register broke up the conference. Prohack passed through the check-out and into the parking lot. But he left Henry's ever-fertile mind busily whirring.

"I don't think that stands up," he said, eyes agleam.

They were back in the car, and Thatcher had not kept pace with his companion's internal monologue.

"What doesn't?"

"This business of Finley not being the type. After all, he's as much the type as Amanda or Eunice. The police theory is that somebody lost his head and acted out of type."

"But Amanda and Eunice might conceivably have a motive for losing their heads," Thatcher objected.

"How do we know about Finley's motives?" Henry demanded unanswerably. "That's what we've got to find out. Why, we don't even know how much he's got riding on Fiord Haven. Or—wait a minute!"

"Yes?" said Thatcher fearing the worst.

"He's from California, isn't he? Maybe Lester and Finley knew each other a lot better than we've assumed. I can see there's a lot of work to be done here."

Thatcher reminded himself that someone else had undertaken the commitment to cleave to Henry for better or worse.

"The first thing to do," he said firmly, "is to tell Ruth about it and see what she says."

Ruth, looking firmly into space, said that she thought it was all very interesting. She personally agreed that the master key must lie elsewhere.

In California.

Or in Boston.

In fact, anywhere—far, far away from Captain Frewen.

"That's right," Henry seethed. "What we should do—"

"What you should do," said Ruth inexorably, "is go down to Boston."

For a moment, Thatcher had feared it would be San Francisco.

"And see what we can find out," Henry finished happily.

"Yes," said Ruth, giving Thatcher a long look.

Like Miss Corsa, Ruth was a virtuoso of wordless communication.

"Boston it is," said Thatcher.

And if that was not performance above and beyond the call of duty, he didn't know what was.

11 UP A TREE

FOR THOSE millions of Americans who pile into the family car and speed across this vast continent via six-lane tollways, the Appalachian Trail is pretty small potatoes. True, it extends a respectable two thousand miles from Maine to Georgia, but it boasts no gas stations, no hot dog stands, no Holiday Inns. In the land of Henry Ford, the Appalachian Trail is, after all, only a footpath.

It is not even an historic footpath. Once upon a time, a considerable stretch of today's trail was paralleled by the Great Indian Warpath, stretching from the Creek territory in Alabama northward into Pennsylvania. But the Creeks were no fools; they traversed valleys and lowlands, not crests. And today, the Red Man has given way to traffic jams, garbage dumps, and the other amenities of civilization.

Indeed, contrary to widespread belief, the Appalachian Trail is not a relic of America's hardier past. It is a mammoth creation of modern man that has generated comparable house-keeping chores. After every winter, after every summer storm, miles of trail must be cleared, then carefully blazed so that no feckless city folk can wander into danger. Apartment dwellers, lulled by air conditioning, have lost their forebears' healthy respect for nature. The Appalachian Trail has to be kept very safe indeed to allow Americans access to a great wilderness, without overloading rescue squads from Mount Katahdin to Springer Mountain.

These onerous responsibilities rest on the combined backs

of many thousands of men and women who themselves value the exhilaration of the trail and who exert themselves to keep it available to others. Naturally, these enthusiasts have formed clubs: the Green Mountains Club, the Susquehanna Club, the Eastern Branch of the Sierra Club, among others. They hold meetings, they enroll members, they offer programs, they dicker with other clubs. But, above all, they maintain the trail.

In a very real sense, spiritual and temporal leadership emanates from the Appalachian Mountain Club, on Joy Street, in Boston. The Appalachian Mountain Club is ninety-three years old, the oldest mountaineering group in this hemisphere. The Club maintains three hundred and sixty miles of the trail and has nearly twelve thousand members.

It is a matter of deep pride, to the Appalachian Mountain Club, that it has preserved many scenic attractions. So, too, is its extensive mountaineering library, open to the public.

"What do you hope to learn at the Club—besides the fact that Lester was a reliable trip leader and a serious hiker?" asked Thatcher as the taxi from Logan Airport finally emerged from the tunnel to a distressing view of the New Boston.

"Don't you worry," Henry assured him. "They won't foist off that Scout's honor stuff on me!"

Henry, Thatcher knew, had an ambivalent approach to the Appalachian Mountain Club. He was, of course, a stalwart in good standing, as he had been these many years. Indeed, Thatcher recalled that Henry was chairman (emeritus) of the Committee on Appalachian Mountain Leadership and Safety, and had guided that body through a hotly fought revision of guidelines. Back in the early days before 1937, Henry, ax in hand, had been one of the pioneers in the field, venturing into uncharted and uncleared territories.

But in the last decade, a change had taken place. Henry accepted, and discharged with brilliant success, responsibility for the maintenance and marking of 3.6 miles of the Appalachian Trail (from Pepperton Gap to Lumley Crossing). This suzerainty had altered his values. His interest in the Appala-

chian Mountain Club had not abated, far from it. But his
view of self had shifted. From loyal club member, Henry had
become a potentate in his own right. The AMC, with 11,500
members, maintained three hundred and sixty miles of the
trail. Henry Morland maintained 3.6 miles. All things considered, he was inclined to feel that this left them just about
even.

Oh well, thought Thatcher, they knew Henry pretty well at
Joy Street.

"New Government Center over there," said the taxi driver,
morosely breaking the silence in the immobilized cab. Whatever else they were doing in the New Boston, they were not
abandoning a street grid resembling a plate of spaghetti.

Without much interest, Thatcher and Henry leaned forward
to inspect a nightmare of concrete stretching, as Henry put it,
in too many directions.

"Tables," said the driver bitterly.

Henry was, inevitably, curious.

"They got new tables in there," explained the driver, starting up Beacon Street with a crash of gears. "Cost seven hundred bucks each."

The Appalachian Mountain Club, although occupying an
ancient building across from the gold dome of Charles Bul-
finch's great State House, promised moral, physical and
spiritual distance from the New Boston.

Thatcher did not look forward to what was coming. Henry
never hared off unprepared. On the contrary, if he had a
fault along those lines, he overplanned. The trip from New
Hampshire to Logan had been spent, from Thatcher's point of
view, learning what Henry hoped to accomplish. Henry wanted
to learn more about the late Stephen Lester. To this end, he
proposed to talk first with young George Philips who had done
Mount Mansfield with Lester last summer and then with one
Harold Downes. At lunch Bradford Ogburn, noted geographer,
conservationist and AMC eminent, would be pumped.

"Then," Thatcher had commented caustically, "I suppose
you propose talking to Lester's secretary and his dentist."

He was alarmed by the effect of these words and reminded himself to curb his tongue. His role on this expedition was to brake Henry, not add fuel to the flames.

". . . real reliable," young Philips was earnestly explaining ten minutes later. "In fact—"

"Yes," said Henry alertly.

Philips looked around helplessly. "Well, for my money, he went by the book a little too much."

"A perfectionist?" asked Henry, himself a perfectionist.

George Philips was abashed and Thatcher took pity on him.

"I take it you mean that Lester was overly rigid."

Philips was better with rocks than with words. "That's it. He was a nice guy, you understand. But if things didn't go just the way he thought they should—well, he'd let you know about it. He was always laying down the law about one thing or another."

By now George Philips was profoundly unhappy. At a guess, Thatcher would say that he was a young man who liked to think well of people. Pressing him for unsavory details about a man now dead, was an unkindness.

It was not one from which Henry shrank.

"Made a lot of enemies, I suppose," he said. "Strange how I never noticed this assertiveness when I was on the committee with him."

Philips grinned at Henry.

"You didn't give him a chance to sound off," he pointed out. "Anyway, I don't say Lester made a lot of enemies. But he was the kind of guy who thought he was the only one who never made mistakes."

"If that doesn't make enemies," Thatcher remarked, "I don't know what does."

Philips was ingenuous. "People just shrug it off," he said. "Nobody bothers."

Somebody, Henry pointed out, had bothered.

But they had exhausted George Philips' meager supply of perceptive insights long before the phone told them that Harold Downes was waiting for them in the library.

"Now we'll really get some information," Henry said confidently as he bustled forward. "This is the man who sponsored Lester for membership. Said he'd known him for twelve years in the application."

But Harold Downes, while admitting the friendship, dashed Henry's hopes. First, he insisted on asking them questions.

"It was a shock, reading about the murder in the papers," he said, earnestly wagging his head. "I couldn't believe it was Steve they were talking about. You must know all about it, since you were there."

Decency required that they provide an abbreviated account of the murder of Stephen Lester. Henry, audibly champing, did his duty.

Harold Downes said he would never understand it, not if he lived to be a hundred. This was not as impressive a confession as it might have been. Downes's kindly, bewildered face made it clear that life presented him with unfathomable mysteries almost daily.

"I'd like to know about the funeral," he said soberly. "Alison and I want to attend, as a mark of respect."

Thatcher suggested that he call the Lester home in Weston for details. This was enough of an opening for Henry.

"That's the second Mrs. Lester out in Weston," he said pointedly. "But I guess you know all about that, having been a friend of Lester's for so many years."

Downes blinked uncertainly. "Well, I don't know that I'd say that," he said cautiously. "You see, I knew Steve when we were both students in Cambridge, graduate students, that is. We were in the Outing Club together. We saw a lot of each other in those days. But, of course, when he went out to the Coast, we lost touch. I hadn't heard from him in years when he called up one day and said he'd moved back East and wanted to join the Appalachian Club. I was glad to sponsor him. He'd been active in the Sierra Club in California, and worked on their conservation committee. And, of course, I remembered what a good rock climber he was—"

Henry moved to forestall yet another dissertation on Stephen Lester's excellence as a mountaineer.

"But then you must have known Lester during his first marriage," he said accusingly.

Downes was certainly anxious to oblige. He frowned harder than ever. "You know, when I was reading the story in the paper about the two wives, I was trying to remember about her. I think, in fact I'm almost sure, that I did meet her at one of the Club's Christmas parties."

"You mean you only met her once?" Henry was outraged.

Downes looked up in mild surprise. "That's right. She never came on any of our trips, or anything. I think she had a job and couldn't get away. Besides, Steve wasn't the type, you know."

Before Henry frightened his fish, Thatcher decided to take a hand. "I'm afraid we don't know, Mr. Downes. We never met Mr. Lester alive. What type wasn't he?"

Downes responded to gentler methods by displaying a surprising aptitude for social commentary. "With married students, one of two things happens. You understand, I'm talking about someone who gets married but moves in a crowd that's mostly unmarried. Either the guy goes domestic and his house becomes the natural clubhouse for gatherings—there's always a refrigerator full of food and drink and a comfortable living room and a wife who'll get out cheese and crackers—or else he keeps his marriage completely apart and comes out for a beer just like anyone else. Steve was like that. I don't think any of us were ever invited up to his place."

Henry obviously disapproved of this mode of life, but whether because it was hard on the wife at the time or because it was hard on the detective years later, Thatcher could not say.

"And you all accepted this?" Henry said sternly.

Downes was not one of nature's warriors. "What would you have expected us to do?" Then he shrugged. "But, hell, sure we accepted it. We didn't know anything about marriage.

I don't think I've ever thought about it until now. And, now, I'm a different person. I've been married for eight years. I've got three kids."

"So now it does seem odd. You don't think that's the way you'd treat your own wife."

Suddenly Downes grinned broadly.

"I'd like to see me trying. You don't know Alison."

En route to their luncheon engagement, Henry tried to summarize. He did it in one sentence.

"Nobody liked Lester."

"I don't think it's that straightforward, Henry. Nobody liked him, but nobody seems to have realized it."

"These outdoor types," said Henry with fine contempt. "You can't expect them to analyze their feelings."

Thatcher opted for diplomacy. "Certainly you have a point there. But I wonder if Lester may not have had some chameleon quality of his own. He seems to have had a talent for being accepted as the conventional norm in any group he moved into."

"It's simpler than that, John." Henry gave a short bark of laughter. "Lester just told everybody he was a man of high standards and they believed him."

But they were about to meet one man who had not.

Dr. Bradford Ogburn, who frequently lectured on Our Ascent of Everest or Twenty Days on Manga Pan, was more critical.

"No, I know you didn't notice, Henry, but Lester was basically not a good committee man. Oh yes, he did his homework but he was stubborn as sin. To be frank, he didn't know how to get along with people."

This cool assessment was made over lunch in the Men's Bar of Locke-Ober's. Ogburn had listened to the details of Lester's dramatic death without particular distress.

"Like him?" he replied to a broadside from Henry. "No, I

didn't particularly like him. That doesn't mean I hit him over the head, Henry. Believe me."

Henry may have believed him. At any rate he plunged into thought leaving Thatcher to make light conversation with Ogburn. It was heavy going.

Ogburn was a professional charmer, with one amusing anecdote after another. He was, Henry had revealed, unsurpassed at fund raising for many excellent causes, from conservation to scientific expeditions.

Oddly enough, he had many similarities to James Joel Finley.

After lunch, Ogburn excused himself as they set off down Winter Place. "Man and Mountain," he explained musically. It was yet another lecture, this time to the Radcliffe Alumnae Club of Brookline.

Henry was not, after all, immune to human atmosphere.

"Going downhill around here," he said, apparently observing in the tawdriness of Tremont Street portents of the decline and fall of the Appalachian Mountain Club. "But I liked young Philips."

Thatcher agreed. "I have never liked the thespian's approach to outdoor activities—"

He had lost his companion's erratic interest. Henry was checking his watch.

"Now what, Henry?" he asked resigned, he thought, for the worst.

Once again Henry surprised him.

12 SECOND GROWTH

HALF-DEFIANT, half-complacent, Henry proceeded to announce that he had seized an idle moment at Locke Ober's to phone Eunice Lester.

"She asked me to keep in touch. Wants to know how things are going, up in Fiord Haven," he ran on glibly. "It seemed like the right thing to do. Remember, John, she's a woman all alone."

Thatcher wished he could duplicate the noise with which Ruth Morland greeted such statements of high-mindedness.

Henry took a deep breath. "Anyway, I promised her we'd run right out to Arlington. Let's find ourselves a taxi."

"Henry!" Thatcher exploded. "Angling for information at the Appalachian Club is one thing. But this goes beyond the bounds of decency. You can't force yourself on Eunice Lester now. She's got enough problems."

"No, no!" Henry protested. "You've got it all wrong, John. Eunice answered the phone as if I were the cavalry coming to the rescue. She really wants us to come."

Thatcher examined him suspiciously. There was no doubt about Henry's sincerity. But how much of Henry's judgment was due to wishful thinking? Unfortunately, there was only one way to find out.

The drive to Arlington was enlivened by Henry's lurid conjectures about the cause of Eunice's current distress. Imminent arrest loomed large in his roster.

"The cops might be with her right now," he said, contemplating the possibility with pleasurable anticipation. "Though in that case, it's hard to see what she expects us to do."

Thatcher grunted skeptically. Eunice Lester had not impressed him as mentally deficient. And that's what it would take to introduce Henry into such a situation.

"Well, maybe not," said Henry, answering the spirit of the grunt. "But then there's always Amanda. Maybe the two of them are having a knock-down, drag-out fight."

"Then, it's even harder to see what she expects us to do." Thatcher's asperity was no longer veiled. "Unless we're supposed to pitch in on Eunice's side. In which case, I'll hold your coat."

Unabashed, Henry progressed to further flights of fancy, but Thatcher was no longer listening. According to the driver, they were now in the immediate vicinity of Eunice Lester's home. The problem was to find Forest Street.

Thatcher examined the neighborhood. The houses seemed to date from the turn of the century. Most of them were straggling two-story frame structures with complicated roofs and wide porches. Their owners seemed too poor to hire badly needed painters and masons. But they were not too poor to be respectable. The yards were neatly raked and the trash cans disciplined. Care and attention had been lavished on shrubberies and flower borders. Eunice Lester's house, finally located, was a model in this respect. Dark shingle walls formed a background for gleaming windows and bright marigolds.

On the porch they found two bells, the upper marked: Mrs. Eunice Lester. Henry's heroic ring produced an immediate answering click which unlocked the front door. As they entered the front hall, their hostess was bending over the banister.

"Come right up!" she called. "I was hoping that was you."

One look was enough to prove that Henry had not been fantasying. Eunice was indeed glad to see them. She ushered them into her living room. A man rose from a chair, the last man that Thatcher expected to see.

"Mr. Quinlan is just leaving," Eunice said firmly, preventing any round of greetings.

Eddie Quinlan shrugged good-naturedly. He even seemed amused. "Sure, Mrs. Lester. I don't want to intrude while you have Mr. Morland and Mr. Thatcher here. But you'll remember what I said?"

"Absolutely," Eunice replied, handing him his hat.

For an apostle of the hard sell, Quinlan proved surprisingly easy to evict. Within minutes Eunice had shown him out.

"Thank God you came," she said, returning. "I never would have gotten rid of him otherwise. And I don't know what he's up to. I don't know what any of them are up to. It's as if everybody is part of some scheme except—"

She stopped, aghast at the sound of her own voice rising out of control.

There could be no denying that, with Eunice, Henry never put a foot wrong. Totally ignoring her outburst, he slowly looked at his surroundings, then turned to say, "You've got a nice place here. I like the way you've fixed it up."

Eunice was momentarily startled. Then her face softened into a smile. She, too, looked around, as if drawing support from the home she had made.

"I'm glad you like it, Henry. I did most of it myself."

Henry's observation had some merit, aside from the strictly therapeutic. The room had dormer windows and sloping ceilings in the corners. But there was no sense of constraint. White wallpaper with an airy green trellis design had been used everywhere; there were crisp white curtains, and the nondescript furniture had been slipcovered in a green and white print. Everything was spanking clean. The room radiated gaiety and good cheer.

"Oh, Henry," Eunice cried impulsively, "I'm so glad you're here. I'll go mad if I don't talk to somebody."

Thatcher fully appreciated the smug glance that Henry cast him. If anybody was entitled to take bows at the moment, it was Henry.

Eunice, suddenly remembering her duties, made offers of hospitality. Hastily declining for the two of them, Henry masterfully thrust Eunice into a chair.

"What did Quinlan want?" he asked baldly.

A sudden thought occurred to Thatcher. "Good God, the man's not trying to sell you a lot *now*, is he?"

Eunice shook her head. "No, he's not doing that. He never so much as mentioned Fiord Haven. That was one of the peculiar things about him."

This unsatisfactory speech raised more questions than it answered. But Henry controlled himself and waited for Eunice to continue.

"All I can tell you is what he said," she began hesitantly. "According to him, he was helping Amanda when she was getting ready to leave Fiord Haven. They were having some kind of discussion about moving the body. Does that make sense to you?"

Both men nodded. It was reasonable that Stephen Lester should be buried somewhere other than New Hampshire.

"All right," Eunice went on. "That part seemed all right to me, too. But then Amanda said something about Steve having died without a will. So she would be executor or administrator or whatever it is, because she was his sole heir. Then according to Mr. Quinlan, he told her that couldn't be right. She couldn't be Steve's only heir because Steve left a child."

"Ah ha!" said Henry happily. "Who benefits?"

Eunice seemed capable of taking Henry's aberrant enthusiasms in stride. "Now that sounds perfectly crazy to me."

Thatcher was genuinely startled. That was no way for the mother of a ten-year-old son to talk. "It makes perfectly good sense," he objected. "Even if there were a will, the existence of a minor child—"

"No," Eunice interrupted unceremoniously, "that's not what I mean. Of course it makes sense. In fact," she paused to smile ruefully at them, "I thought of it right off. But it didn't seem like a healthy subject to mention to the New Hampshire police."

Thatcher's original impression was confirmed. Eunice Lester was no fool.

"Then what *is* crazy?" he persisted.

"The way Quinlan is behaving," Eunice answered roundly. "He swears this little piece of information just slipped out. Then, when he saw the effect it had on Amanda, he thought it his duty to race around to me and offer his apologies and support."

"Support?"

"For a minute I thought he was just touting for legal business. He is a lawyer, after all. Now I wonder if he isn't trying to stir things up."

"You have a point," Thatcher agreed. "But of course, Amanda would have found out in time, anyway."

Eunice nodded energetically. "Oh, I know she would have. Indeed I would have had to bring it to her attention. But in a natural sequence, if you know what I mean. I would have gotten a lawyer. Amanda would have, too. Then the lawyers would have gotten together. Nothing would have happened for weeks or months. Instead Quinlan is throwing himself into things. Do you think he could be trying to get back at Amanda?"

"Why does he want to get back at her?" Henry demanded. "What's she done to him?"

"I don't think he was very happy about the way she denied Steve bought a lot. Of course she backed down, when she heard Quinlan's story. He probably didn't realize she was just being spiteful to me. He may have thought she was a chronic troublemaker, and he couldn't resist the temptation to toss a little trouble her way." Eunice sighed unhappily. "Oh, how I wish he hadn't interfered. Whatever he had in mind, he's just going to end up making things harder for me."

Thatcher sympathized with Eunice's reaction, but he wanted to clear up an earlier statement. "Let's go back a minute," he suggested. "You say Amanda lied simply in a malicious attempt to throw suspicion on you. You don't think she might have more substantial reasons for diverting police attention?"

Eunice's eyes widened. "You mean because she murdered Steve herself?"

"Well, somebody did," Thatcher reminded her.

Eunice was not the crisp businesswoman she had been at Fiord Haven. Partly it was because her severe suit had been replaced by slacks and a shirt, partly it was because she was confused and permitting herself to show it. At the moment, she might have been as young as Amanda.

"It just doesn't make sense," she said at last, frowning in concentration. "I still can't believe Steve has actually been murdered. It's so unreasonable. But I'll tell you the police are right about one thing. He must have been killed in a burst of exasperation."

Henry arched his eyebrows in silent protest. Eunice defended her statement. "Oh, I know that sounds impossible. But exasperation was the kind of emotion Steve aroused. To the *nth* degree."

"And the logical person to be exasperated by someone is his wife," Thatcher said. "Isn't that so?"

"Not Amanda." Eunice sounded regretful but sure. "In fact, that's one of the reasons Amanda gets to me the way she does. I was having trouble with Steve within six weeks of our wedding. I couldn't take that habit of his of making high and mighty moral judgments about everyone else—while he did exactly what he pleased. He was driving me up a wall long before he walked out on me. Then I saw him doing exactly the same sort of thing to Amanda, and it didn't ruffle her a bit. She's destroyed an illusion of mine. I liked to think that no woman could live in peace with Steve. And goddamit, there she was, pulling off the trick without batting an eyelash."

Thatcher, while reminding himself to relay this information to Ruth to help broaden her view of the first-wife–second-wife relationship, was moved to protest.

"Come now, there's some difference in your positions, isn't there?"

Eunice thought she understood. "You mean, there's nothing like money for sweetening the temper? I admit that Steve got under my skin most of all when I came home from work after stopping at the market. While I was making dinner, he'd lean back and tell me how worried he was about the atom bomb. Or, how he was having a crisis of conscience about being in a university with defense contracts. He never had a crisis of conscience about letting me do the dishes. Okay, when he married Amanda, he was a self-supporting adult with a good salary. I think you're suggesting I have a petty mind, and I won't admit it."

"That wasn't exactly what I had in mind," Thatcher corrected her. "I meant that Amanda wasn't committed to anything except her husband yet. She hadn't undertaken any of the adult major responsibilities, primarily children, where she might have found herself in conflict with him. She could afford to be good-natured and tolerant."

Henry shifted restlessly. "I don't like the way this conversation is going," he confessed. "If you cross Amanda off, who's left? Eunice, that's who. Just because of those big, adult responsibilities, like children."

"I didn't kill Steve. The only time I was ever likely to was when I was living with him. That's when people really exasperate you."

"Not when they try to take your child away?" Henry asked with what Thatcher regarded as foolhardy courage. But Eunice did not go up in flames.

"That didn't exasperate me. That made me mad as hell. Mad enough to do something about it. It was Steve all over. A lot of talk about the best interests of the child, coupled with a total avoidance of his son until he had some use for him."

Thatcher hoped that Eunice's indulgence didn't operate exclusively for Henry. "What could you do? I gather that your husband had acquired some damning information about you. You, yourself, said he was single-minded, regardless of cost, when he wanted something."

Eunice lost her look of youth. "You weren't listening very carefully. Steve was regardless of the cost to others. He was always mindful of any cost to Stephen Lester. He attacked me by playing the odds. He knew it was unlikely I would remain absolutely virtuous for ten years. Well, I played the odds, too."

Henry shook his head dubiously. "You mean Steve was unmarried for seven years? But courts don't pay much attention to that, do they?"

Eunice's answer came as a surprise. "I didn't waste any time on Steve. Amanda was in college four years ago. When she first met Steve they were both part of a swinging crowd. Two months ago I hired detectives to investigate Amanda. And I told them exactly what I wanted. Any record on any police blotter anywhere, particularly with reference to smoking pot."

Henry was a little shocked and did not trouble to conceal it. Thatcher, on the other hand, was moved to admiration.

"Yes, indeed," he said. "You were playing the odds. Did you get anything?"

"She was at a party that was raided for smoking marijuana. It would have been enough. For a corporate executive, that is. Steve's public image didn't include a drug addict for a wife."

Henry's voice was stern. "That girl? She's no more a drug addict than I am!"

"Of course not!" Eunice snapped impatiently. "She probably smoked one joint in her life. But, then, I'm not a streetwalker either. I wasn't concerned with winning a court battle. I can't afford one. But I knew my Steve. If there were likely to be any casualties on his side, he wouldn't be interested in fighting. He'd forget about Tommy and start thinking about adopting."

Thatcher could not help feeling that Amanda would have been out of her depth in any confrontation between Eunice and Stephen Lester. Although, he suddenly remembered, not one of the many witnesses to their encounter at Fiord Haven had described Amanda as outclassed.

He awoke to discover a plot in the making.

"You could find out, couldn't you, Henry? If you went to see Amanda yourself?" Eunice was definitely up to something. There was a roguish gleam in her eye.

Thatcher, seeing Henry sit forward alertly, quickly intervened, "Why should we go see Amanda?"

Now Eunice was openly cajoling. "Because you understand about wills and estates. Oh, I know I'll have to put my lawyer on to this eventually. But it would be wonderful if Amanda and I could agree not to fight about this. You could give her your advice, couldn't you?"

Henry burst into speech.

Publicly, Thatcher would later claim that he had yielded to the two-pronged blitzkreig launched by Eunice and Henry. But, as Miss Corsa could have predicted, it was his own curiosity that hooked him.

He had, he discovered, one small question of his own for Amanda Lester.

13 ROOT AND BRANCH

It is a long way from Arlington, Massachusetts, to Weston, in more ways than one.

"About twenty miles," the driver had told Thatcher and Henry.

The streetcar suburbs fell behind. The car sped out the Massachusetts Turnpike in the direction of one-acre zoning. And it became clear that twenty miles was delivering them to another world.

Five minutes off the turnpike and they were on a tree-lined lane, winding through a carefully contrived rural scene past very large homes. Most of them were postwar colonial, flaunting costly appendages to the austere architectural form once hallowed by plain living and high thinking.

The street number of the Lester home was proclaimed in black wrought iron. A gas light guarded the long driveway.

"Well," said Thatcher when they had debouched onto a flagstone walk, "now we know the reason for that ruthless determination to get custody of a child only Eunice seems to have wanted before."

"Yes?" said Henry.

Thatcher indicated their surroundings. "The photographic effect, Henry. You remember, Eunice said the same thing. This setting calls for a large dog and children, as well as a station wagon and a GE kitchen."

"Don't forget the Porsche, too," said Henry grumpily. He followed Thatcher's gaze. "It's sure a far cry from that dump in Arlington."

Thatcher reminded himself of Henry's fatal tendency to wax fiercely partisan in any controversy. It was not going to make this visit any easier.

An overweight golden retriever, lying on the porch, blinked incuriously at them. The owner of The Pepper Mill studied the brass doorknocker before he let it sound.

"Cheap reproduction," he muttered. "I'll bet they paid plenty for it."

Thatcher wished that he, himself, were as incurious as the dog. But he was beginning to follow the bad example being set by Henry. There was, in the first place, the question of how Amanda was reacting to the suggestion that ten-year-old Tommy Lester had certain rights. Amanda, no doubt, had always thought that the Lester worldly goods were provided by Providence for her comfort. Whether her husband was dead or alive.

Then too, Thatcher was wondering about Henry's immediate tactics. The jaunt to Arlington had been camouflaged in a socially acceptable way—by sympathy for Eunice who shared Henry's status as police suspect and who had other claims on his compassion.

But Henry was now going to be hoist by his own petard. He had been much moved by Eunice Lester's lot in life.

Just how would a partisan—and transparent—Henry behave here in Weston?

But when the door was opened by a youthfully middle-aged man, it became clear that Thatcher was not destined to see Henry's response to this challenge. The play had already begun. He and Henry were, for the time being, only latecomers in the audience.

For audience there was. Eunice Lester might be alone in the world. Amanda was surrounded by supporters. In the round of introductions, Thatcher identified Amanda's father, who had opened the door for them, and Amanda's mother, who was a slightly blurred version of her daughter. Two other men sat on the sofa near the fieldstone fireplace. They looked like official mourners: Thatcher deduced they were lawyers. Reasons for the dourness were not slow to emerge. Amanda was having trouble with her retinue.

". . . but of course I understand what you said about Steve not leaving a will," she assured the sofa emphatically. "What difference does that make? Steve didn't want her to have his money. He meant for me to have it."

This reasonableness touched something obscure in Amanda's mother.

"Of course he did, darling," she said lovingly. "When I think of how happy you both were˙ when you were building this beautiful house together . . ."

Amanda kept her guns trained elsewhere.

"So, you'll have to do something about it."

The sofa dwellers, a Mr. Clive and a Mr. Plassey it developed, listened to these commands with admirable self-control. There was, Thatcher reflected, something about the Boston legal profession lacking in New York. That cod-like look of frozen suffering was not something you saw everywhere.

Mr. Clive, carefully ignoring Mr. Plassey, leaned forward.

"As we explained to you earlier, Mrs. Lester—"

Mrs. Lester tossed her head. "Explanations? You explained why you weren't going to do anything. Even after I told you what Steve really wanted. All you say is that you can't do anything. Don't they, Daddy? There must be something to do. This isn't fair."

Daddy, otherwise Mr. Trainor, was torn. On the one hand, a man among men, he had to deprecate such feminine illogic. On the other hand, he, too, did not think it was fair. He cleared his throat and, in a grave baritone, said:

"Now Mandy, honey, don't get yourself upset—not on top of everything else."

Amanda set her jaw.

Her father turned to the lawyers. "But, Clive, I admit I don't see why we don't have a strong case. After all, Amanda *is* the widow. Steve hadn't seen these other people for years."

"Oh dear, it's all so terrible." Amanda's mother lapsed into gentle sniffing and dabbed at her eyes. It was not emotional abandon but it was too much for Amanda. She jumped to her feet to get a cigarette from the small china cup on the mantle. If she had said it aloud, it could not have been more emphatic: "Oh, Mother!"

"There, there, Rosemary," said Mr. Trainor, patting Rosemary's shoulder.

The lawyers surveyed the whole Trainor family with impartial hostility.

Mr. Plassey, it seemed, had a shorter fuse than Mr. Clive. He eschewed the *As I have explained before* road.

"It is certainly very unfortunate," he said, closing his briefcase with a snap that made Thatcher wonder how long this consultation had been going on, "that Mr. Lester neglected to take the precaution of making a will."

"Better than vaudeville," whispered Henry. For Mr. and Mrs. Trainor, as well as Amanda, took immediate exception to Plassey's words.

"I certainly do not think this is the time to be criticizing," said Mrs. Trainor.

"How could Steve imagine that that woman was going to go crazy?" Amanda blazed out.

"In the prime of life," said Mr. Trainor meaninglessly but firmly.

Both lawyers were human enough to glance involuntarily toward Thatcher and Henry. Then, glassy-eyed with control, they launched into a duet clearly performed at least once before.

". . . confer with Mrs. Lester's attorneys on Monday morning . . ."

"Possible compromise settlement . . ."

"I will not compromise with that woman," said Amanda awfully.

"Look at their expressions," said Henry softly.

Thatcher had to do so quickly.

Clive and Passey rose as one, delivered another round of instant counsel, then, with more haste than is usual, withdrew.

They were probably not yet out of earshot, when Amanda spoke.

"Daddy, I'm going to get new lawyers."

"Now, baby," he said, looking over his shoulder to be sure that the door had shut.

Fortunately, at this juncture, Mrs. Trainor relapsed into her decorative sorrow.

Mr. Trainor, the picture of masculine protectiveness, bowed his head over hers, then indicated to Amanda that he would take charge. He led his wife solicitously from the room. Was it base, Thatcher wondered, to suspect that the Trainors, like others, found Amanda rather overpowering?

Among those others, he decided, he could number himself. About Henry he had no real doubts.

"It is all so unfair," Amanda said, virtually ignoring her family's retreat. "That woman—"

"You mean Mrs. Eunice Lester?" Henry interjected.

The lovely young face hardened.

"Yes, I mean that bitch Eunice!"

In a world of four letter words, it is no novelty to hear young women use language that would have called forth apologies from their grandfathers. Thatcher was quite certain that Henry, who after all dealt with the public at large, regularly heard far worse. Nevertheless, he was not surprised to see Henry immediately become an eminent divine.

"Now Mrs. Lester," he said, more in sorrow than in anger.

But Henry miscalculated. Amanda Lester never played audience to anybody else. Ignoring the Vicar of Wakefield, she said, "And—I just realized! That explains it." Suddenly her eyes shone with excitement. "When the police find out about this . . ."

Caught between Henry, gathering steam, and a woman obsessed, Thatcher felt bound to intervene.

"The police probably already know about your husband's estate," he said.

"Are you sure?"

There was a hungry note in Amanda's voice that caused Henry to mutter something under his breath. Hurriedly, Thatcher tried to lead her away from this topic.

"I should think so, Mrs. Lester. Now, we don't wish to keep you from . . . er . . . your own concerns. We have intruded at this time simply to ask you about one small point. Your husband had an exchange of words with James Joel Finley. It's a minor thing—but we were wondering if you knew anything about it."

"That's right," said Henry, who had forgotten all about Alec Prohack in the light of later developments.

Amanda, too, had forgotten. "James Joel Finley?" she repeated, not recognizing the name.

Understandably enough, thought Thatcher. James Joel Finley, Fiord Haven, indeed the whole distant world before Stephen Lester's murder, could now seem very remote.

Except for the fact that Amanda Lester was not visibly numbed by her loss. If she was in the grip of any emotion, Thatcher was not convinced that it was grief.

"Oh, you mean that architect up *there*," she said after a moment or two. "I don't really know. Steve did say something about the roof up at that lodge. I wasn't really paying much attention—"

Henry momentarily put aside his colors as champion of Eunice and became Yankee sleuth, pure and simple. "You see," he said earnestly, "witnesses have informed the police that Finley and your husband had a quarrel of some sort. Naturally, you can understand why we—they—want to track it down if we can—"

Amanda had put her money elsewhere.

Bluntly, and quite honestly, Thatcher thought, she said, "But why on earth would anybody quarrel over a roof? That's just silly."

Quite suddenly, Amanda seemed exhausted. Exhausted, in fact, to the point of incapacity. With a quick signal, Thatcher kept Henry from continuing and indicated the desirability of departure.

Amanda saw them to the door in some private fog, that did not altogether blanket her automatic responses to Henry's courtesies. But even allowing for great emotional strain, thought Thatcher as they strode back to the car, it was striking how indifferent Amanda Lester seemed to everything concerning her husband's death. Everything, that is, except Eunice.

"All right, all right," said Henry forthrightly when they were once again car-borne. "I apologize. It was a waste of time. I admit it. And damned unpleasant, to boot."

"Oh I don't know," said Thatcher slowly.

Henry turned to glare at him. "Good God, John! That selfish, cold-hearted—when I think of a woman like that trying to take Eunice's boy—well, words fail me."

"I agree that it was unpleasant," said Thatcher, reflecting it was unlikely that words would ever fail Henry. "I meant that it may not have been a waste of time."

There was silence while Henry digested this. Finally, finishing his review of the preceding hour, he said: "Exactly what do you mean by that?"

There are times when it is politic to dissimulate. So Thatcher was not being evasive when he tailored his reply.

"Among other things, Henry, this roof business. If Lester argued with Finley about a roof—well, I, for one, think it might bear looking into."

Henry was projecting hopefulness.

Thatcher continued. "As long as we're down here, it might not do any harm to see Fiord Haven's Boston operation. I think it might be useful to talk with Quinlan about James Joel Finley—among other things."

"That's the spirit!" Henry applauded.

As Thatcher had feared, Henry thought he had recruited an ally.

14 WAVING PALMS

IF ANYBODY stood in need of allies, it was Charlie Trinkam. Charlie, who took charge of the sixth floor of the Sloan Guaranty Trust during Thatcher's absences, was currently beleaguered.

The State Banking Commission had forwarded a second communication to the Sloan; the stock market was seesawing up and down wildly; the air conditioning of the Sloan's magnificent new temple on Exchange Place had developed a kink during one of New York's brutal autumn heat waves.

Even Charlie, a congenital optimist, had to concede that the situation was deteriorating.

While inadequate fans blew documents off desks, the trust officers were showing the strain. Their combativeness was no less exacerbating for remaining perfectly polite.

". . . now Chet, the way I read the situation, there's a possibility of a sixty percent drop in GGB . . ."

". . . no, Mrs. Sibley. We are not recommending major portfolio shifts . . ."

Unfortunately, here and there, politeness cracked.

"Now let's face facts, Bowman," said Ingersoll in an unwise assault on the research department. "Your earnings estimate for Gloman's is way off. Have you seen what *Barrons* says?"

Walter Bowman, enormous in shirt sleeves, resembled an outraged Kodiak bear.

"Way off? Let me tell you—"

Charlie had barely left the ensuing arbitration session when he was waylaid.

Everett Gabler, tie in place, coat buttoned and impervious to temperature, was a living rebuke to his disheveled colleagues.

". . . said it once, and I shall say it again."

"What was that, Ev?" asked Charlie, insincerely responsive.

Everett was at his bleakest. "The State Banking Commission," he said icily. "You have seen the latest questionnaire, I trust?"

Charlie groaned to himself. "Sure, I've seen it, Ev. I can't waste time on routine. I've been pretty busy trying to figure out what's up with the market. You know, according to the random-walk boys—"

Everett Gabler was not interested in the random-walk boys. "I don't believe I can agree that it is routine," he said. "I feel strongly that we should discuss the entire matter."

"Sure, sure," said Charlie, swallowing other retorts. The next forty-five minutes were not made easier for him by Everett's open contempt for the fans and iced drinks showing how Charlie had knuckled under to the environment.

When Charlie entered John Thatcher's office a little later, he felt entitled to relax.

"Whew!" he said, settling himself in a chair. "I feel like a lion tamer."

Miss Corsa waited for something more specific.

"Still, we may get through the day without anybody actually taking a punch at anybody else," said Charlie brightening as he always did. "I defy John to do better. Rose, do we have any idea when they're going to get that air conditioning working?"

Miss Corsa, ignoring allusions to Mr. Thatcher and to fisticuffs at the Sloan, was cooperative about the common enemy. The Sloan's maintenance engineer reported that a flaw in a duct had been located and would be repaired by morning. Then, since she was only human, she added that the U.S. Weather Bureau predicted that the heat wave would break some eight hours earlier.

"Naturally," said Charlie. "Just pray that the market doesn't break, too. You said that John called? Where is he? I thought he was far, far away—on some mountain or other."

Miss Corsa had no information on Mr. Thatcher's where-abouts. "But," she went on, "he told me to ask you and Mr. Bowman for some details."

Meticulously she consulted her dictation book, and Charlie listened to a hodgepodge of items that Mr. Thatcher would like the staff to check: there were inquiries for banks in California; there were the names of New York specialists in second-home building; there were legal opinions concerning the custody laws of the Commonwealth of Massachusetts.

"I'll start rounding things up," said Charlie good-naturedly. "But what do you think he wants them for?"

Miss Corsa could have made a good guess, but she did not feel it her place to do so. Charlie continued:

"Of course there was that trouble up in New Hampshire, wasn't there?"

"Yes," said Miss Corsa. News of Stephen Lester's murder had filtered down to the Sloan, but not enough to give it much prominence.

"I thought John and this Henry Morland only stuck around long enough to call the police," Charlie muttered, studying his notes. "Oh well, maybe John just got interested. After all, what else can you do when you're tramping through the woods? He probably just wants something to pass the time. I'll see what I can dig up, Rose . . ."

Charlie left behind him a deeply suspicious Miss Corsa. Like everybody else at the Sloan, Miss Corsa respected Mr. Thatcher's passion for factual minutia and had interpreted his telephone message in that spirit.

But the picture Mr. Trinkam painted brought her to her senses. Experience had taught Miss Corsa it was highly unlikely that Mr. Thatcher would be tramping away from anything that interested him.

Mr. Thatcher, of course, was not tramping through the woods. He was alighting from a cab in Kenmore Square, Boston.

While Henry engaged in complex severance pay negotiations with the cabby, Thatcher inspected his surroundings. Kenmore Square, like most of downtown Boston, had been affected by two great forces. Affluence was evidenced by new façades on old buildings, by a large glass and concrete motor-hotel, by boutiques and coffeehouses. Yesterday's baby boom, however, had produced the streams of college students now surging in and out of the vast Bauhaus compounds of Boston University.

"Highway robbery," reported Henry cheerfully, as the taxi pulled away.

"Literally or figuratively?" Thatcher inquired, but Henry, hot on the trail, did not dissipate energy.

"There it is," he said, hurling himself across waves of miniskirts, blue jeans, long hair, and sandals.

Obediently, Thatcher followed. NORTHERN LAND DEVELOPMENT CORPORATION proclaimed a sign in one of the many stores, six steps down. Its immediate neighbors were a liquor store and something called Uhuru, Inc., which seemed to specialize in objects made of wicker, leather or polystyrene—or some combination of the three.

FIORD HAVEN said a magenta and saffron poster. A NEW CONCEPT IN COUNTRY LIVING.

Next to it was a large-scale model of YOUR VACATION DREAM HOME, cross-sectioned so that one could study the cathedral-ceilinged living room, the fur rugs, the freestanding fireplace. It was furnished down to a ski rack in the hallway complete with skis.

Finally, there was an enormous photographic mural with four panels: MAGIC SEASONS AT FIORD HAVEN.

But Henry was not the man to linger over imaginative renderings of SUMMER FUN ON FIORD LAKE, or WINTRY WONDER AT FIORD MOUNTAIN. He trotted down the stairs, and Thatcher followed him into an office which consisted of six desks, each deep in brochures and folders. The occupants of each desk were either scanning lists, typing furiously or hunching over a telephone.

The young woman nearest them abandoned her typewriter to look up inquiringly.

"Is Mr. Quinlan available?" Henry began. He discovered that informality reigned at Northern Land Development as insistently as at Fiord Haven.

"Phil!" the young woman called to a neighbor. "Is Eddie back from the Sheraton yet?"

Phil cupped a hand over the phone. "Yeah," he said. "Got back while you were getting coffee. Yes indeed, Mrs. Bell. No, of course there is absolutely no obligation. We just want you and Mr. Bell to see . . ."

The young woman pointed to the rear of the room. "That's Eddie's door," she informed them before returning to her work.

Fortunately, before Thatcher and Henry could debate the propriety of marching in unannounced and possibly unwelcome, the door opened. Eddie Quinlan himself appeared.

"Say, Frank, has anybody double-checked with the hotel about honoring the parking tickets? We don't want to have anybody charged for parking tonight the way they were last August—"

"I just fixed that up, Eddie," said a voice from behind Thatcher and Henry.

Ralph Valenti had entered on their heels. He pumped hands, then led the way.

"Be with you in a minute," said Quinlan who was bending over the desk and studying a much penciled chart. "Better arrange to have another table available if we should need it, Max."

Valenti hung his coat on a rack and gestured his guests into the inner office. It was a spartan affair of table-desks, a sofa, a large round conference table, and colorful FIORD HAVEN posters on the walls. A wastebasket near them bristled with rolls of blueprints.

"Eddie," Valenti said as Quinlan joined them, "before I forget. The Davidsons are coming tonight."

Quinlan grinned. "We're going to end up feeding those kids forever. Maybe she hasn't learned how to cook yet."

Valenti, settling himself across from their guests, was serious. "Remember, we did decide to invite repeaters to our big night at the Prudential Center. Of course, only if they're really good prospects for Fiord Haven . . ."

"Okay, okay," said Quinlan.

By now, both Henry and Thatcher realized that their descent had coincided with one of Fiord Haven's non-stop promotional efforts. A question from Henry gave them the dimensions; two hundred prospects—this time invited on the basis of safe-deposit boxes in selected Boston banks, Eddie having a nephew in the commissioner's office—were to be Fiord Haven's guests at dinner tonight, in the Sheraton Hotel at the Prudential Center.

". . . and after dinner," Valenti finished, "we're showing a new film we've just got. Eddie, did you get Sid to run it for you?"

Eddie nodded. "Great," he said.

Valenti agreed. "Sid's got a lot of talent."

Neither Quinlan nor Valenti was curious about their visitors, and Thatcher knew why. This whirlwind of details to be checked, of arrangements to be made and, above all, of people to be contacted, was no last-minute push. It was the way business was regularly done at Northern Land Development. Tomorrow would see no letdown; the phones would still be ringing, as the one on Quinlan's desk was ringing now. The young men outside would be going over other lists, making other calls. What with dinners and films, with weekends and ads, time cost more at Fiord Haven than at most places.

This was a pace John Thatcher had seen in other operations. He was not hidebound enough to think that the Sloan's was the only way to do business. So, he did not conclude, as many of his Wall Street colleagues would have, that this was commercially suspect. Hard sells and strong pitches have earned a bad name, but Thatcher could list many respectable and profitable firms—from encyclopedia publishers to mutual funds —that relied on them.

It was, however, a way of doing business that left Quinlan and Valenti with no time and no inclination to ask themselves why Thatcher and Morland were intruding themselves on this assembly line. They had too many other claims on their attention.

"Feldman," Quinlan reported as he left the phone. "The Rentners have just signed."

"Good!" cried Valenti.

Thatcher would have liked to have known how many of Fiord Haven's lots were sold. But, he thought, he was more likely to get a realistic answer from one of Charlie Trinkam's contacts than from either of these frenetic promoters.

Henry felt no qualms. "Did you sell any lots to the crowd at Fiord Haven the weekend they found Lester's body?"

"Not so far," said Quinlan with that sardonic smile. "There were a lot of second thoughts."

Valenti did not enjoy gallows humor. "The Davidson couple," he said, almost vehement, "they're really interested."

The partners were strongly contrasted, Thatcher thought, as Henry finally launched into an intricate explanation of their interest in James Joel Finley. Quinlan was the man equipped by nature to sell. He had a taut air that was not, Thatcher would guess, the result of business pressures. Fiord Haven kept him busy, on the phone, planning, scheming, persuading—but Thatcher's impression was that he would be doing just that anyway.

Valenti was something else again. Unlike Quinlan, he did not evince nervous exhilaration. He was tired and, when tired, he became depressed behind his mask of easy cheer. It cost him an effort to keep his attention concentrated on the task of selling Fiord Haven. He did it because success would make him rich. And, Thatcher suspected, he might become one of the many rich men who discover they have sacrificed too much for wealth.

". . . discussion between Lester and Finley," Henry was saying with elaborate nonchalance. "Something about the roof . . ."

A troubled look between Quinlan and Valenti indicated that he had touched a sensitive spot.

Speaking with clipped care, Quinlan said, "I'm not sure that the police want us to talk about that, Mr. Morland."

Henry dismissed this. "The police told me all about it," he said, conveniently forgetting it had been Alec Prohack, not the police. But, since it was Prohack who had probably informed the police, it no doubt all came to the same thing in Henry's mind. And Thatcher was not sure that he was far wrong at that.

Quinlan was still frowning in thought. Valenti, however, was not a man to keep his own counsel. He made an indeterminate, unhappy sound. Thatcher thought that a nudge would do it.

"Tell me, have they resumed work on your lodge yet?" he asked.

Valenti looked even unhappier and, for once, there was no smile on Quinlan's face as he replied, "You know just as much as we do."

Having let down his guard, he continued, "I don't know what the hell it means. First, Finley's suddenly got to make some changes, so all the work gets held up. Then somebody tells this story about Lester chewing him out because of the roof."

"What is the matter with the roof?" Henry interrupted to ask.

"Finley wanted to make some design changes," Valenti answered vaguely.

Eddie Quinlan was not vague. "Nothing's the matter with it," he said with a snap. "We sent a construction engineer up to Fiord Haven this morning to make sure."

A nasty implication, Thatcher thought. Ralph Valenti still intended to defend Fiord Haven and everyone associated with it.

"The police are crazy," he said. "James Joel Finley is a world-famous architect. He couldn't—"

Eddie Quinlan's defensive instincts were more finely-honed.

"James Joel Finley isn't Fiord Haven. And Fiord Haven is guaranteeing that everything built up there is first-class."

Unspoken was his corollary: If James Joel Finley had anything to do with Stephen Lester's murder, that was his problem, not Fiord Haven's.

Henry did not leave things hanging. "How much would you be hurt if Finley is implicated?"

This bluntness made poor Valenti choke. Quinlan only smiled and said, "It would hurt. We've featured James Joel Finley in all our promotion. And hell—this has got to be some mix-up. To show you what we think—well, Finley's coming to the dinner tonight. But, in the last analysis, if worst comes to worst—well, Fiord Haven isn't selling because of any architect."

This cool optimism depressed Valenti still further.

He struggled to remain as detached as Quinlan. "Do you know if the police seriously suspect Finley?" he asked Henry.

Henry was not quick enough off the mark.

Once again, Quinlan's guard slipped. "Ralph," he said, "forget about what the police are doing. They can take care of their business, and we should concentrate on ours—which is Fiord Haven."

"I know, I know," Valenti said, troubled. "But I can't help worrying."

"I know it's not easy," Quinlan said. "Hell, I'm just as bad as you are. This afternoon, when we've got a million things to do, I went out of my way to try to help Mrs. Lester." He glanced at Thatcher and Morland, including them in his comment. "And it was a mistake. A waste of time. So I've learned my lesson. None of this is our business. The police will take care of it—and we'll go on selling Fiord Haven."

Before they could see if Valenti had been convinced, the phone rang again. A young woman opened the door and demanded an instant decision about radio spots on WHDH.

"You see what I mean?" Quinlan said.

The selling effort of Fiord Haven had a momentum of its own. Thatcher and Henry withdrew.

Kenmore Square was a riot of snarled traffic and bad-tempered jaywalkers. Henry ignored both.

"Do you believe that?" he asked in a conspiratorial tone. "That Quinlan was just trying to help Eunice?"

He was disappointed when Thatcher replied temperately that he did not know.

"And as for forgetting about the murder . . ." Henry continued with scorn.

"If Quinlan and Valenti can forget about the murder," Thatcher agreed, "then they will be the only ones who can."

15 GROUND COVER

THATCHER AND Henry set off on foot for the Ritz where they had reserved rooms for the night.

Henry, engaged in internal struggle, remained silent. Thatcher was not surprised. Henry had come gallivanting down from New Hampshire with high hopes of unmasking Lester's murderer. By now those hopes had been dashed.

"I suppose," said Henry suddenly, "that we should take Quinlan's advice ourselves."

Thatcher abandoned the scenery on Commonwealth Avenue for his companion.

"I mean," said Henry doggedly, "we should probably forget about the murder. Get back up to the Trail."

"This doesn't sound like you, Henry," said Thatcher cautiously.

"It's simply a matter of will power," said Henry with dignity. "I shall put the matter entirely from my mind."

And, for the rest of the afternoon, he did.

James Joel Finley was not so fortunate. He would have given his eye teeth to forget Stephen Lester and Fiord Haven. But it was not possible. Even while Henry and Thatcher were strolling back to the Ritz, Finley was descending on the premises of Northern Land Development.

His initial reception was flattering. James Joel Finley was the nearest thing to distinction ever to have visited that office and he commanded the devotion of the entire clerical staff. Like acolytes, young girls swarmed around him ready to anticipate his wishes, run his errands and provide for his comfort. Normally, Finley relished this round-eyed homage. Today, it interfered with his plans.

"I told Mr. Valenti's secretary that you had to speak with him," a messenger reported. "But she said he's in conference with Mr. Quinlan about our radio promotion."

Finley frowned.

"I could get him out for you, Mr. Finley," the girl volunteered.

Finley was gracious. "That won't be necessary, my dear."

"I'd tell him it was important," she persisted.

"No! I don't want to make an issue of it." Finley heard the snap in his voice and recovered control. His smile was strained. "I can very profitably use the time myself. I have some telephoning to do."

This evasion merely produced another assistant. "Oh, Mr. Finley, I'll put through your calls for you," said a small pert redhead. "I'm going on at the switchboard now."

Finley, with that old-world courtesy that had won him his admirers, took an elbow in either hand and ushered both girls to the door. "No, no," he said, indulgently firm, "these are private calls."

Amanda Lester, whatever her faults, was nobody's acolyte.

"No, Daddy," she announced firmly, "I'm going to handle this myself."

Her father stared in astonishment. In twenty-six years Amanda had never done anything for herself. To the best of his knowledge she had never even contemplated doing so. If there was one thing he and Rosemary prided themselves on, it was bringing up a simple, old-fashioned girl.

"Now, honey," he began uneasily, "do you think Steve would have liked to see you acting this way?"

Amanda's reply was withering. "Steve isn't here to see how I'm acting. He's dead, remember?"

David Trainor's face went blank.

He thinks I'm being brutal, she thought suddenly. He doesn't realize I'm just being realistic.

The trouble, she knew, was that her father couldn't believe she was a widow. He saw her as a child. By stretching, he could make it a young bride. But that was as far as he could go. Probably nobody considered a woman adult until she became a mother.

"Everything is Eunice's fault," she said obscurely. "You know it is."

"Well, we can't be certain about that, can we?" her father temporized. His voice assumed a specious authority. "The police will find out who murdered Steve, Mandy. Let them do it their own way."

"Their own way! You saw that letter from California. Somebody's been digging up that old marijuana party. You know it was Eunice. She's probably giving the police an earful. And you expect me to take that lying down?" She glared.

Mr. Trainor was helpless. Amanda was making him remember that terrible time with the call from the police station at three o'clock in the morning. They had Mandy—his Mandy— in a cell. All his instincts were to forget that night as completely as possible.

Meanwhile, Amanda was acting. She dialed a number scribbled on a pad. As she waited for the connection, she turned to her father again.

"And Daddy," she said almost threateningly, "don't tell Mother."

Then the receiver squeaked and her voice held nothing but hard impatience.

"This is Mrs. Amanda Lester. Please put me through to Mr. Quinlan, at once."

Eddie Quinlan hung up the receiver and stared at it incredulously. Then he shook his head and blinked once before speaking.

"Either she's going crazy, or I am."

Ralph Valenti looked more worried than ever. "That was Amanda Lester, wasn't it?"

"She's coming to the Pru," Eddie said baldly.

"My God!" Valenti exploded. "Who was fool enough to ask her?"

Quinlan shrugged. "No one as far as I know."

"Her husband was just murdered the other day." Valenti's ideas of decorum were shaken. "That girl doesn't know how to behave. This is no time for a widow to be coming to parties."

Quinlan leaned back in his chair and stared at the ceiling through narrowed eyes. "Amanda's not out for pleasure. She says she has to speak to us urgently. So that we can straighten out our stories to the police."

"Another one!" The shadows were back on Valenti's face. "That's all I need."

"Ralph, we've got to handle her carefully. She may have come up with something new. She sounds as if she's nerving herself for something."

"I say we shouldn't have anything to do with her," Valenti said stubbornly. "She's a troublemaker."

Quinlan looked up swiftly. He heard a new note in Valenti's voice. "Everything's up to you, Ralph. I'll let you call the shots."

"If it weren't for Fiord Haven—" Valenti was fervent.

"Fiord Haven means a lot to you, doesn't it, Ralph?" Quinlan asked seriously.

"It means everything."

Eunice Lester was staring hopelessly across the table at Peter Vernon. She could see he was going to be difficult.

"I don't understand you, Eunice," he was saying. "I really don't. Of course, the whole thing is unpleasant, there's no denying it. But your problems are over. It would be silly not to recognize that. In the long run, this makes things easier for you."

"Easier?" Eunice gasped, hysteria nearly displacing the sarcasm she intended.

Vernon's slow, grave explanation did not falter. "Yes. This means an end to that custody suit. I never did like the idea of going into court."

"I told you I was taking care of that," Eunice said abruptly.

"Of course. But this solves everything."

"Does it occur to you, Peter darling," Eunice asked with dangerous sweetness, "that the police are arguing along exactly the same lines? In their eyes, it gives me a motive for murdering Steve."

"That's nonsense," Peter said predictably. "And they'll soon see it themselves."

Oh, thought Eunice, if only she knew what Peter was really thinking! Was he being tactful? Was he being sincere? Was there new reserve in his attitude toward her? It did not help that his avowed opinion was that she was a creature of unbridled passion. Until two weeks ago, this assessment had been flattering. But now? This was no time to resemble a tigress lashing her tail. Consciously she tried to create an atmosphere of cool, common sense.

"I'd like them to see it as soon as possible," she said calmly.

Peter was reassured. "Then the thing to do is cooperate when they ask for cooperation. Otherwise, have nothing to do with the whole affair. Forget about it as much as possible. It's not as if you were involved."

Eunice flinched. There was a shade of reserve in his last statement. She played her trump card.

"Not involved! Do you realize that it was Tommy's father who was murdered? Do you realize that Tommy is old enough to read newspapers? That he knows his mother is a murder suspect?" Now she did not attempt to control the trembling in her voice.

Her attack put Vernon on the defensive. He was a widower who had been married for twenty years. He knew about feminine nerves; furthermore he respected all displays of maternal anxiety. For the next ten minutes Peter Vernon was unstinting with both apologies and reassurances.

When he had gone, Eunice cleared away the glasses and decided she was a fool.

Why were all the men in her life totally without protective instincts? For that matter, what was the deep similarity which made them all demand their eggs scrambled hard? And, most unanswerable of all, why was life a vacuum unless there was a man to cook scrambled eggs for? What she needed was a man who ate in restaurants and was occasionally of some help to her. Someone she could turn to when she needed . . .

Suddenly she stopped emptying an ashtray and froze in thought. Her eyes brightened as a name came to mind.

"Of course," she whispered to herself.

Eunice was not the only one having trouble with her man.

"I tell you, Alan," Sukey declared, "it could be important!"

"I didn't say it wasn't important," Alan replied bearishly. "I said we shouldn't get mixed up with the police."

"You make it sound as if we were going to live with them. I just think they ought to know. I could stop by the station house tomorrow morning. For heaven's sake, Alan, if you like it better, I could write to the police up in New Hampshire."

"The fuzz are the fuzz anywhere," Alan declaimed, "and you know how we feel about them."

Sukey did indeed know. Had they not both belonged to SDS at Brandeis?

"That's different, Alan. We don't believe in allowing police on campus; we don't believe in allowing them to oppress underprivileged minorities. That's because they're acting beyond their jurisdiction. But the New Hampshire police have a right to investigate a murder in New Hampshire, don't they?"

The voice of sweet reason was making Alan sullen. He had a grudge against the New Hampshire State Police. Never had he recoiled from flying wedges of police, from nightsticks, from riot cars. But he had been disoriented that day on the Appalachian Trail, spiritually as well as geographically. He had greeted the police as deliverers. He had meekly answered all their questions. He had not once reminded them that he was too socially responsible to allow them to jackboot their way across his civil rights. They had tarnished his image of Alan Davidson, and he wasn't going to forgive that easily.

He shifted ground. "What difference would it make if they knew?" he demanded. "It doesn't change anything."

"Oh, yes, it does," Sukey said roundly. "Mr. Valenti wasn't scheduled to speak to us after dinner the night Steve Lester was murdered. But somehow he changed the schedule around. You can see why he did it. He didn't expect the murder to be discovered so soon, and he wanted an alibi for that night."

"You're just imagining all that. Anyway, if the police are so bright, they'll find out themselves. We aren't the only ones who know, and I don't like the idea of being a patsy for the fuzz."

Sukey sat up straight. "And I don't like being a patsy for a murderer! If you want to know, I liked Captain Frewen!"

Alan sucked in his breath sharply. He did not realize he was witnessing a development foreseen by someone else a long time ago.

Sukey as campus radical had appalled her father, dismayed her faculty adviser, and terrorized her roommate. Sukey's mother, however, had—in her husband's opinion—remained preternaturally placid. She had made one visit to SDS headquarters and noted the large number of attractive young men. Without doubting Sukey's sincerity for a moment, she had decided that nature, as usual, had found the shortest distance between two points. The path was tiresome, of course. But a good deal less tiresome than young couples throbbing sympathetically to Maeterlinck's *Blue Bird,* which had been the path obligatory for nineteenth-century romantics.

"Sukey will grow out of it," she had assured her fulminating husband. She might have added that the growing-out process would furnish Alan with the education he had missed in college.

Alan's reaction to this opportunity was momentarily deferred. Just as he was about to castigate Sukey as a cop lover, an establishment hireling and an apostate, the phone rang. He knew something was up when he heard her young-matron tone.

"Yes, this is Mrs. Davidson . . . why, Mr. Finley! Of course I'll help."

Henry Morland continued his demonstration of the power of mind over matter during the walk to the Ritz. He raised, discussed, and dropped many topics of great importance, never once reverting to Stephen Lester or murder. By the time he had said what little there is to be said about the space program, water pollution and the urban crisis, Thatcher was regretting the old, unregenerate Henry.

He was relieved, therefore, when a telephone call removed Henry from the Ritz's cocktail lounge, and even more relieved when Henry returned to announce: "Sorry to run out on you, John, but I felt that I might as well make up for wasted time."

"Yes?" Thatcher inquired.

"We'll get back on the Trail tomorrow," said Henry, in what seemed to be a non sequitur.

"Fine," said Thatcher.

"So tonight, I thought I'd get a little business done, if you'll excuse me." Henry had made an appointment for dinner and a business talk with an artisan in Roxbury who had developed an interesting new technique for producing wormholes in wood.

"Fake antiques, Henry?"

"Certainly not," replied Henry with dignity. "We certify that these are modern pieces and price them accordingly. What people tell their neighbors when they get them home—that's up to them."

With Henry off on this new wrinkle in duplicity, Thatcher

consulted his conscience. A rapid review of many professional and personal contacts in Boston and Cambridge produced only one obligation so overriding that he was helpless before it.

Supported by a first-rate meal, Thatcher took to his feet again, this time to Beacon Hill.

Beacon Hill is no longer the home of the Brahmans, but it remains a good address in a more eclectic sense than it once did. Many of the homes built for an Otis or a Bancroft are now devoted to good works, like the American Girl Scouts, the Red Cross, and, up on Joy Street, the Appalachian Mountain Club. But here and there are some vestiges of a golden past. One of them, a house on Cedar Street, was Thatcher's immediate goal. He was paying an evening call on Mr. and Mrs. Forbes Thorndike.

With Mr. and Mrs. Forbes Thorndike, Thatcher now, and for many years past, had nothing in common. And yet, he reflected as he plodded across the Public Gardens, the years had provided their cement.

Mrs. Thorndike had been godmother to Thatcher's late wife. So, she and her husband had sent a very handsome wedding present. Silver, Thatcher seemed to remember. Laura, his daughter, must have it now. They had sent equally handsome presents for the birthdays and weddings of each of the Thatcher children. They had often dined with the Thatchers before one of their regular voyages to Europe. And they had, although quite elderly by then, attended the funeral.

It was nothing in common, Thatcher realized, or alternatively a lifetime in common.

The melancholy tenor of his thoughts was sharply terminated by the Forbes Thorndikes themselves. In earlier years, they had seemed simply indeterminate. Now in their nineties, they were reverting to type with a certain astringency. They were also unaffectedly and unsentimentally pleased to welcome Thatcher to the house with its notable oval dining room, its kitchen garden, and its authentic violet windows.

Quite contrary to his expectations, John Putnam Thatcher

spent a thoroughly entertaining evening. Although advanced in years, Forbes and Abigail Thorndike retained full possession of their faculties. Furthermore, a far-sighted nineteenth-century Thorndike was still contributing to their comfort. Not only was there a staff to keep the sideboards dusted and the flower vases filled, there was a housekeeper with a nursing degree.

"Quinlan? Quinlan?" asked Forbes Thorndike, pouring brandy with a hand as steady of a youth's.

"Edward J. Quinlan," said Thatcher who had described his visit to Boston in anecdotal, but accurate, terms. "And a Ralph Valenti—"

Forbes Thorndike snorted. "Sounds like an election ticket. Get an Italian from the North End and somebody green—"

Abigail Thorndike could give her husband a year or two, but she ventured farther from Cedar Street these days than he did.

"There is a Quinlan who was head of the Port Authority a year or two ago," she said.

"If it wasn't a Quinlan," Forbes said, "it was a Flynn. Have I ever told you, John, about that lunch I had with Mayor Curley?"

He had, but Thatcher listened again. Or half listened.

There was something timeless about the Thorndikes, frail as they now were. He was glad to have lived in at least part of their era. Once they were gone, their like would not be seen again. Their own children, Thatcher knew, did not resemble them in the least. One was a lawyer on State Street whose entire professional career consisted of lending the luster of his name and connections to firms where the real work was done by others—others frequently named Quinlan or Flynn. The Thorndike girl, although she must be a grandmother by now, had married somebody named Swenson and made a life for herself in Minneapolis.

But with the Thorndikes senior, in their house on Cedar Street that was not much changed since the first Thorndike had brought home his bride, one could sense the triviality, even the ephemerality, of the most painful hornet's nest of the moment.

Henry notwithstanding.

Thatcher, matching Forbes brandy for brandy, found himself mellowly reflecting that by tomorrow afternoon, or the day after at the latest, he would be back on the Appalachian Trail. Stephen Lester would be one more ripple in the placid ocean of time . . .

Strong drink is a deceiver. At just about the time Forbes Thorndike was rounding out his story (". . . beautiful voice . . . would you believe it, I had tears in my eyes when he sang 'My Wild Irish Rose' "), life in the New Boston was proceeding apace.

In the special function room of the Sheraton Hotel at the Prudential Center, the lights went up.

Sukey Davidson loosed a scream that bounced off the walls like a fusillade.

"Look," she gurgled before collapsing into Alan's arms.

For, after the movie, *Fiord Haven—Your All-Season Home,* the guests of Fiord Haven were still blinking slightly. But Sukey put an end to the blinking. All eyes swerved to the man she was pointing at.

He lay slumped forward like a drunk, hands aimlessly dangling.

But he was not drunk. From his back projected one of the Sheraton's long, sharp carving knives.

16 PRUNING KNIFE

IGNORANCE IS bliss. The dramatic events occurring at one hotel in Boston did not disturb John Putnam Thatcher's slumbers at another. Protected by his dislike of pre-breakfast television, he sallied forth the next morning in search of nourishment.

The dining room of the Ritz in Boston is on the second floor. Its spacious elegance includes a wall of windows overlooking the Public Gardens and Boston Common. On a clear, sunny morning in late September it seems suspended among the treetops, the multi-colored leaves affording glimpses of gliding swan boats and frolicking children.

Idyllic, thought John Thatcher approvingly, as he laid down his morning papers and prepared to join Henry Morland, who was already at a corner table. Thatcher himself was flushed with the sense of well-being that comes from a blameless evening followed by a night of refreshing repose. He gave his order to a hovering waiter, picked up *The New York Times* and, as befitted his calling in life, turned to the financial page. Here he remained engrossed by Dow-Jones averages until his orange juice arrived. Casually he glanced up. Instantly he realized that something was wrong.

Henry, like many men of small, wiry build, had a ferocious appetite. Normally he approached the breakfast table like a powerful vacuum cleaner, absorbing every crumb of toast, scrap of marmalade, or pat of butter within reach. But not

135

today. He was still broodily pecking at the same egg which had been occupying him five minutes earlier.

"John," he asked plaintively, "aren't you ever going to turn to the news?"

Deferring useless questions, Thatcher unfurled the front page. It held no surprises for him. The peace talks were bogged down, salvos has been exchanged across the Suez Canal, and the trade unions in England were attacking the latest austerity measures designed to shore up Britain's flagging economy.

Henry used his knife as a pointer. "The other one," he directed.

The *Boston Globe* had apparently abandoned the international situation. A two-column spread, in tones not far removed from hysteria, described a local event:

MURDER AT THE PRU
BUSINESSMAN STABBED TO DEATH
Fiord Haven's Second Killing

BOSTON, September 12—Yesterday evening at the Sheraton Hotel in the Prudential Center, Ralph G. Valenti, a prominent Boston realtor, was stabbed to death. The murder occurred during a hospitality evening sponsored by Fiord Haven, a resort community in New Hampshire of which Valenti was a promotor. Last Saturday, Stephen Lester, a business executive from Weston, Mass., was murdered at Fiord Haven during a weekend organized for prospective residents.

Over a hundred people were present last night at the dinner and subsequent film showing which culminated in the discovery of Valenti's body. Valenti was stabbed in the back with a carving knife while the lights were out in the special function room. At the conclusion of the movie, the body was discovered by Mr. Alan Davidson of

Cambridge who was sitting next to
Valenti.
"It was just awful," Mrs. Alan
Davidson told our reporter. "The
lights went on and I heard Alan kind
of choke, so I turned around and I
saw him."

But the *Boston Globe* was not prepared to waste time on
Sukey Davidson or, indeed, on any of the participants. Its passions had been roused by the desecration of the Prudential
Center. The financial history of the complex was recalled. Its
dimensions were retailed with pride. The urban renewal un-
leashed by its erection was painstakingly reviewed. At the
bottom of the page, Thatcher was not much wiser than at the
end of the second paragraph. He looked at Henry inquiringly.

"Turn to page nine," said the martyr's voice.

On page nine, it all came out. Among those present,
Thatcher learned, were Mrs. Amanda Lester, widow of Stephen
Lester, Mrs. Eunice Lester, ex-wife of Stephen Lester, James
Joel Finley, prominent architect, and Henry Morland, owner
of The Pepper Mill in Pepperton, New Hampshire.

"So that was your business appointment last night," said
Thatcher, unable to mount much surprise. Somehow it was inevitable that, if the personnel of Fiord Haven were to be as-
sassinated, Henry would manage to be on the spot.

"I went with Eunice," Henry confessed.

"Who cares what your excuse was? Have you told Ruth?"

"I called her this morning."

"And?"

"Women," Henry complained evasively, "get so excited."

Sternly Thatcher tried to suppress the memory of Ruth's
placidity in the face of Henry's vagrant enthusiasms. Henry
was continuing gloomily, "but she says Duncan is bound to
find out."

Duncan was the eldest of the Morland children. He was
thirty-five and putting on weight. Of late, he had begun to feel
it was his duty to give his parents the benefit of his mature
counsel.

Thatcher cast around for comfort. "He's not likely to come anywhere near New Hampshire," he offered.

All three of Henry's children were married, respectable and well-settled. Nonetheless they represented bitter failure. Henry had justified his move to New England many years ago on the grounds that the children could be raised close to nature. Accordingly, the three young Morlands had spent their high school and college vacations humping supplies up mountainsides, clearing trails, and instructing novices in the arts of the woodsman. Upon achieving emancipation, the three fled to large cities and established residence in skyscrapers. From these aeries, they were in the habit of extending warm invitations to their parents. Not one of them, so far as was known, had seen a blade of grass in years.

"That won't stop Duncan from coming to Boston," Henry pointed out.

"Then leave Boston," Thatcher said sharply.

"I can't," Henry groaned. "Not yet anyway. I have to turn up at some police station at eleven."

Thatcher had been hoping that Henry and Eunice might have spent the evening cheek by jowl, thereby providing each other with an alibi. He should have known better.

"Perhaps, Henry," he suggested, "you had better tell me about it."

With a coherence indicating he had already told the tale several times, Henry obliged. Thatcher gave him a lead.

"Start by explaining why Eunice went. I thought she was through with Fiord Haven."

"It was a last-minute decision," Henry replied. "She found out that Amanda was going. That made her nervous as hell. She figured something was up. After all, Amanda had a lot more reason to remain in seclusion than she did. So she decided Amanda was going to pull something, and she'd better see what it was."

"Did Amanda pull anything?"

"Not unless she murdered Valenti." Henry was dispirited.

"Go on," Thatcher directed.

It developed that dinner had been served at an immense, U-shaped table. Old Fiord Haven prospects and new prospects had been intermingled. Henry and Eunice had sat with unknowns. They did not even spot Amanda until dinner was almost over.

"And she was sitting with a bunch of strangers, too. Then, we were all herded into the next room to see movies. I was pretty disappointed. It looked as if we were going to sit through a couple of hours of sales pitch in the total dark, and that would be that."

Thatcher could imagine the frustration. Henry, of course, had sneaked off to this function in order to continue his detective activities among the participants of the murder weekend. Instead he had been forced to eat a bad dinner with strangers, then sit in silence for the remainder of the evening.

"But things turned out not to be so bad." Henry brightened at the memory. "I guess they figured that program would be too stiff to put people in the mood to buy. So they had a series of movies. Then, while the operator was changing reels, they brought in a trolley of drinks and encouraged everyone to move around and chat."

Thatcher nodded. He could see what was coming.

"The first one they showed was a real shortie. Couldn't have been more than a couple of minutes. It was about opening and closing one of their houses and how little there is to it. That time I went to the trolley and got drinks for us and came back to Eunice. She was talking to some couple from Newton. The second film was a ski movie. You know, filled with dramatic shots of some athlete pivoting in a spray of snow. That wasn't too long, either, and the photography was interesting," Henry said, giving credit where credit was due. "That time Eunice didn't want anything. So I went to get some soda water and I started to talk to one of those salesmen. Burt—you remember him. The lights went down while I was still talking to him, so I just took the first empty chair I could find. In the third film they really gave us the works. It was called *Year 'Round Fun in New Hampshire*. It went on and on with a sound track. The pictures, naturally, had to be of some place else. I think they used a development that's already open. But the track was all about Fiord Haven. They told us how they had to choose between putting the houses close to the ski tow or close to the lake and how clever they'd been to decide on the tow. That way people wouldn't have to get their cars started in the winter. They'd be right there, close to the base of the runs. But what would be even better would be the summer. The lake was on the other side of the mountain and the kids would be using it all day with speed boats and water-skiing and lifeguards. It sounded like the prelude to hell, if you ask me," Henry said, suddenly diverted.

"They must think so, too," Thatcher replied, "if they're bragging about how far away it is."

"They're going to run a bus, right after breakfast. That way they figure to keep the kids out of everyone's hair all day—or anyway until dinnertime. Meanwhile the parents get a heated pool with a clubhouse bar and no noise. Not a bad idea," Henry said handsomely.

"Keep to the point," Thatcher growled, uninterested in Henry's reaction. "What about Valenti's murder?"

"After this thing had run on for what seemed like hours, the lights went up, people started to mill around and Sukey Davidson screamed."

Thatcher drew a deep breath at this dramatic termination of Henry's recital.

"I suppose the police have been concentrating on where people went between the films," he said slowly.

"Have they ever!" Henry said feelingly. "Of course, at first, they were concentrating on Valenti's movements, but that didn't help them much. You see, Valenti had been at the trolley with everyone else at the intermission. But he was one of the first to take a seat. He went and sat down next to the Davidsons long before they blacked out for the third movie. That was in the next-to-last row of chairs. Plenty of people had time to see where he was and plenty of them didn't go back to their seats for more punishment until the lights went out. So almost anyone could have slipped into the last row, stabbed Valenti and then shuffled off to a seat on the other side of the room."

"Just what do you mean by that *almost anyone,* Henry? Do you really mean the whole room of a hundred people was surging around?"

"Hell, no! I suppose quite a few of them never got up at all. But you don't have to be a mind reader to see how the cops are thinking. It's only natural. The first thing they did was ask about the repeaters from the murder weekend. When they couldn't produce anyone who held their hand throughout the entire third movie, the cops lost interest in the newcomers." Henry spread his arms helplessly. "That boils down to Eunice, Amanda, me, Quinlan, that Finley, and a couple of the salesmen. A short, choice list!"

Thatcher abandoned his role as comforter in search of information. "What about the other people at Fiord Haven for the weekend?" he demanded. "One of them could have been a long-lost enemy of Lester's. And their alibis were all provided by spouses who were changing for dinner with them. You can't tell me the police have entirely lost interest in them."

"If they hadn't before, they have now." Henry was the picture of gloom. "None of them were at the Pru last night."

"Are you sure?" Thatcher demanded. "After all, Valenti said they were letting in repeaters. Who made up last night's list, anyway?"

"There seems," said Henry temperately, "to be some question as to how these invitations were issued."

At the police station three hours later, that question was still not being answered.

"I don't care," Amanda snapped defiantly. "I wasn't going to attend. But when Sukey told me that woman was going, nothing could have stopped me."

It became apparent that her father, her mother, and her

lawyers had certainly not been equal to the task. They had all tried; they had all failed. When she left, Amanda was still breathing fire.

The next witness had the same story.

"I've told you once. I'll tell you again," Eunice declared with iron control. "I hadn't even heard about it until Mrs. Davidson told me that Mr. Finley had persuaded Amanda to go. Then I decided I'd have to look after my interests."

Eunice had, at last, decided to produce support more effective than Henry's had proven. She was accompanied by a lantern-jawed attorney. But not by Peter Vernon.

"But why are you all blaming me?" asked a tearful Sukey. "I just did what Mr. Finley asked."

Sukey was fighting on two fronts. In the intervals of fending off the police, she was trying to cope with reproaches from Alan. Why, he wanted to know, hadn't she told James Joel Finley to run his own errands? With burning indignation, she reminded her husband that he had been enormously pleased and flattered to learn that one of our well-known modern architects was looking to the Davidsons for assistance.

Eddie Quinlan seemed past fighting. White with shock, he asked more questions than he answered.

"You don't have to tell me something's been going on at Fiord Haven. I figured that out myself. But what the hell is it? First this guy Lester—and now Ralph . . ."

He listened to the police ask about the invitation list almost blankly.

"I don't know how those women got on the list. They weren't on it yesterday morning, I know that much. But anybody could have put them on after that. Maybe Finley did it. Hell, maybe Ralph did. But one thing is sure—they didn't do it to help sell Fiord Haven. Who wants a bunch of widows around?"

Least temperate of all was Finley himself.

"Well, Mr. Finley?" the police asked with limitless patience.

"They're lying," Finley said flatly. "I never talked to the Davidson girl. Why should I want Lester's wives to come? I don't know what they're up to, but they're all lying."

The police produced Sukey Davidson's statement. James Joel Finley had called her up and asked her to invite Eunice and Amanda Lester to Fiord Haven's party. He had even told her how to bait the hook.

"I know who I called and who I didn't." Finley sounded more stubborn than ever. "It's her word against mine. And besides, her story doesn't make sense!"

Unemotionally, the police recorded his words. Unemotionally, they broke new ground.

"And what about the program for last night, Mr. Finley? Do you deny you selected it?"

"Of course not," he snapped. "What selecting there was, was done by me. We have a stable of fifteen or sixteen films. We always show a selection of three. I chose the three."

"So you knew there would be a lot of milling around?"

"I would have known that anyway." Finley was snarling his defiance. "There always is. You can't keep people chained up for three films."

"And during that last film, Mr. Finley? You didn't leave the drinks trolley until the lights went out?"

"The whole point of having a bar is to enable the Fiord Haven staff to socialize with the clients. We all exchange a few words with as many people as possible."

"So it would be very hard for anyone to say where you had been at any moment?"

Finley was beginning to look very tired.

"You're trying to make my actions look mysterious, when they weren't. Everything I did was predicated on an evening whose purpose was to bring together our guests and tell them about Fiord Haven. That was everyone's reason for being there."

The policeman looked up.

"Not this time, Mr. Finley. Someone had a very different reason this time."

17 EVERGREEN

It is one thing to be holed up in New Hampshire, as Thatcher informed Henry. Boston was something else again.

"In fact," he said, reaching for the phone, "unless you want me to go to the police station with you, I think I'm going to let you stew in your own juice for a while."

Henry's essential bounce had reasserted itself. No, he saw no need for Thatcher. But where, he asked, was John planning to spend the interval?

"New York," said Thatcher, adding to himself that he could always fly back instantly if Henry got in over his depth.

"Aha!" said Henry.

The trouble with Henry, Thatcher decided on the shuttle flight to LaGuardia, was that he was such an unpredictable combination of the antic and the shrewd. It would have been satisfying to leave him in the dark. Unfortunately, Henry not only fathomed Thatcher's intentions; he approved of them. Thatcher had a strong presentiment that Ruth would not.

Because Thatcher had decided to opt for some hard information. True to his instincts, he was sure that hard information would not come to light in Weston, in Arlington, in Boston or in New Hampshire. Hard information was to be found on Wall Street.

It had not occurred to him that his arrival at the Sloan Guaranty Trust would require justification.

"No, Miss Corsa," he remarked casually. "I'm just down for the day. Can you ask Bowman to drop by?"

"Certainly, Mr. Thatcher," said Miss Corsa, somehow suggesting that she deplored his presence.

Thatcher was mildly taken aback. Then, when Walter Bowman, the Sloan's energetic chief of research, bustled in, he was confronted with another trying response.

"No, I'm still on vacation, Walter," Thatcher explained. "There were just one or two things . . ."

But Bowman was still frowning. He was never happy until he had unraveled any small problem in his immediate vicinity and, for some reason, Thatcher's appearance seemed to constitute such a problem.

"Why didn't you call?" he inquired, seeking enlightenment.

John Putnam Thatcher prided himself on a firmly reined temper, but limitless patience had never been his forte.

"Now listen, Walter," he began.

Bowman raised a pudgy hand.

"I was just wondering," he explained disarmingly.

Thatcher, who had reason to value Walter's disinterested passion for any and all information, was willing to accept this.

"Fine," he said crisply. "Now, what I want to know is this . . ."

During the flight down, Thatcher had catalogued the areas where he felt further information might be useful. Certainly there were enough heated emotions and ambiguous personal relationships to keep Henry, and possibly the police, occupied for weeks. But to a banker, certain other questions leaped to mind quite automatically. In all honesty, Thatcher could not see that the answers would identify the double murderer. But given Henry, he knew he was going to be asked to think further about the murders of Stephen Lester and Ralph Valenti. He had decided to equip himself with some meaningful data.

Unfortunately, assembling this data brought him into contact with more members of the Sloan family than Walter Bowman and Miss Corsa; each of them, so it seemed to Thatcher, mildly questioned his appearance on the premises.

"But I thought you couldn't be reached," exclaimed Everett Gabler. "Really, John, if I'd known that you were coming in, I would never have allowed Charlie to send that memorandum to the State Banking Commission. I thought at the time, and I still feel, that it was most unwise. Now, let me explain to you . . ."

Charlie took the larger view. "You mean, after all this, you're going back up north tomorrow? You're still going on with that hike? Boy, John—okay, okay. But before you go, it would be a big help if you tried talking to Everett about this Banking Commission testimony . . ."

Bradford Withers, the eminent world traveler and president of the Sloan, simply looked hard at his senior vice president.

"Thought you were away," he said. Or accused.

It was a lesson learned, Thatcher concluded ruefully several hours later. Either he was at the helm of the Sloan or he was not. Clearly, his subordinates and colleagues—and Miss Corsa, who was in a category apart—were not happy with a John Putnam Thatcher present at the Sloan but not setting the course. Although he was soberly attired, he might just as well have come clumping into the Trust Department in hiking boots and backpack. Henry Morland might embrace the unexpected, but the rest of mankind liked their firmaments well charted.

So, since Thatcher was both thoughtful of the comfort of others and interested in the efficiency of the Sloan, he removed himself as rapidly as possible to the privacy of his apartment in the Devonshire. There could be no doubt, he realized as he left Miss Corsa straightening the chaos he had introduced onto his desk, that his departure was a great relief to all concerned.

"About the schedule of where you can be reached . . . ?" Miss Corsa said half-heartedly as Thatcher reached the door.

He braked. "I don't know, Miss Corsa. We'll probably have to cut short some of the trip. I'll call in—at intervals."

It was a pleasure to get back at least some of his own, he reflected, as the elevator bore him streetward.

At his apartment, he dismissed this petty triumph and concentrated on what the Sloan and other sources had brought to light. At first glance, it did not amount to much.

About the vacation home industry, Charlie Trinkam and Walter Bowman had been helpful.

"Boy, is that a wide open field," said Charlie. "You know, these second homes are selling like hotcakes. And the latest thing is this development bit. Hundreds of them. We own Buller Corp., out in Washington, and Orlando Homes in Florida—"

"But you've got to pick the company carefully," Walter interrupted. "There are all kinds. You know—developments aimed at older people. Or second homes for skiers—or swimmers. There are private clubs and public resorts. There are lots of different gimmicks. But you have to be careful."

Walter Bowman realized that his companions knew this much and more. He was simply warming to his subject. Charlie interrupted to ask about soft spots.

"Hell, yes," said Walter darkly. "A couple of the biggest developments have run into trouble. Bad planning. Not selling. Not enough capital—you remember that place near Washington. They took a big risk and lost—"

Thatcher decided that he wanted less theory and more detail. He asked about Northern Land Development and Fiord Haven.

Saddened, Walter shook his head. "Never heard of it."

Neither had Charlie. But, of course, he knew someone who would have. Even more predictably, that someone was a Miss Hazen and she was free for lunch.

"I can break my appointment with Berman and join you," Charlie said.

Was this the offer of an official escort? Thatcher could not be sure. In any event, he said, "I think I can handle Miss Hazen on my own, Charlie. Thank you, anyway."

In a matter of minutes, he was discovering that he had done Charlie a serious injustice. Miss Hazen was waiting for him at the bar of the Pierre. She was smoking a slim black cigar.

Thigh-high boots reached thigh-low pearls; green-rimmed sweep-around sunglasses echoed a brief emerald shift.

On the stool beside her, she had deposited a crash helmet and a briefcase.

Ah well, thought Thatcher, another new experience.

"Miss Hazen?" he inquired blandly.

It was. Miss Hazen, associated with Fontana, Goldsmith & Hazen, did not waste time on preliminary niceties. Thatcher was barely seated before she was proving that she had done her homework. In brisk, staccato phrases, interrupted only by four martinis, she gave a real estate specialist's view of Fiord Haven. And once they reached their table, she plunged on.

"Now, what is it you want to know?"

In spite of conspicuous appurtenances of femininity, Miss Hazen favored a distinctly man-to-man approach.

Thatcher tried to prove worthy of it.

"About some of the financial details—" he began.

"Right!" said Miss Hazen, thrusting the menu at a waiter like a rapier. "You know that Quinlan and Valenti incorporated, don't you?"

"Yes—"

"But that's a technicality," Miss Hazen went on, rummaging through a large purse for another pair of glasses. "They didn't sell stock to the public, so we don't have the real dirt on them—"

Although he was in danger of being mesmerized, Thatcher knew she meant that Fontana, Goldsmith & Hazen did not have the information about capital and earnings they automatically filed on any corporation selling stock to the public.

Miss Hazen was disposing of an oyster. Thatcher seized his opportunity.

"How did they raise the money for Fiord Haven?" he asked. It was an investment that must have run to several hundred thousand dollars. And Fiord Haven's many promotions were not cheap. Eddie Quinlan and Ralph had not seemed like rich men—and Thatcher's eye for this was acute.

Miss Hazen's back-up glasses were hexagonal and studded with small pieces of reflecting metal. They were, if anything, more opaque than the first pair.

"Passed the hat," she said. "Friends and relatives—that sort of thing. Valenti's father-in-law is a dentist—and you know what that means."

Thatcher knew this suggested money, but he was not altogether sure he accepted Miss Hazen's certainty on the point.

"Anyway, they parlayed it with those apartments in Boston. Then they sank everything into the New Hampshire deal."

"And they have enough capital?" Thatcher asked.

Miss Hazen was offhand. "None of these vacation-home babies ever have enough capital. Everything they do eats up money. So it all boils down to the big question—are they selling lots? If they are—they're in gravy. If not, they're in big, big trouble. Feast or famine—that's about it."

"And since Fiord Haven is not a publicly held corporation, we have no information about their sales?" Thatcher suggested.

Sylvia Hazen weighed his comment. "Right. You've got it in one. But there is something we've heard in their favor. When they bought the property, they took an option on another four hundred acres—in case they want to expand. That's a pretty smart move, and it should keep them from hitting the wall the way a lot of the other boys have."

"You know," Thatcher said, "the frenzy of their selling efforts suggested to me that they might be in difficulties."

Only after the words were out of his mouth did he realize that he might have been tactless. Miss Hazen, and by extension, Fontana, Goldsmith & Hazen, obviously were not above forceful techniques. But in this instance, the lady identified with tradition. She abandoned the *prosciutto*.

"That's how it grabs a lot of people," she told him kindly. "But they all operate as if there was no tomorrow. I just came back from an operation in Puerto Rico that charters jet planes from Cleveland and Chicago, and takes hundreds of prospects out to this thing called Paradise Island. And Ed and Larry Fish out in Nevada offer you a weekend in Las Vegas, complete with stake. They've got about five thousand acres of desert to peddle."

With the end of lunch, Miss Hazen unfurled another cigar. Thatcher was thanking her for her cooperation when she suddenly dropped her businesslike manner. She removed her glasses to reveal wide-spaced green eyes.

"Yes, yes, I'll keep an eye peeled for whatever turns up about Fiord Haven," she said. "Of course, this murder business won't help . . ."

Thatcher's look of inquiry drew forth information.

The Daily News," said Miss Hazen. "In this business, you've got to watch them like hawks. Well, anything that passes my desk, I'll shoot over."

"Thank you," said Thatcher.

"And Mr. Thatcher," Miss Hazen added when they were ready to part at her Vespa. "Tell Charlie I'll keep in touch, won't you?"

Thatcher denied himself this pleasure. Who was he to chaff Charlie on unorthodox methods?

Instead, he consulted another member of the Sloan. Answell Briggs, of the real estate department, had no Sylvia Hazens up his sleeve.

"Say," he said boyishly, "I thought you were on vacation."

With asperity, Thatcher explained his pro-tem status to the phone. He then repeated his request for information.

"Oh sure," said Briggs. "James Joel Finley. He's one of the big names in architecture these days, you know."

"It's not a field I keep up with," Thatcher admitted.

"Lucky devil," said Briggs. "Finley's had a lot of publicity about some library he built in Hawaii—a big play in *Time.* You know the sort of thing. But he hasn't designed any buildings here in New York."

"So at the moment, he's more famous than rich?"

"Put it this way," Briggs explained. "He can make it big,

but he hasn't so far. Is that the sort of thing you want to know?"

"In part," said Thatcher. He went on to explain James Joel Finley's association with Fiord Haven and asked for comment.

"We-ell," said Briggs, "it could be almost anything. They could be giving him a straight fee for designing this lodge, and maybe one or two model homes."

"What are the other possibilities?" Thatcher asked.

Briggs thought for a moment.

"He could be profit sharing, John. But to tell you the truth, I'd bet that they've worked out some deal where Finley lets them use his name and farms out the work to somebody else. That way he gets the publicity he wants, and it doesn't cost them so much."

Here was another line of inquiry to hand Henry, if he needed one, thought Thatcher. Aloud he said:

"Tell me, Answell, just how good an architect is James Joel Finley?"

"Good?" the phone repeated. "John, I can see you don't keep up with the field. If, by good, you mean inventive or even proficient, you're fifty years behind the times. The big names in architecture are comparable—oh, say, to dress designers. It's all a matter of line and looks. You make a name by designing an all glass house, or a house that's built under a highway. Or a house that revolves—"

He had, Thatcher saw, struck a vein.

"Yes, yes," he said. "But tell me, Answell, what makes it safe for us to go into the buildings these distinguished architects design?"

"In many cases," said Briggs firmly, "it is not safe. But if it is, it's because of some engineer—possibly an engineer employed by the Sloan. Or by the labor unions . . ."

This alliance lost Thatcher.

"Nobody else may give a damn," Answell explained, "but the people who put up the money—like us. And the construction gangs are interested, too. When they see something that's likely to collapse on them—well, they look out for their own necks. Between the two of us, we introduce some elementary safety."

There is such a thing, thought Thatcher, as too cold a critical eye. Answell, he knew, had been involved in financing some of the more extraordinary edifices now disfiguring Manhattan. Perhaps he was constantly frustrated by the triumph of profit motives over loftier values.

But suddenly Thatcher was reminded of James Joel Finley—and Alec Prohack.

What is true in Manhattan may well hold true elsewhere. Another point to keep Henry busy.

Or, as Henry put it, more loose ends. As if there were not enough already.

Thatcher being as much of a perfectionist in his way as Henry Morland, he persevered. His last query required only one brief telephone call. An hour later Miss Corsa, who had taken down the telephoned reply, deposited the findings on Thatcher's desk.

"Thank you, Miss Corsa," he murmured.

"Not at all, Mr. Thatcher," said Miss Corsa, eyes averted.

He understood. As far as Rose Teresa Corsa was concerned, Mr. Thatcher was still away.

Amused, Thatcher stuffed the report into his briefcase, to be studied in other surroundings. But not before he absorbed its gist. The credit rating of almost everybody connected with Fiord Haven and the two murders was excellent, from Stephen Lester to Eunice, from Eunice's fiancé, Peter Vernon, to Eddie Quinlan and Ralph Valenti. Even Alan and Sukey Davidson were no threat to a potential extender of credit.

There was only one man whose personal financial position was precarious enough to merit warnings to the world at large. That was the distinguished architect, James Joel Finley.

18 FRAMEWORK

WHEN THATCHER returned to Boston late that evening, it was to discover a downcast Henry awaiting him.

"The police weren't really interested in what I had to say," he announced self-pityingly.

"For your sake, Henry, I wish you were on death row," Thatcher replied. "It's only because of Ruth that I can't really sympathize."

Henry was impervious to such shafts. "So far as I can see, nobody's making any progress at all."

The pile of newspapers at his feet bore him out. Thatcher glanced idly over them. The police were withholding comment. The principals were in seclusion. Inquiries were proceeding.

"Although why you expected to learn anything from the *Christian Science Monitor* eludes me," Thatcher commented.

Absently, Henry replied that he had just ordered all available papers. Mary Baker Eddy, complete with a Polish editorial, had been scooped up in the newsie's net.

Thatcher was relieved to discover that the strain had not caused Henry to forget everything he ever knew.

"I tell you, John," he said, waking from a brown study, "I don't have a lot of confidence in the Boston police. I don't think they'll ever find out who killed Valenti."

Thatcher resisted the temptation to point out that New Hampshire was not making stunning progress in the matter of Stephen Lester. He realized that these words really meant that the local police had not evinced deep interest in Henry's implausible hypotheses. And on balance, he preferred not to contemplate what they might have been.

"Tell me," he said instead. "Did anything ever come to light about that invitation list?"

"What? Oh, you mean getting Eunice and Amanda Lester to the Pru? No. Everybody's sticking to their story. Including Finley, who denies everything."

"How do you know, Henry?" asked Thatcher, beginning to see light at the end of the tunnel.

Henry was restrained. "After I finished with the police— and let me tell you John, I could put my opinion of them in much stronger terms—I naturally made a few calls."

"Oh naturally," said Thatcher, to whom all was now clear. Henry had gone haring out of the police station full of frisk and eager to pursue his own investigation. He had been surprised, and possibly hurt, to discover that not everybody shared his innocent taste for drama. Perhaps someone had even told him that he was intruding.

"I think, John," said Henry, confirming this reading in every wounded syllable, "I think now is the time for us to go home."

Home was not what it had been.

"Well, so here you are. Fresh from another murder," said Ruth Morland with a noticeable lack of enthusiasm.

Thatcher was fond of his hostess, but not fond enough to let this pass.

"You recall, Ruth," he replied coldly, "whose idea this trip to Boston was. I think we all agree it was not an unqualified success."

"Oh, I don't know about that," Henry intervened. "After all, we did find out there's nothing sinister in Lester's background. He was just another one of those loudmouths, full of his own moral superiority."

Henry's jauntiness had revived the minute he set foot over

his own threshold, where he was monarch of all he surveyed, including 3.6 miles of the Appalachian Trail.

Ruth ignored him. "There have been quite a few phone calls this morning," she went on implacably. "The State Police want to see both of you again. And a Miss Corsa called, from the Sloan."

Thatcher felt a momentary qualm. Was this what had ruffled the usually placid Ruth?

"What did she want?" he asked cautiously.

"She was just making sure she could keep in contact with you. She seems to be a very sensible young woman," said Ruth, like Queen Victoria bestowing tempered praise on a sister sovereign.

Henry had no difficulty hacking his way to the nub of the problem. "I suppose Duncan has been on your neck."

Ruth's voice was hollow. "He wants to come up for the weekend. Bringing a lawyer with him."

"All right," Henry barked, suddenly going on the offensive. "Tell him, it'll be a great help having him here for a couple of days. Say the Trail needs a lot of work, and I haven't been able to get round to it. That'll fix his wagon," he chuckled at high glee. "And when do the police want to see us?"

"At one-thirty. Oh, dear," she sighed in uncharacteristic despair, "I suppose you have to go."

Henry stared at her. "Of course, we've got to go. Anyway, why shouldn't we?"

"Because," his wife said with returning tartness, "on the basis of past performance, the minute you step inside the station the desk sergeant will slump forward, riddled with machine-gun bullets."

The desk sergeant did no such thing. The personnel of the station remained in robust good health throughout their visit. What's more, the general air of camaraderie and the casual treatment of their formal affidavits suggested that

Henry's status had dwindled to that of a potential prosecution witness. A very minor witness.

"The Boston police seem to think they'll be ready for a warrant in a couple of days," was the genial parting. "Guess they want to show us hicks how you do things."

Henry's excitement bubbled over as they returned to their car. "They must be planning an arrest on the basis of Lester's murder," he speculated, prepared to revise his opinion of Boston officials.

"Yes." Thatcher, too, had noticed that their affidavits covered the discovery of Lester's body and only one other point. "All they wanted from me was testimony to the effect that Finley was prominent in the cocktail lounge the evening of the murder."

"It's easy enough to see what they're heading for. Finley killed Lester, then Finley rushed back to give himself an alibi. You and Ralph Valenti both talked about something like that when we couldn't figure out why the murderer didn't simply tip Lester's corpse off a cliff somewhere."

Thatcher nodded slowly as he recalled earlier conversations. "The official theory must be that Finley intended to go back after dinner. Then his plans were frustrated by your premature discovery of the body."

"Fine. But what difference does it make what Finley intended to do and then didn't?" Henry bounced impatiently in his seat as they waited out the town's only red light. "What I want to know, is why he did it. Why bash Lester in the first place?"

"For that matter," said Thatcher, falling prey to a habit of orderly thought, "why then go on to stab Valenti? The police aren't thinking in terms of two different murderers."

Henry's eyes were gleaming. "I'll tell you what. We could stop by at Fiord Haven. Ruth said Alec Prohack has finally got his crew back on the job. They'll know all the dirt."

Thatcher agreed at once. Experience had taught him that it was useless to deny Henry his excitements. One should remain by his side, eyewitness to his non-homicidal conduct, and let the bodies fall where they might.

Meanwhile Henry had turned into a wily D.A. "If that fight between Lester and Finley about a roof is our motive, then Alec is bound to be one of the prosecution's star witnesses. A lot would depend on how he saw things. That kind of fight, whatever it was about, can cover anything from a mild difference of opinion to a murderous rage."

Whether Henry's reading of the situation was right or wrong, it became apparent, as soon as they pulled into the construction lot, that it was shared by at least one other person. The police had already had their innings with Alec Prohack. Now James Joel Finley was having his.

The architect and the builder were standing apart from the activity swirling around the unfinished lodge. Neither of them acknowledged the arrival of the Morland car.

"I've got to tell it the way it happened, Mr. Finley," Prohack was saying. "You know that."

Finley no longer looked like the great man of modern architecture. When he had been riding high, his flowing white locks, his mannered stateliness, his immense assurance had made him seem an exceptionally vigorous sixty. Curiously enough, his troubles had taken years off his apparent age, but not for the better. Now he looked a bewildered and ineffective fifty. His clothes hung limply from his shoulders as if they were a size too large. He was having difficulty with his voice.

"I'm not asking you to do anything else, Prohack. I just want to make sure you keep things in proportion."

Prohack's eyes focused on some distant horizon. "I wouldn't know about that. They asked me if you had a fight with Lester. You did, and I told them so."

"I've already admitted I had words with him." Finley ground the sentence out. "That doesn't make it a fight, not in their sense. Every architect has trouble with clients at some stage of the game."

"I guess that's right. So there's nothing to worry about." Prohack looked hopefully at the lodge where a gang of men had swarmed onto the roof. "If that's all, I could go check—"

"No, it isn't!" Finley tried for a more placatory tone. "For God's sake, man, you're a contractor. You've been around building sites all your life. How many times have you known an architect to murder someone who didn't approve of what he was building?"

"Well, if you put it like that—never," Prohack conceded. "But that isn't what the cops are asking me."

"You know what cops are like. They'll make a mountain out of any molehill." Finley brandished the roll of drawings he was clutching. "After all, what is there to say? Lester and I had a difference of professional opinion, that's all. Anyway, I was being professional. God knows what he thought he was being."

"Look, Mr. Finley. I'm not out to get you. But you've been down at the station, too. You know that isn't good enough for the cops. They want to know everything that happened, everything that was said. And that's what they're getting. What else can I do?"

Finley's hand crushed the drawings into an hourglass. "You can make it plain to them that Lester was simply another nut!"

"You can't very well expect me to do that." The builder looked at the architect with open dislike. "I told you that roof wasn't safe long before Lester did. You know we were right. That's why you're changing it."

Finley slid away from the subject of the roof. "All right, so you told me. You're still alive, aren't you?"

"Maybe," Prohack suggested softly, "that's because I didn't threaten to make it public. I didn't say I was going to write to the Architectural Society. I didn't threaten to make a stink from here to California."

"He never could have gotten to first base," Finley blustered.

"That wasn't the way you reacted then," Prohack reminded him sharply. "Sure, you were high and mighty with him at first. Just like you were with me. But you changed your tune damned fast when you saw what you were tangled with."

Finley made a last despairing effort to salvage the situation. "I've admitted I was annoyed with him."

"Who do you think you're kidding? You were seeing red!"

"My God!" Finley howled. "The man was out to destroy me. For no reason at all!"

"So tell that to the cops and see how they like it!"

But James Joel Finley, white-faced and shaken, refused the challenge. "You can't tell them that," he protested.

"I don't have to. You're telling the whole world."

For the first time, Finley became aware of his audience. Swiveling, he stared at the car and its passengers. Then, without another word, he shambled off.

Henry's whistle was the first sound to break the silence. It occurred to Thatcher that the sight of Henry, chin on hand and agog with curiosity, must have been the final blow for Finley.

"Well, now," Henry chirped, "that sounded interesting."

"That smug bastard has had it coming to him for a long time," Alec Prohack stated roundly.

Henry showed no disposition to quarrel with this assessment. "What was wrong with the roof?"

Prohack was relieving his feelings by savagely jabbing tobacco into a stumpy pipe. "It was one of those flat roofs that are the big thing in California. You know, Finley has done most of his work out on the Coast. I didn't like it when they handed out the specifications, and I told him so. I kept telling him so after I got the job, too."

"Why?" asked Thatcher, entering the spirit of forthright question and answer. "Your only responsibility is to build according to the specifications, isn't it? If they're wrong, that's not your fault."

Prohack replied that it didn't do a builder any good to become identified with roofs that fell in, accompanied by extensive property damage and personal injury.

"Yes, yes, I can see that," Thatcher agreed. "But was Finley's roof that bad?"

"Hell, I don't know. I haven't had a lot of experience with these flat roofs. He was using steel beams, and he said that would be good enough. I still wasn't crazy about the idea. Of course, his big pitch was that the money for the lodge had been allocated. So Quinlan and Valenti weren't going to be sweet about spending more than they'd bargained for." Prohack puffed vigorously to induce a kindle before continuing in an aside, "If you ask me, they weren't in any shape to ante up more for the lodge. They didn't leave enough room in their budgets for last-minute changes."

"You're dreaming of another world, Alec," Henry replied to this piece of Yankee conservatism. "Everybody builds before they've got enough money these days."

Thatcher regarded his companions without favor. They were both making substantial livings out of modern America's haste to acquire possessions. How much would either of them relish a world in which young couples did not buy a home until they had the entire cost in their savings account? Or, for that matter, a world where you did not open The Pepper Mill until you were above the need to finance?

"Let's agree that nobody is financially prudent these days," he said sternly, "and get back to this roof. Did Lester know any more than you did? Or was he making idle accusations?"

"That's the whole point." Prohack removed his pipe to underline the seriousness of his observations. "You know they had a big winter two years ago down around Boston. A lot of the fancy buildings in the new shopping centers couldn't stand up. When this guy Lester went to build himself a house last year, he wanted a flat roof like he had in California. He made such a pest of himself, his architect gave him a short course in roof framing. Explained to him why those flat roofs had collapsed under the snow load, even with steel beams. And finally, of course, made him see reason. The beams would have to be centered so much closer than in California that it would push the price way up. So, Lester had all the facts at his finger-tips. He knew that Finley was planning exactly the same kind of framing that hadn't stood up two years ago."

"Finley must have loved that," Henry remarked ironi-cally.

Surprisingly, Prohack dissented. Possibly he was now sorry he had goaded Finley. "You may have gotten the wrong idea about Finley, seeing him go to pieces just now. He wasn't bad with Lester at the beginning. Of course, he pulled the great man stunt. That's his style. But he was listening, I'll say that for him. In fact, I was kind of pleased. I thought maybe Lester was going to manage what I hadn't. But then Lester pulled that business about making the whole thing public."

Henry was the keen-eyed detective. "You mean they struck sparks off each other? Natural incompatibles?"

"No," Prohack insisted, "that isn't what I mean. This Lester wasn't mad. He just said it was a matter of duty. The public had a right to be informed about incompetence that was creating safety hazards. He made a little speech, sort of con-gratulating himself. You know what I mean. He said the main trouble with our society was the let-George-do-it atti-tude. If more people acted like him, then we'd have a better society. No incompetence, no indifference, no crime in the streets. Doesn't seem to have worked out that way, does it?" Prohack concluded, looking around his own particular street.

"It's astonishing Lester survived as long as he did," Thatcher observed.

"You remember what Eunice said about him," Henry said darkly.

"I don't know about this Eunice, but Finley was ready to split a gut. You can't really blame the old geezer either. One minute he's condescending to some stranger. Hell, Lester hadn't even bought a lot. The next thing Finley knows, he's going to be flayed alive in public."

"How did this exchange end?" Thatcher inquired. "We heard you say Finley saw red."

"If you ask me, he was looking for a way to back down. He

was sure-as-hell willing to go over Lester's numbers. But Lester just strolled away, as if he couldn't wait to get to a typewriter and start telling the world. That's when Finley exploded. I don't know what happened next. I was the nearest target and I decided to make myself scarce." Prohack nodded to himself, as if only his sagacity had saved his life.

"But when did this happen?" Thatcher asked sharply. "You said Lester hadn't bought a lot yet. So it wasn't Saturday afternoon."

"That's right. All this happened during the morning tour. The rest of the crowd was over on the hillside looking at where the ski tow is going to be." Alec Prohack brightened into his first display of enthusiasm. "Over there. The trails are supposed to start right at the crest. And, of course, the lake is on the other side. Makes a tidy amount of work for us."

Henry refused to be diverted into construction details. "But Alec," he said, disappointed, "then Lester wasn't murdered for seven or eight hours."

Prohack did his best. "The police are thinking that maybe Lester and Finley met at the site before dinner and Finley made an effort to get Lester to see reason. From what I saw, that could easily lead to Finley's picking up a hammer and letting fly out of sheer . . . sheer . . ."

"Exasperation," Henry supplied. "Eunice really had a point, didn't she?"

Thatcher was not so swift to draw obvious conclusions. "Whether she did, depends on what Finley was doing before he showed up for cocktails at the motel. Does anybody know? Or does he simply say he was alone somewhere?"

A grim smile appeared on Alec Prohack's roughhewn features. "It's neater than that. The police asked him just that question on Wednesday afternoon. He told them he was with Ralph Valenti. Then, when the police were through with him, he went down to Boston to have a talk with the developers and attend that big dinner of theirs. That night somebody takes a knife and shuts Valenti's mouth for good."

19 TRIMMING THE TREE

OTHERS MIGHT marvel at the tragic vulnerability of a renowned architect and the macabre annihilation of his alibi. But not John Putnam Thatcher.

A long and observant life had all but destroyed Thatcher's capacity for surpise. This, he knew, tended to set him apart from his fellowmen. On Wall Street, for instance, he was surrounded by colleagues who were stunned and shocked with monotonous regularity by a sag in IBM, by a rise in the interest rate, by a presidential address, or even by antitrust suits launched with elephantine secrecy by the Department of Justice. In many ways, the telephone in his office on the sixth floor of the Sloan Guaranty Trust was a conduit for pained yelps:

"My God, John! Have you seen the latest?"

"You won't believe it, but—"

"I tell you, I thought I was seeing things!"

Wall Street is, at bottom, a collection of endearingly child-like innocents, always expecting the good, the beautiful, the true, and the profitable. The shrewd eyes, manly handshakes, and expensive tailoring that deluded the public (and a goodly portion of the financial press) did not fool Thatcher for one moment; he was one of the few men on the Street not constantly surprised by the turn of events—*any* turn of events.

This immunity was the by-product of other rarities: an observing eye and a long memory. Thatcher was not the oldest financier in New York but, he was willing to bet, he was one of the few who remembered some of the more lunatic moments of the Great Crash. Of course, he did not expect a mass defenestration of fund managers. Far from it. But, if it came, he would not be rendered speechless with shock and wonder.

Similarly, he had seen great firms go bankrupt and large banks collapse. He had seen excellent lawyers become alcoholics, Secretaries of State, and worse. He had known dowagers who had eloped with youthful chauffeurs.

So, while he was frequently interested and curious, he rarely found himself overwhelmingly surprised. Yet that was exactly his state of mind in Pepperton, New Hampshire on the morning after Alec Prohack's disclosures.

The source was, of all people, Ruth Morland. They were sitting in the kitchen over an ample breakfast. And, indisputably, Ruth was angry. Not resigned. Not amused. Not even humorously indignant. No, Ruth was mad as hell.

Considering, Thatcher thought, what he had seen Ruth endure—and this included backpacking in the Rockies with three small children, two summers during which Henry experimented with wild nuts and berries as a source of food, and one winter, many years ago, when Henry had been smitten by the charms of the coach of the U.S. Ladies' Field Hockey Team—the cause seemed, to a mere man, disproportionate to the effect. Nevertheless, the effect was enough to make him wish himself elsewhere.

"You said *what?*" said Ruth, coffeepot ominously suspended in midair.

Henry, Thatcher regretted to see, did not recognize storm signals when they were flapping in a high wind.

"I said to come on up. We could put them up for a few days." Henry, returning from the phone, reseated himself and reached happily for more toast. "Seems there's some fuss about that Porsche of Steve Lester's. So Eunice has to clear it up. And I'm glad to say that this Willy of hers—"

"Peter," Thatcher supplied, a wary eye on Ruth. "Peter Vernon."

"That's right," Henry rattled on. "Well, Peter Vernon's finally decided to lend a hand—"

"Henry Morland!" said Ruth. She was quiet. But she got through. "Do you mean to tell me that you've invited two house guests, at a time like this?"

God knew, Henry had never been a pourer of oil on troubled waters. But Thatcher had not realized that he was fool enough to try answering such a question.

"What do you mean by a time like this, Ruth? After all, everything's just about wrapped up. I expect the police will be arresting that nut, James Joel Finley, any minute now. We told you what Prohack had to say. No, Ruth, all that trouble is just about over now. And, of course, Eunice doesn't care to stay at the White Mountains Motel. You can understand that, after what happened. So, I said we'd be delighted to put them up. Probably it will just be overnight."

Ruth looked steadily at her husband. Then, without a word, she put down the coffeepot and walked out of the kitchen.

Despite a brilliantly clear autumn afternoon, the atmosphere was not happy.

"I don't understand it," said Henry crossly when the two men were preparing scratch lunches some hours later. "Ruth's taken the car and gone someplace. Now, why on earth . . .?"

Thatcher had no desire to intervene in marital discord. He did, however, suggest that the lady of the house might feel she had a right to warning, if not veto power, over forthcoming houseguests. Particularly when the link with those houseguests remained two as yet unsolved murders.

Henry waved this aside, recalling his descent with six stranded members of the Dartmouth Outing Club and his unannounced arrival with a visiting delegation of Englishmen. He described Ruth's splendid and unstinting acceptance of these challenges.

"Ruth," said Henry with simple assurance, "loves company."

Thatcher had once known a man, a staid investment banker, who felt a periodic need to seek out some deserted location, throw back his head and scream as loudly as possible. He would then wend his way back to civilization and function as impeccably as usual. Nor did this need for catharsis in any way disable him; it grew no more pressing with age or tension. Simply, and to the end, Brooks Sargent had to scream aloud every two or three months.

Life with Henry, Thatcher reflected, might induce similar needs.

It was not a train of thought he proposed to discuss with Henry.

"Exactly why is Eunice Lester coming up, did you say?" he asked as Henry peered helplessly into the well-stocked refrigerator.

"Just have to be sandwiches, I guess. What? Oh, it seems that the police hauled off that Porsche of Lester's. And, now that this question of Lester's estate has come up, Eunice decided that it would be wise to get up here and attach it. Her Boston lawyer got in touch with Guy Villars."

Thatcher wondered if this attention to relatively minor detail was in fact the result of Boston legal advice.

Possibly it was the fiancé, until now conspicuous by his absence, who had remembered the expensive car still in New Hampshire.

Henry was now a man cast adrift by the woman who had vowed to love, cherish and feed him.

"I can't find any pickles," he said plaintively.

Thatcher silently removed three jars of pickles.

"Henry, has it occurred to you that this Vernon fellow is something of a dark horse? You know, he may explain some of Eunice Lester's tension. Granted, she has been in a difficult position . . ."

"She certainly has," said Henry stoutly.

"But not as difficult as . . . say, Finley," Thatcher continued.

Henry, who had succeeded in laying as unappetizing a luncheon as possible in Ruth's kitchen, protested, "But Eunice didn't murder anybody!"

Thatcher let that pass, noting however that Henry had weighed the evidence against Finley, and found it sufficient. And was it?

Henry was still waiting.

"I agree," Thatcher said slowly, "but since Mrs. Lester did not murder anybody, she seems to have been unnecessarily . . . er . . . apprehensive."

"She was a suspect," Henry corrected him. "I wish Ruth would remember to stock rye bread."

The afternoon seemed interminable. Henry dithered around but showed no inclination for forays to Gridleigh, to Fiord Haven, to Boston, or even to his own office not two miles away. Amused, Thatcher understood. Henry was a gadfly who needed a secure base of operations. And with Ruth gone, Henry was more than helpless. He was rootless. How many miles on the Appalachian Trail had been traversed only because Ruth was securely placed in the Pepperton kitchen?

She reappeared at four-thirty, serene as usual. She also had several large paper bags.

"Well, Henry," she replied to a fusillade of questions, "if we're having houseguests, we have to feed them, don't we?"

"Oh, good," said Henry, inspecting the contents of one of the bags he had transported from the car. "I'm glad they had pumpkin ice cream."

Did Henry ever suspect that occasional need to scream? Thatcher doubted it.

By the time a large Cadillac was nosing into the Morland driveway, peace and harmony reigned within. Already, appetizing aromas were beginning to fill the kitchen; upstairs, flowers had been placed in the bedrooms, the bathrooms held full complements of fluffy towels. Henry, spruce in a sports jacket and respectable slacks, was readying an extensive array of bottles.

Eunice Lester, although she seemed thinner than Thatcher recalled, was relaxed and charmingly apologetic to Ruth Morland.

"I do realize that we're imposing on you," she began.

But Ruth, looking trim in a skirt and blouse, did not let her finish.

"Not a bit of it," she said with warmth. "We're delighted."

And, Thatcher saw, Ruth meant it.

If there were any surprises left in life, it was a sure thing that women would provide them.

Men, or at least, Peter Vernon, most assuredly would not. He proved to be a solid, middle-aged man without much to say. Or so it first seemed. Over cocktails, or the fearsome concoctions Henry regarded as cocktails, he responded readily enough to questions and even joined the general conversation. But he was reserved, almost self-conscious.

This was not altogether surprising, thought Thatcher. Within minutes, Henry, Ruth and Eunice might have been lifelong friends, so unconstrainedly were they exchanging views on current events. Not everybody has the gift of instant intimacy. Then too, being the houseguest of total strangers is not conducive to ease and relaxation in most adults. Furthermore, only very young men can carry off the role of fiancé with any real aplomb.

"Wholesale liquor importer," Vernon replied to one of Henry's direct questions. "You should drop in on us when you're in Boston. We have one of the finest cellars on the East Coast."

"I can hardly believe it," Eunice was saying as Henry lavishly poured refills. "Although I know that Steven could make himself obnoxious about almost anything, including architects' plans. Still . . ."

Peter Vernon cleared his throat. "I don't know much about the details," he announced, unnecessarily to Thatcher's way of thinking, "but a mistake like that is important, isn't it? A defective roof. That's dangerous. An architect might kill anybody who found out."

Ruth Morland, reappearing from the kitchen with a second tray of cheese savories from the oven, disagreed. "I should have thought Finley would be grateful. Surely it would be worse for his reputation if the mistake weren't found. Then the lodge might have collapsed and killed people. This way, he had the error corrected before the building was up. That couldn't hurt his reputation. After all, how many people would learn about it?"

It was Henry who responded.

"More people know about it than you might think, Ruth," he said. "All the local people, like Alec. Actually, I expect half of Gridleigh knows all about the mistake the great architect made. Then, too, there were Quinlan and Valenti. And they were paying Finley . . ."

Ruth looked unconvinced and Ruth was a woman of admirable common sense. How important would this have been to James Joel Finley, who was building a national, not a New Hampshire reputation? Thatcher wondered.

Again Vernon, almost hesitatingly, commented. "That's true, of course. But then you have to take into account that Finley might have wanted the best of both worlds. Without . . . er . . . without Lester around, he could quietly alter his plans. Then no one would ever know he had even made an error in his plans—let alone that he designed a building that was dangerous. This might be enough to cause him to commit murder."

The fireplace was casting flickering shadows through the living room. Outside, the suddenly quickening dusk promised that summer was passing and the long New England winter was just around the corner.

"That suggests a pathological ego," Ruth remarked. "To commit murder for such a reason, and then a second murder to cover it."

"God knows the man was an egotist," said Henry.

But James Joel Finley's vanity, it had seemed to Thatcher, was far from pathological. It seemed soundly based in dollars and cents. All his affectations were calculated to pay off.

"Of course, I didn't know Finley," Vernon remarked almost apologetically.

These reminders that Peter Vernon knew very little of what

had happened at Fiord Haven, these withdrawals from small points carefully made, added up to the portrait of a cautious man. Perhaps too cautious.

Suddenly, after a long silence, Eunice burst forth:

"Oh, that doesn't make any sense—not about James Joel Finley, at any rate. That wasn't why it happened. I know it wasn't. What happened was that Steve was so offensive, he was so goddam superior . . ."

"Eunice," said Peter. She ignored him.

"This poor fish lost his head and swatted Steve. And I understand it. Oh, God, how I understand it."

"Eunice," said Vernon once again.

Ruth was more effective. "I think," she said rising, "dinner should be about ready. Just bring your drinks to the table."

By general consent, the subject of murder was dropped for the rest of the evening. Naturally, this involved deflecting Henry more than once. But Peter Vernon shook off his constraint to display insatiable curiosity about the Appalachian Trail. How had it been established? What about the right of way? Who used it? He had so many questions that Henry could barely keep up. On the whole, dinner featured Peter Vernon, talking steadily.

Was this because he felt that Eunice Lester's feelings about her late husband were too intense for prudence? Whether or not someone else had murdered him?

Possibly. It was possible, Thatcher decided, that Peter Vernon was simply conventional to an unnatural degree.

At any rate the evening passed pleasantly if unexcitingly. The ladies retired early leaving the gentlemen to nightcaps at an hour suggesting that no one had a burning desire to prolong the occasion.

"Vernon," said Thatcher, suppressing a yawn, "do you know anything about Eddie Quinlan or Ralph Valenti?"

Vernon was, after all, a Boston businessman.

"I wish I had never heard of them," he replied with the first hint of real feeling Thatcher had heard in his voice. "Then none of this—" he broke off. When he continued, it was more temperately. "When Eunice and I decided we might be wanting a vacation place, I thought of building one of our own. But I don't know if you know about the labor situation here in New Hampshire . . ."

For five minutes, he gave them a description. It was accurate, detailed and dull. Henry put another log on the fire with unnecessary violence.

" . . . so," Vernon continued. "I looked into the better developments. Some of them are pretty cheap operations, you know."

"Yes," said Thatcher, recalling Miss Hazen's lecture back in New York.

"Quinlan and Valenti are newcomers," Vernon said. "But they did build those garden apartments on the Jamaicaway, and I happen to know they've been a success. I asked around, and people who should know assured me they were bright, young and ambitious—but they did things with quality. No corner-cutting. No cheap shortcuts. I know their advertising made them sound like some of these fly-by-night deals, but people who dealt with them in Boston, and that includes their general contractor, told me that they really did hold out for the best."

Something stirred in Thatcher's mind, something beyond the sudden realization that there was more to Peter Vernon than met the eye. Eddie Quinlan, and the late Ralph Valenti, prided themselves on their imaginative selection of prospects. They thought they had enticed Peter Vernon. Instead, coolly and after some effort, Peter Vernon had singled them out. As, perhaps, Stephen Lester had?

"Well," Vernon wound up. "It wasn't one of my brighter ideas. Not that I could have foreseen exactly how bad it would turn out to be. I hope to God that, when this business gets cleared up, Eunice and I never have to see New Hampshire again. Hell, if we need a vacation house, we can get one in Vermont. Or Maine. Or Florida, for that matter."

It was a measure of Henry's apathy that he uttered no protest.

The next morning, it appeared that the opportunity to leave New Hampshire forever might be at hand.

"That was Mr. Villars," Eunice announced returning from the phone. She looked radiantly happy. "He says I have to go down to the state police with him and sign some papers. Then we can leave . . ."

"Oh, can't you stay for another day or two?" Ruth protested.

Eunice smiled affectionately at her. "We'd love to, Ruth. You and Henry have been just wonderful. But—you understand."

Ruth understood. Thatcher understood. Peter Vernon understood. Everybody understood. Everybody, that is, except Henry.

Henry had fallen deep into thought. And Thatcher knew why. The warhorse, dormant for fully twenty-four hours, had just heard the bugle.

And Thatcher knew exactly what had sounded the alarm: the words *State Police.*

Ruth did too.

"Before you set off," she said, casting Thatcher an eloquent look, "let me get you all another cup of coffee."

"Fine," said Henry alertly. "And don't worry, Ruth, I'll be back soon."

20 LOGGERHEADS

"So THIS is where you like to spend all your time," Ruth Morland observed, her disenchanted gaze inspecting the State Police Barracks.

Curiously enough, it was not Henry's burning desire to play detective or Eunice Lester's need for additional support which had propelled the entire house party thirty miles down the road. Ruth Morland and John Thatcher had fallen afoul of Peter Vernon's determination to repay hospitality with hospitality.

"Look, you said you had errands in Gridleigh this morning anyway," he had urged. "And Guy Villars says it will only take a minute to sign the papers. Then we could all have lunch together before Eunice and I head back to Boston."

The result was inevitable. Thatcher and the Morlands were cooling their heels in the reception room, while the legal detail served its writ of attachment over at the State Police garage. The desk sergeant greeted Henry like a long lost friend while Ruth looked on ironically. Unabashed, Henry exploited the intimacy.

"At the gas station they were saying you'd pulled in Finley," he prompted eagerly.

"Talk about tom-toms! They've got nothing on the grapevine around here. All you've got to do is sneeze in one county, and everybody in the next county is ready to lend you a handkerchief," the sergeant said. "That's right. We picked him up last night."

"Then you're building your case on the basis of Lester's murder, not Valenti's?" Henry pursued.

The sergeant became heavily sarcastic. "Oh, there's no talk about a murder charge. Finley was booked as a material witness. Not that we can get away with that for long. The big shot from Fiord Haven is already down here—you know, the one who's a lawyer in Boston—so the judge will spring Finley in twenty-four hours unless the VIPs decide to go ahead with a murder charge."

Henry sighed happily. This was life! "And will they?" he asked, agog with curiosity.

The sergeant shrugged fatalistically. "Who can tell what the brass will ever do?"

Henry was willing to speculate, but Thatcher nudged him sharply as the back door opened to admit Eddie Quinlan with a young couple. The girl recognized them instantly.

"Oh, Mr. Thatcher! And Mr. Morland, too. Don't you remember me? Sukey Davidson."

Sukey seemed to be the only member of her party capable of rising to conventional cordiality. Her companions nodded somberly in the background. It was, Thatcher realized, not difficult to assign a cause to Quinlan's moroseness.

The promoter rapidly confirmed this diagnosis.

"I suppose you've heard that they arrested Finley," he said gloomily. "God knows what this will do to Fiord Haven."

Mentally Thatcher reviewed the blows raining down on that potential Garden of Eden. First a customer murdered. Then a developer murdered. And now the architect arrested. Offhand, he would have said that was more than enough to dissipate the fun-filled image which Eddie Quinlan had spent so much money to fabricate. But he was the first to admit that he did not understand the attraction of Fiord Haven. He decided to eschew the commercial for the personal approach.

"How is Finley taking this? I suppose you've seen him."

"Oh, sure, I've seen him. He's scared as hell. Who can blame him?" A tight, nervous smile glinted briefly. "I've got a lawyer coming out from Concord. We'll see how long this charge holds up. Not that it isn't going to do us a lot of damage, no matter what happens."

So much for the personal note. Eddie Quinlan was prepared to discuss lawyers, calculate courtroom probabilities and invite sympathy for his own predicament. But, Thatcher noted, he was not saying one word about James Joel Finley's innocence.

It was almost a relief to hear Henry galloping into the fray.

"I understand what Eddie Quinlan's doing here," he was saying brazenly to Alan Davidson. "But what about you two? I thought you lived in Cambridge?"

"We came up here to have another look at Fiord Haven," Alan said grudgingly.

"There's a building lot that Alan is interested in," Sukey said, disassociating herself from her husband.

There was a long pause. Alan broke first.

"And then Sukey insisted on coming here to the barracks with this damn silly story of hers," he burst out.

Everyone understood there had been a divergence of opinion between the young couple. It's nature was not so apparent. Sukey had denounced Alan's objections to cooperation with the establishment. They came poorly, she insisted, from someone infected by a bourgeois propensity for property accumulation. The accusation still rankled.

"Silly or not," she said firmly, "the police have a right to know." She turned toward Henry for support. "You wouldn't know this, but on the night of Mr. Lester's murder, Mr. Valenti changed the entertainment program around. He wasn't supposed to speak to us that night. He wasn't on the program at all. But at the last minute he announced a change."

"What difference does that make?" her husband complained. "We didn't even have the program that night. Not after Captain Frewen told everybody about the murder."

Sukey's lips set in a stubborn line. "Mr. Valenti didn't know the body was going to be discovered. He wanted a lot of witnesses to what he was doing that night. He probably came to cocktails with blood on his hands!"

"Crap!" Alan snapped. "That just shows how much you know. First of all, there wasn't any blood. Second of all, he wouldn't have had the time. I'll prove it to you. Just before we cut out from the rest to go hiking, I asked Mr. Valenti if their three-bedroom chalet could be cut down to one bedroom. When we went into cocktails he showed me some plans that had been all worked over. The plumbing lines were changed and everything. He wouldn't have bothered with something like that if he'd been murdering someone in the meantime."

"And third of all," Eddie Quinlan cut in, his voice suddenly rasping, "you might remember that Ralph was murdered himself. This isn't just fun and games, you know. I've spent the last two days with Ralph's wife. And I'll tell you this. I've got my shirt riding on Fiord Haven but, if that Finley bastard stuck a knife into Ralph, I'll let it all go down the drain—to see he gets what's coming to him!"

There was a painful pause. The Davidsons both flushed darkly. How they would have responded to this outburst remained doubtful, because at that moment the main feature began. The back door once again opened. This time it was Eunice Lester, turning to address a remark to Peter Vernon over her shoulder.

Simultaneously Amanda Lester strode in through the front door. She gave one brief look at the gathering, then carefully elevated her chin and advanced on the desk. She was, Thatcher noted apprehensively, swinging a chain of car keys from her finger.

"I am Mrs. Stephen Lester," she announced distinctly. "You told my lawyer you were through with my car. I've come to pick it up."

The desk sergeant, who could see trouble looming, abandoned the larger philosophical pose and became an anonymous official.

"Well, Miss," he said vaguely, "I'm afraid there's going to be some trouble about that."

"Mrs." Amanda was arctic. "What trouble?"

"This Mrs. Lester," he gestured toward Eunice, "has just attached the car. We can't give it to anybody."

Amanda did not let her eyes follow the gesture. As far as she was concerned, Eunice did not exist.

"Don't be silly. It's my car."

The desk sergeant was too cunning to try to argue. "I expect the best thing would be to see your lawyer. It's a shame you came up here today. You must have just missed the notice."

The facts were slowly sinking in. "Do you mean to tell me that you're giving my car to her?"

"Maybe you'd like to talk to Captain Frewen," the sergeant suggested cravenly.

Amanda decided to notice Eunice with a vengeance. "You can tell this bitch that it's my car. And I mean to have it."

"You've got it wrong, Amanda." Eunice was opting for a steely sweetness that brought sweat to the brow of every man in the room. "That car belonged to Steve. Now it belongs to Steve's estate."

"And that belongs to me. You've got delusions of grandeur if you think Steve left anything to some tramp of an ex-wife."

Eunice's voice dropped a full octave. "He doesn't seem to have done much about leaving things to his tramp of a present wife."

Amanda's eyes widened. "Who the hell do you think you are? I've had just about enough from you. Every time I turn around, there you are trying to get to me. Don't think I don't know about your slimy investigators crawling around California."

"And what about your slimy investigators crawling around Boston? Did you think you were on a one-way street? Is there something sacred about your dirty little past that nobody's supposed to ask any questions about it?" Eunice's breath was beginning to come quickly. "While you run wild destroying everybody else's life?"

"Oh, so that bugged you, did it?" Amanda jeered. "I suppose you're trying to pass yourself off as some sort of lily maid to him." She waved derisively toward Peter Vernon. "Let me tell you that Steve had every right to find out what kind of woman was bringing up his son."

"And I had every right to find out what he was planning to substitute."

This stung Amanda.

"You wouldn't understand. You're not capable of it. Steve and I wanted to have a child. We wanted one of our own. When that didn't work out, it was only natural for Steve to want his son."

Eunice laughed bitterly. "What did you and Steve know about wanting a son? Did you want to change his diapers and nurse him through mumps? Did you want to toilet train him and teach him how to walk? You just saw a pretty picture. You wanted a son the way you'd want a collie dog."

"That's not true," Amanda fired up. "You talk as if he's your exclusive property. He was just as much Steve's son as he was yours."

"Remember *that* when he takes his share of Steve's estate."

"Oh, now we come down to it. He's not Steve's son, but he's Steve's heir!"

Eunice's eyes narrowed into slits. "You're so contemptible, you're not worth talking to. You and your *Steve wanted a son.* He didn't want one when it would have done Tommy some good to have a father. He didn't want one so long as it would cost him a cent. He didn't get the urge until he was in the market to buy luxuries. Sure, Tommy's his heir. It'll make up for the ten years that went before."

"Tell us about those ten years you spent as a devoted mother," Amanda gritted through clenched teeth. "The ten years you spent bringing men back to the house. I'll bet Tommy knows all about substitute fathers. Or did you make the big sacrifice and wait till he was asleep before you pulled down your hot pants? It must have gotten inconvenient when he was big enough to notice what was going on! By now, he knows what his mother is."

"Well, three cheers! Now we get Amanda, the protector of the young. You'll have to give us a minute to adjust. Up till now, all we've gotten has been Amanda the swinger, Amanda the girl who's too with it to give up smoking pot. And who's being the lily maid now? Tell us about how you and Steve courted. Holding hands on the porch while you drank lemonade, was that how it was?"

Amanda for some reason had gone a brilliant crimson. "That's none of your filthy business!" she bellowed with surprising depth for so slight a girl. "Do you think that you had some kind of lifetime license on Steve? Or have you forgotten how normal people act?"

As Amanda grew less controlled, Eunice became more so. "You're mixing your lines," she almost purred. "Nothing less than absolute chastity can come near our young. I've got to hand it to you. You were willing to turn over more than a leaf. You were going to throw the whole book away."

Amanda was being backed into a corner. Perhaps Eddie Quinlan was inspired to raise his voice by some remembered ideal of gallantry. Thatcher was more inclined to suspect sheer nervousness.

"Oh, come on, Eunice!" he pleaded ill-advisedly. "And Amanda, too. You're both saying more than you intend. Why don't we all just—"

Amanda sighted a new target. "You!" she said in tones of loathing. "What the hell do you think you're doing? You talk about poor Mr. Valenti. And about poor Mrs. Valenti! You know as well as I do where you have to look for your killer. But you didn't want to go with me to the police. Oh, no, not you! You were too worried about your two-bit little business."

Quinlan defended himself. "What you wanted was a little perjury in the night," he replied shortly. "I can't help it if your husband forgot to talk to you about the lot he was buying."

"He didn't forget!" Amanda declared roundly.

She was almost beaten to the gun by Eunice. "Still pushing me as a murder suspect, Amanda? And not too fussy what means you use? My God, I probably made the mistake of my life thinking the dirty work on that custody suit was Steve's idea. He was willing, but he wasn't very imaginative. I suppose he had to rely on you for that."

"You hated Steve! And you murdered him!"

Eunice smiled pityingly. "Get this through your head, once and for all, Amanda. Steve wasn't interesting enough to inspire much emotion in anyone on a long-term basis. Hell, the only reason you were still waltzing around him was because he was your meal ticket."

"I don't sell myself! Take a good look at me. I'm probably a foreign animal to the likes of you," Amanda invited.

"I'll say one thing," Eunice conceded. "You don't sell yourself cheap. You want a lot more than the going price."

"Why, you . . . how dare you . . . you can't say that to me!"

Surprisingly enough, Amanda seemed to believe what she was saying, although she had just received proof that Eunice would talk any way she pleased.

"You're playing with grown-ups, now," Eunice warned. "Either be a good girl or get ready to hear a lot of unpleasant things."

Tears began coursing down Amanda's face, but she was still young enough to make a last desperate stab at dignity.

"I don't have to stay here and be insulted. You're just flailing around, trying to make everybody forget. Well, I won't forget. And don't think you're getting away with any of this. With the car, with the estate or with murder."

Amanda had been retreating as she spoke. Her final comment was a thunderous slamming of the door.

Silence should have reigned longer than it did.

"Now, Eunice honey," Peter Vernon began, "I think you were a little hard on her. After all, somebody did murder Steve Lester."

Eunice might have been warming up for this moment.

"Oh, you think I was a little hard, do you?" she asked with savage mimicry. "Your standards shift around so fast, it's not easy for me to follow, Peter."

"Eh?" Vernon was genuinely startled at drawing fire. "What in God's name do you mean?"

"It was your idea to attach the car."

"Sure it was," he protested. "For Christ's sake, she's trying to get herself declared administratrix. You'll never see a cent if she can start unloading assets."

Eunice smiled alarmingly. "And it's perfectly gentlemanly to worry about disappearing assets. Amanda doesn't have to be protected against attachments or anything like that. But let her start calling me a streetwalker, let her start accusing me of murder, and then we all have to be very careful of Amanda's feelings."

Vernon was belatedly scenting danger. "Oh, now, I didn't say that, Eunice."

"You didn't have to! You've been acting it out for the last two weeks. Well, let me tell you, it's time you started worrying about *my* feelings. I can get pretty upset at little things like being accused of murder, being questioned by the police, and being left, always, without fail, to go through everything by myself."

"If you wanted me," Vernon blinked unhappily, "you only had to ask."

"Well, I'm asking now! Either you're on my side, or you're no damned use to me. I'm not going through the rest of my life like this. I'm not something you bought C.O.D., on approval."

Peter Vernon at this point proved that age and experience do after all leave their mark on a man. He abandoned the contest of words as one in which he was a sure loser. Instead he marched up to Eunice, held out his arms and said, "I'm here. Right beside you. In case you haven't noticed, that's the important thing."

Eunice looked up at him, seeing him for the first time. The words she neither heard nor understood, although they would come back to her later. But everything else was clear as crystal.

Suddenly she crumpled, and the sobs burst forth like a torrent.

At that point, Peter Vernon earned John Thatcher's everlasting approval. Looking over Eunice's head at the remaining company, he spoke with unabated dignity, "I think the rest of you people had better go on without us. I'm going to look after Eunice."

21 FOUR BY SIX

SUKEY DAVIDSON was first to speak after the combatants left the field.

"Well," she breathed on a long drawn-out sigh. "That's some marriage those two are planning. Do you think he knows what he's letting himself in for?"

"That woman must be plain hell on wheels," agreed Alan, still round-eyed. "I can understand her going after Amanda. But why make a dead set for that Vernon? I tell you, I'm glad she didn't get me in her sights."

Henry bristled. "Vernon has been asking for it for a long time," he said shortly, giving every evidence of being willing to pick up where Eunice had left off. "It's made me sick, watching him and his hands-off policy. Where was he when Eunice was being grilled by the police? Where was he when Eunice was at the Prudential Center? Either she's been alone or she's been with someone else. I've been with her. Hell," he said, swinging around to Eddie Quinlan, "I've seen you with her. Probably John has seen more of her than this so-called fiancé."

Eddie Quinlan had learned a lesson. He muttered that he didn't know anything about all that. John Thatcher was equally prudent. The cudgels were picked up in an unexpected quarter.

"You know," Ruth Morland said thoughtfully, "I think you're being a little unfair to Peter Vernon. I don't think it's entirely his fault."

"Ruth!" Henry had been betrayed. "You can't approve of the way he's been behaving?"

"Not approve, no," Ruth conceded slowly.

"I'd like to hear what you'd say if I behaved that way. I can tell you what the trouble is, Ruth. Just because you've fed the man in your own house, you automatically spread your wing over him."

"And whose fault is it that I've been feeding him?" Ruth asked cogently. "But I'm not simply being protective. I do think a lot of this is Eunice's fault."

Henry was thunderstruck.

"Eunice's fault? How can it be her fault?"

Undaunted by Henry's incredulity, Ruth composed her thoughts. "First of all, do you think Eunice has asked him for any support? I know if you hadn't gone with her to that dinner where Mr. Valenti was murdered, she was planning to go alone. Do you think that Peter even knew that there was a dinner, let alone that Eunice was going?"

"He knew she was being questioned by the police," Henry said doggedly. "It was in the papers."

"Yes, but did he know where or when? Or did he just read about it when it was all over?"

Henry squinted at his wife suspiciously. "I don't see what you're driving at."

"I'm willing to bet that Eunice never asks him for support because she's afraid he'll refuse. Then, when she has to go through things by herself, she blames him for not being there."

"Now, look, Ruth," Henry said in the tones of a man who was not paying out any more rope. "Regardless of what Eunice has been asking, he could guess that she needs help, couldn't he? Hell, even I could!"

Ruth was exasperated. "I'm not claiming that Peter Vernon is a perceptive man. Probably when his first wife wanted something, she said so, loud and clear. After twenty years of that, he doesn't react unless he hears the signal."

"Poor Eunice," Henry lamented. "She has a real gift for picking lemons."

"That's where the trouble is. She positively expects her second husband to act as badly as her first." Ruth had become sibylline. "She lost confidence when Steve Lester walked out on her. All she knows is that she desperately wants to marry Peter Vernon. I expect it's never occurred to her that he feels the same way."

"He hasn't given her much proof," Henry ground out resentfully.

"Well, he has his chance now. It's probably the best thing she could have done, blowing up at him that way. She's given him his loud, clear signal. If he doesn't respond, then she's better off without him. But he will. A man of his age doesn't propose to a woman of her age unless he wants the kind of home she can give him. He wasn't just swept off his feet for a solid year."

"So you think they're making it up now." Henry's ever-alert imagination was limning the scene all too vividly. "I suppose they've checked into a hotel by now. I suppose—"

But Ruth was a conservative product of her generation. "And whatever they're doing," she interrupted firmly, "is none of your business." She rose and shook herself. "I think it's time we all went and had that lunch Peter Vernon has forgotten about. We could go to Thelma's Restaurant. She has very nice home-cooked food."

At last they had reached a point where John Thatcher dared venture an opinion.

"This lunch is on me," he said. "And we are going someplace with a bar. I don't know about the rest of you, but I could use a drink."

Quite a lot of people felt the same way. The cocktail lounge and dining room of the Gridleigh Inn were crowded.

"These people are all locals now," Henry explained on entry, nodding to the right and left. "We all stay away once the ski season starts."

Eddie Quinlan looked startled and asked why.

"Everybody wants tourists to have a good time and spend a lot of money," Henry said ruminatively, "and somehow it spoils the atmosphere to have a bunch of men in business suits at the bar."

Thatcher nodded comprehendingly. He had seen the same phenomenon from Cape Cod to Aspen, Colorado. These resort communities all specialized in creating elaborate auras—everything from Tyrolean Gemütlichkeit to old salts putting to sea in whaling ships—and the permanent residents did their bit to sustain the illusion by appearing in ski boots and sou'westers, or not appearing at all. Henry probably had a wolfskin parka stowed away somewhere.

By the time the intercom summoned them to a center table in the thronged, noisy dining room, most of the gathering had successfully put the problems of Peter Vernon and Eunice Lester from their minds. True, Sukey was still wrapped in silent abstraction. But the older members of the party realized that she was formulating silent resolves about the loud clear signals she would transmit to her husband in future life.

Alan Davidson, happily, was following his own line of thought. "What I'll never understand," he said, "is why Finley got Sukey to call Amanda and Eunice and get them to go to the Prudential dinner. Why did he want to involve Sukey?"

"I don't think he cared about Sukey," Eddie Quinlan said in an unguarded moment.

"Then, what was he up to?" Alan demanded.

Quinlan shifted uneasily as the implications of his speech came home to him. He reverted to his support of Fiord Haven's architect, "Look, you know as well as I do that Finley claims he didn't call Sukey. All I'm saying is that, if he did call her, he was trying to involve Lester's wives." His lips clamped firmly shut.

But tactful hints were lost on Alan. He was genuinely puzzled. "Why would he want to do that?"

Quinlan glared at him.

Thatcher came to the rescue. "I think Mr. Quinlan means

that the police would be so occupied trying to work out the marital tangle that they would underestimate other motives. After all, Amanda Lester tends to thrust that motive forward whenever she's on the scene."

Slowly but surely, Alan was coming up the homestretch. "You mean that everybody always thinks marriage is the best motive for murder?"

It was a genuine search for enlightenment, the kind of activity that is supposed to be encouraged in the young. Nobody at the table was very encouraging and they were happy to be diverted.

"Ruth! Ruth Morland!"

An elderly woman, tidy in a suit and hat and accompanied by a large festive party, had paused by their table.

"Elvira Tilley!" Ruth beamed. "How nice to see you. When did you get back from Florida?"

"Last night. And Mr. Morland too!" Punctiliously Mrs. Tilley shook hands with Henry. "Sally has been telling me about all the excitement I've missed. Imagine, I live here for sixty-five years and nothing happens. Then I go away for ten months and you have a murder."

Ruth agreed that it was unfair.

"And I hear that they've locked up this poor architect. Trust Donald Frewen to mismanage things!"

A gleam of mischief appeared in Ruth's eyes. "You think he's locked up the wrong person, Elvira? Do you know something we don't?"

Mrs. Tilley permitted herself a ladylike snort. "When a man is murdered with two wives on the scene, I don't have to know anything else! But there's Guy Villars and Edith, too. I must run over to their table. I'm trying to say hello to everybody."

After Mrs. Tilley had left, Ruth looked across the table at Alan. "There's your answer. That's how most people feel about motives for murder."

Alan was unhappy and Henry looked none too pleased.

"But, look at Mr. Quinlan," Alan insisted. "I don't want to

embarrass him or anything, but he doesn't seem to think that Mr. Finley is automatically innocent because he wasn't married to Steve Lester."

"Some people," said Quinlan, goaded, "might be murdered by almost anyone they meet."

Alan had his own defenses against sarcasm. "You mean you think Lester was like that?" he asked earnestly.

"I don't know anything about Lester! I don't know all that much about Finley! He just came into Fiord Haven last year." Quinlan took a deep breath and looked hesitantly at Henry. "But if a wife of Lester's finally lost her head and went for him, say Amanda just for argument's sake, then I'd expect her to go temporarily insane and batter him to pieces. This was a . . . almost a restrained murder."

"Now that is really interesting," observed Henry, who had not blanched at the picture painted. "And you're right, you know. If Eunice caved in after ten years of hating Lester, it would take more than one whack to let off her steam."

Alan was proving surprisingly squeamish for a rebel accustomed to jousting with police mercenaries. Thatcher decided that it was the domestic context of the discussion that was putting the boy off.

"Sukey," her husband said accusingly, "if you could only be definite about that phone call, it would answer a lot of questions."

Sukey emerged from her private reverie. "What's that?"

"Everybody here has doubts about Finley being the murderer because they think only marriage drives people to extremes. They don't see Finley swatting Lester just because of a business disagreement."

Sukey's expressive face became reflective. "It wasn't just a business disagreement. Not the way I heard it. Mr. Finley was willing to back down and change his roof. But Mr. Lester said that wasn't enough. People had to be warned about his dangerous building practices." She leaned forward intently.

Thatcher was kind. "You mean that Lester was imperiling

Finley's career? That makes him more of a menace, but the motive would still be a business motive."

Sukey shook her head decisively. "No, I'm not talking about motive alone. After all, everybody here knew the story of the Lester triangle within two hours of the meeting between Eunice and Amanda. No matter how you felt about it, Steve Lester didn't look good. Then he pulls this holier-than-thou act. I think that could drive someone into a frenzy. I mean, having someone who you know has got plenty of faults of his own"—was it an accident that her glance rested momentarily on her husband?—"taking a high-and-mighty line about some sin of yours. I think that, for five minutes, it might almost be the same as being married to him."

Whether he had noted that glance or not, Alan was prompt to lead the conversation back to proper channels.

"But that's all guesswork. If you knew who talked to you on the phone, that would be proof."

"Well, I just don't." Sukey looked at the others for support. "You've got to understand that we spent hours here, that first weekend, listening to voices drone on and on—about recreational opportunities and lakes across the mountain and rising land values. We heard the same thing over and over again. From Mr. Valenti and Mr. Quinlan and Mr. Finley and Burt O'Neil, until it all just blended into one voice. Then that phone call came. It asked me to get the two Mrs. Lesters to come to this dinner—about fine recreational opportunities. Of course, it sounded familiar. Tiny Tim would have sounded familiar too."

And on that note the party broke up. Quinlan and the Davidsons were rushing back to yet another tour of Fiord Haven.

"Although how he can have the gall to break out another spiel after what Sukey just said, I'll never understand," Henry observed as the three of them made their way to the parking lot.

"If he didn't have that kind of gall, he wouldn't be in this business, Henry," Thatcher said acutely. "But I'd like to go back to what Mrs. Tilley said. Did she just get back from Florida, Ruth?"

"That's right. She's been there since last December."

"And already she's on to this business about Amanda and Eunice. That's fast work."

Henry could be acute, too. "You forget that Amanda's been in town all day today. She's probably been organizing a lynching party for Eunice."

Thatcher ignored frivolity. "Would Mrs. Tilley be up on all the gossip, Ruth? Who is she anyway? That was almost a royal progress she was making through the dining room."

"Elvira Tilley would know everything within two hours of hitting town. She has a private hot line to all the gossip. You see, she's a lifelong resident and very active. She was head of the women's division of the Grange, and big in the Ladies Aid. She's also one of the first beneficiaries of the land boom started by Fiord Haven."

"Ah ha!"

"I thought that would interest you, John. After the price of land went way up, Elvira sold an option on her farm. She hadn't really planned to sell yet. She was going to hang on and leave it to Sally, that's her daughter. But the offer was too good to pass up. So she treated her arthritis to a year in Florida. If Northern Land Development exercises the option, then she plans to go south for the winter every year. It really has done her a world of good. She looks fifteen years younger than she did after that last winter she spent here."

"And this Sally is her mother's daughter?"

Ruth laughed outright. "Indeed, she is. She's following right in the family footsteps. Ladies Aid and all."

"Then Mrs. Tilley is echoing what everyone is saying. That should make for a very interesting trial here. You realize that the jury will be composed of Mrs. Tilley's neighbors."

Henry was pleased to see that the case of Steve Lester's murder had not become a foregone conclusion.

"They can say all they want, John. I've heard Frewen talk about the motive Finley had. And I just heard Sukey tell me that maybe Steve Lester could drive you up the wall almost as much as a wife. But I still don't see it. So Lester was going to publicize Finley's mistakes. Who was going to listen to him?"

"More important, where was he going to find a forum?" Thatcher asked.

"That's right," Henry rejoined. "Lester might write to the architects' association, but you can't tell me that they were going to give a lot of space to their failures. Their pitch is that you hire an architect to prevent the roof collapsing."

Thatcher shouldered his responsibilities. "Well, Henry, the trial may be a bare twenty miles from Pepperton. If so, you'll be able to follow the whole thing then. Right now, the important thing is to get our stuff packed up. You've forgotten that we're going to be back on the Trail tomorrow."

22 STUMPED

HENRY HAD not forgotten. On the contrary, for the rest of the afternoon and evening, he put up a good show of enthusiasm for returning to the Appalachian Trail. After dinner, he heartily unfurled maps and AMC guides. Before dawn the next morning he was downstairs, repacking the Svea stove. When Thatcher joined him, he was counting fruit-and-nut bars with a vengeance. Stephen Lester and Ralph Valenti might never have existed.

Henry's good intentions, however, required verbal outlet.

"Morning, John. We have a glorious day for getting back to the Trail. I hope you're looking forward to it as much as I am. What was that, Ruth? Yes, yes I did make certain we have extra socks. Oh, John, do you realize that we could have been halfway through Connecticut by now, if we hadn't—oh, well. No use crying over spilled milk. But this time, no sidetracks —right? By the way, John, have you looked through your pack again? I would, if I were you . . ."

Possibly a stranger might have been deceived by this unflagging zest, but John Thatcher and Ruth Morland were not.

So, when he and Henry were once again trudging south on the Trail, silence was not the least of its charms. As Henry had reported, the morning was sunny and unclouded. But winter had moved nearer. There was a new bite in the air. And whole mountainsides blazed with color where previously single fingers of crimson had touched the valley to the west. Autumn's leaves were falling fast since they left the Trail, and they had broader views of the magnificent sweep of the White Mountains.

"Five-minute break," announced Henry from up ahead, stern with authority. Even on informal outings with friends, he believed in team-and-leader. And there was never any doubt in Henry's mind about who was the leader-born. Amused, Thatcher had never demurred. The way to handle congenital organizers, he had long since realized, was to give them their heads.

Almost immediately, Henry shed his Himalayan-team-leader incarnation. Contrary to the principles of sound mountaineering, promulgated by many authorities including himself, he unslung his rucksack and squatted on an inviting slab of granite.

"I've been thinking," he confessed.

"Yes?" said Thatcher, with an internal bet on the subject. Even the best intentions can carry a man only so far.

"James Joel Finley," said Henry. "It's all very well to arrest him, I suppose. But I've been thinking, John. And honestly, I don't believe he has the guts to murder two men. You remember the kind he is. You remember the clothes he wears. Now, does it seem likely that a man like that . . . ?"

"Mmm," said Thatcher evasively. He did not subscribe to Henry's implied theory that a double murderer must possess unusual qualifications and, hence, strengths. Furthermore, while clothes might make the man, they did not necessarily make the murderer.

Yet undeniably, Finley's arrest did not write a satisfactory finis to the Fiord Haven tragedies, even in minds other than Henry's. If, and Thatcher was carefully neutral when he used the word even to himself, if James Joel Finley had murdered Stephen Lester and Ralph Valenti, then he had done so with a simplicity that was almost breathtaking. Indeed, the script read like a primer.

Lester had threatened Finley's reputation, his pride, and his livelihood by uncovering a flaw in the design for the roof of Fiord Haven's main lodge. As a result, Finley had taken advantage of a chance encounter at the building site. He had struck Lester down.

Put that way, Thatcher reflected, it sounded almost biblical. No doubt defense counsel would argue that Finley was mentally unsound, afflicted with delusions of grandeur. Would the prosecution, he wondered, look up credit standings?

At any rate, after this act of retribution, Finley's behavior grew even simpler, if that were possible. Once he realized that Ralph Valenti might withdraw his vital alibi, Finley had used the confusion of the Fiord Haven gala at the Prudential Center to murder Valenti.

Really, despite those confused attempts to involve Eunice and Amanda, James Joel Finley's motives and methods seemed outstanding for their primitive directness.

"A man like that . . ." Thatcher skeptically repeated aloud.

Henry, to all intents and purposes, was concentrating on the valley where a string of large ponds gleamed like pearls in the morning light. Nevertheless, he pounced.

"What was that?"

"Just another anomaly," said Thatcher without elaborating. Then, to give Henry something else to brood over, he added, "We ran into the Davidsons just about a mile or two ahead, didn't we?"

"That's right," said Henry, stiffly. "I guess we'd better push on."

He was on his feet and moving.

Referring to Sukey and Alan Davidson did not distress Henry, Thatcher knew. No, his pique came from another source. He had been reminded of the contretemps that had marred preparations for this resumed trek.

The night before, Henry, a purist among Philistines, had maintained that the only proper behavior for a true Appalachian Trail buff was to start from scratch.

"But Henry," Thatcher had protested mildly, "why retrace our own steps? After all, we're not out to set any records, or even to get mentioned in footnotes. Why not simply pick up the Trail where we left it?"

Ruth had looked up from her knitting to second him.

Naturally, this was enough to spark Henry's demon of perversity. In exalted terms, he held forth on standards and excellence, on man and mountain, on nature and the integrity she demanded from those who serve her.

It made a nice change from murder, but his audience remained adamant. He and Thatcher had rejoined the trail some miles north of the tree beneath which they had first encountered the weeping Sukey. When they camped tonight, it would be several miles south of that ill-starred spot, and free from all unhappy associations.

Or so Thatcher hoped.

Yet even while he was steering Henry away from recent events, Thatcher found his own attention circling back, to the Davidsons, to Fiord Haven, to Eunice, to Amanda Lester, even to Finley. If the police thought they had a case against Finley, no doubt they did. Alec Prohack, and possibly others, might well prove it. But Finley's arrest left unsolved many problems that had come to light. Thatcher had a feeling that Finley's conviction might do so, as well.

What, for example, explained the conflicting accounts of Stephen Lester's purchase of a Fiord Haven lot?

And if it was understandable why Ralph Valenti had given Finley a false alibi, what had later induced him to do an about-face?

For that matter, was the naked hatred crackling between Eunice and Amanda entirely credible?

And Peter Vernon . . . ?

Thatcher found himself wondering if the police had been reviewing Vernon's movements over the last few days. Lester's death had removed a threat from Finley, but it had removed a greater threat from his ex-wife. And it had left Eunice with a windfall—a windfall that some men might regard as a dowry.

Thatcher, automatically following Henry, had to take himself in hand at this point. There is such a thing as going too far. The banker's bias stood him in good stead nine times out of ten. But there was always the danger of falling into Henry's error: thinking that, at any given time or place, there was only one correct way to view the situation. Fiord Haven had certainly been the cockpit for enough basic passions to explain violence and murder. Possibly his niggling questions proved, as Henry had ringingly declaimed more than once, that Wall Street diminished the human spirit.

Just then, the human body reclaimed his attention. A careless step on a loose stone almost cost him his balance. Thatcher called himself to order. Only fools strolled along the Appalachian Trail with wandering wits. Better let the dead bury their dead, and the living keep their secrets, if he hoped to return to Wall Street no more flawed than he had left it.

Henry, forging effortlessly ahead, stopped to wait.

"Here," he said, pointing out a tree identical to the thousands surrounding it, "here is where we first came across the Davidsons."

Thatcher was not going to argue. Among other things, this was Henry's way of showing that he was too generous to harbor a grudge. It also signified that he was still determined to put recent events behind them. This was particularly praiseworthy since they now stood exactly where they had when Henry plunged into the brush, first to find James Joel Finley's lodge, then Stephen Lester's body.

"I believe you're right," Thatcher replied.

With covert amusement, he watched Henry struggle against the temptation to prove incontrovertibly that there could be no doubt about it. But when Henry was magnanimous, he was magnanimous in a big way. After a visible struggle, he kept the conversation general.

"You know, it's a damned good thing you can't see Fiord Haven from here," he observed. "It hadn't occurred to me before, but that would spoil this section of the Trail."

From here, the view lay westwards, to the valley with the pond large enough to be called a lake anywhere but in New England. The slope eastwards toward Fiord Haven was gentler and heavily wooded with the growth that had been so difficult for Sukey Davidson.

Yes, Thatcher agreed, it was just as well that Henry and all other defenders of the Appalachian faith should be spared a clear view of the eruption of civilization, as exemplified by Fiord Haven, into their beloved wilderness.

"I wonder if Fiord Haven will survive, after all," he said. "They're going to get more bad publicity during Finley's trial. And yesterday I rather thought that Quinlan's optimism was fraying at the edges."

Henry put mannerisms aside. "Yesterday was hard on him. On top of Finley's arrest, there was that scene between Eunice and Amanda . . . But in the long haul, John, there is no such thing as bad publicity. Quinlan will remember that—if he's not remembering it already. There are millions of people jammed between Boston and Washington—and that's what will save Fiord Haven and the rest of these places. Everybody wants to get out to the country where there's space. Of course, none of them realizes that all they're doing is spreading the blight. They'll build their cottages, and in ten years, this will be another rural slum, a blot on the landscape. There will be drive-in movies and hot dog stands . . ."

"You're old-fashioned, Henry," Thatcher interrupted to say. "You're right in essence, but wrong in detail. Drive-in movies and hot dog stands are for renters. Up here, there will be pretentious French restaurants with huge parking lots. A summer theater. And quaint stores, selling candles and homemade jam—"

"Don't forget sandals," Henry added savagely. Then, his normal spirits returned. "God knows what these sandal makers do all winter! Oh well, let's get out of here."

As they moved on, Thatcher conceded that he had been unjust to Henry Morland. Along this portion of the Appalachian Trail, everything conspired against forgetting what had happened. Just when memory had been bullied into quiescence, when a banker's fascination with money had been beaten down, here was Fiord Haven (A NEW CONCEPT IN COUNTRY LIVING) casting a long shadow over the Appalachian Trail itself.

And despite the best intentions in the world, the quiet of the forest was not broken only by the chatter of jays, the quick scudding of chipmunks, the bubbling of rivulets soon to be frozen. There were also echoes of remembered voices.

Sukey Davidson, talking to a salesman. "Here," he had said persuasively, "let me show you the photographs . . ."

That youngster in Boston. ". . . he was the kind of guy who thought he was the only one who never made mistakes . . ."

And a man, now dead. "I wish I had been the one to find Lester's body . . . because if I had, I'd have rolled it down a mountainside, that's what I would have done."

There were more recent voices. A proper New England lady, yesterday exchanging courteous greetings with total strangers. And Henry, waxing philosophic . . .

"Good God!" Thatcher exclaimed abruptly. His attention had strayed so far afield that the branch lying across the path was his undoing. After a brief flailing, he crashed earthwards, face down. The fall was noisy enough to silence not only the forest murmurs, but those distracting voices, as well.

"John!" Turning, Henry hurried back. Bending over, he demanded, "Are you hurt?"

Clearly, he was horrified.

Thatcher righted himself and laughed aloud. Henry's emotion was half concern and half censure. Of the two, Thatcher knew which was exercising Henry more.

"No," he said, ruefully brushing off leaves as he rose. "I am not hurt. And don't worry. This is not a symptom of premature senility."

"Good, good," said Henry dubiously.

This was not the time or the place, Thatcher decided, to share his thoughts.

"You're sure you feel all right?" Henry pressed, still uncertain.

Thatcher reassured him and the day proceeded without further mishap. They reached the Wilburn Shelter in very good time.

It was over their second cup of coffee that Thatcher judged it prudent to present the case to Henry.

"I've been doing some thinking about Finley," he began.

Henry became virtuous. By superhuman effort, he had kept himself from reverting to the subject. This, he felt, rendered him superior to those incapable of similar self-denial.

Nonetheless, he listened intently as Thatcher ticked off the items that he had been weighing as they moved along the Trail that afternoon. When Thatcher finished, there was a long silence, broken only by the hiss of a dying fire. Overhead, thousands of stars shone coldly in a black sky.

Then Henry exploded.

"By God!" he roared, jumping to his feet. "You've done it! You must be right, John. You've got everything down—"

He broke off, looking around dementedly. Thatcher saw his problem plainly. Henry wanted to take action immediately and a rustic mountaintop shelter, deep in the New Hampshire woods, at ten o'clock at night, was nobody's ideal of a starting place. This did not stymie Henry long.

"No," Thatcher was forced to cut in some moments later as Henry went from forced midnight marches to more ambitious commando tactics. "I think I have a better idea."

It took time to sell Henry on anything so tame, but in the end Thatcher prevailed.

Early the next morning, they left the Trail to hike four miles to Route 84 and the Kitt's Crossing General Store. And while Henry prowled up and down, Thatcher made one telephone call. It took a full forty minutes and, oddly enough, was not to the New Hampshire State Police, to Boston, or even to Ruth. It was to the Sloan Guaranty Trust.

"All set?" asked Henry conspiratorially.

"I hope so," Thatcher replied. "Now, we'll just have to wait and see."

"And in the meantime—?"

In the meantime, John Putnam Thatcher and Henry Morland had plenty to do.

23 WOODLAND PLOT

DURING HER tenure as Thatcher's secretary, Miss Corsa had received many bizarre instructions. Fortunately, she was by nature unexcitable; experience had simply reinforced instinct. No matter what Mr. Thatcher's requests, Miss Corsa took careful notes, asked only what was necessary and, insofar as possible, did as told.

This suited Thatcher very well. On occasion, however, it maddened the rest of the Sloan. As Miss Corsa communicated with the subordinates Mr. Thatcher had named during his latest call, the subordinates were variously shaken, startled or outraged. In each and every instance, Miss Corsa's composure added fuel to the fire.

Kenneth Nicolls, for example, was nonplussed. A junior member of the trust department, he was a serious-minded young man, eager to fulfill his responsibilities. The trouble was that the nature of these responsibilities, as defined by John Thatcher, kept catching him off base.

"But what am I supposed to do?" he demanded.

"You are," Miss Corsa quoted accurately, "to keep your eyes open, express real interest and, as late as possible, purchase a lot."

Ken recognized Thatcher's words. Since they were not emanating directly from Thatcher, he protested.

"Purchase a lot?" he shouted. "How the hell . . . ?"

Miss Corsa had already moved on.

Everett Gabler was indignant. "More delays. I foresaw them. Indeed I did. Yes, of course I have made notes, Miss Corsa.

But you say that John, himself, will not be there? I suppose I should have expected that. When anybody in this bank is going to give the State Banking Commission the attention it requires, is what I would like to know."

He was still fulminating as Miss Corsa departed in search of Charlie Trinkam.

Here Miss Corsa encountered her first real resistance. Trinkam, normally the least difficult of Thatcher's staff, raised an objection. Moreover, to her extreme discomfiture, he insisted on telling her about it.

"Sure, sure," he said absently after hearing her out, "but I don't buy it. This business of registering at the motel as Mr. and Mrs. Trinkam, I mean."

This aspect of affairs had not occurred to Miss Corsa. It left her without a word to say. Miss Corsa had high principles and, not even for Mr. Thatcher, would she lend a helping hand to any occasion for sin. Worse was yet to come.

Charlie Trinkam, as he made clear, had no objection to occasions for sin. Other things troubled him. "Now, the one thing I've always been straight about is marriage, Rose. But you start playing house like this and people get the wrong ideas. And Sylvia Hazen—well, with Sylvia, you have to watch your step. No, we'd better make a change or two—"

This time Miss Corsa did not withdraw. She fled.

Very few security systems outside the government (or within it) are absolutely money-proof. Two calls by Sylvia Hazen to what she described as "buddies in Boston," plus a promise of one hundred dollars, persuaded a clerk in an office in Kenmore Square to make additions to a list of names. As a result, on Friday night, Mr. and Mrs. Kenneth Nicolls, Mr. Everett Gabler, Mr. Charles Trinkam and Miss Sylvia Hazen found themselves in the lobby of the White Mountains Motel, surrounded by predatory young men.

". . . let me show you to your room," said Gerry Wahl to

the Nicollses. "On the way, we can stop to look at the various models, in case you're interested in building. We've got some architect-designed beauties."

Jane Nicolls, who had red hair and an enchanting smile, shot a mischievous look up at her husband and said, "Is that the architect who was arrested?"

Undeflected, Wahl drowned her out. "Oh, I want you to meet Mr. and Mrs. Davidson. They know as much about Fiord Haven as I do, ha ha!"

A similar voice, aimed at Everett, had progressed further, possibly because of the total lack of response. ". . . cocktail party, courtesy of Fiord Haven, Mr. Gabler."

Everett compressed his lips. ". . . talk by Mr. Quinlan about the philosophy behind Fiord Haven after dinner tonight."

Charlie closed the door behind his tormentor and examined a brochure: YOUR FUN WEEK END PROGRAM. Scanning a virtually unbroken two-day schedule of activities, he wondered if he had not perhaps demonstrated an excess of caution. After lectures by Quinlan, slides shown by somebody named Ivor, tours of building sites, sociability hours, buffet dinners and question-and-answer sessions, would he have energy to do anything but collapse into a solitary bed?

Miss Hazen, meanwhile, was demoralizing Burt O'Neil. It was not the slim cigar. It was the terrifying knowledgeability.

". . . protection and privacy," he faltered, fascinated.

She blew a smoke ring. "Great. Now what's the fallout from the police investigations? How do your sales charts look?"

Burt floundered and Miss Hazen passed rapidly on. "And when does the bar open? I wouldn't say no to a drink."

The relationship between salesman and customer is complicated. Car buyers and housewives might be chagrined to realize how quickly and accurately good salesmen size them up. Escorting Fiord Haven's guests to their motel units gave the salesman a chance for a preliminary inspection. Then, while the Nicollses and thirty-four other people unpacked, Eddie Quinlan held a sales meeting.

". . . this guy Gabler," a salesman named Lou summarized. "Sure, maybe he's interested in a retirement home, but he's the kind who looks as if everything smells bad. He'll be tough . . ."

"Let Gus take a crack at him," Quinlan decided. "What about Trinkam?"

Trinkam's man grinned. "Could be a looker, but if there's any chance for a sale, Yvonne's the one to make it."

There was a general laugh. Yvonne was a deceptively angel-faced blonde whose specialty was melting male sales resistance.

"Fine," said Quinlan, "now Burt . . . ?"

The Nicollses were pegged as standard. Sylvia Hazen, Burt reported, was anybody's guess.

After the rest of the party had been reviewed, Quinlan looked at the staff. The strain of the last weeks had sharpened his features.

"Any feedback?"

Reluctantly one salesman spoke up. "One old lady asked if this wasn't where the murder took place. But she was interested, Eddie, not scared. That isn't what worries me. I don't like having the Davidsons up here again, Eddie. They're bound to shoot off their mouths—"

Quinlan impatiently interrupted. "Can't be helped," he said shortly. "They may buy, don't forget that. Anyway, we're clean. Finley went nuts, but Finley's in jail. That's all over, and it doesn't have anything to do with Fiord Haven. But let's not remind people. Don't mention architects, don't put a lot of emphasis on safety or protection. Stress fun and relaxation, okay? And I'll keep an eye on the Davidsons, to be sure they don't make trouble."

A gong sounded and the sales force scattered. No Fiord Haven guests were going to drink alone in the Pine Cone Lounge. Slowly, Eddie Quinlan followed.

Forty-five minutes later, Everett Gabler, clutching a tomato juice that disheartened Gus, was inspecting Fiord Haven much as he might inspect a zoo.

". . . very little upkeep. For people on fixed incomes, it's wonderful not to have to pay rent."

Gus was trying to spark Gabler's interest. He was lucky he failed, since Everett was quite capable of reading him a blighting lecture on elementary real estate economics. But Everett was absorbing the passing scene.

The piano was playing softly in the background. Circulating through the room were waiters with drinks, followed by salesmen, moving with ballet corps precision.

"Good to meet you, Mr. Gabler," said Eddie Quinlan, appearing beside him. "I understand you're from New York. Lots of New Yorkers retire to New Hampshire."

"So I understand," said Everett. Gus had faded away to lend a hand elsewhere.

"One of the advantages of Fiord Haven," Quinlan continued fluently, "is that you won't be isolated. We're going to have stores and recreation areas. Actually, Fiord Haven will be self-contained, almost a small city."

After more smooth comments, Quinlan excused himself and moved on. It was a remarkable performance, Everett had to admit. Particularly in view of what Eddie Quinlan and Fiord Haven had been through.

Another salesman materialized. "Let me tell you about our low taxes," he began.

Everett carefully placed his glass on a nearby tray and made his move.

"What is the fishing like?"

The salesman was taken aback. Gabler did not have the look of a sportsman. But, since you never can tell, he replied:

"We will have one of the finest lakes in New Hampshire . . ."

Everett, who knew nothing about fishing, was gambling that the salesman did not either.

"I'm looking forward to seeing that lake on the tour tomorrow," he said. "You can get a good idea of what the fishing is like, if you keep your eyes open."

"Uh . . . yes," said the salesman, as if this made sense.

"I hope we're going to be seeing it early in the morning,"

Everett continued, hazily recalling that anglers rise before dawn.

"They're ready for us in the dining room," the salesman pointed out.

Everett smiled to himself. Prying anything negative out of Fiord Haven was like pulling teeth. "What time will we be touring the lake?" he asked inexorably.

Involuntarily, the salesman looked around for assistance. Then, "Unfortunately, the access roads aren't in yet, so we can't show you the lake itself. We do have photographs."

"Hmph," said Everett Gabler.

Yvonne and Charlie were sharing a table with Sylvia Hazen and the hapless Burt.

"You don't mind if I call you Charlie," Yvonne suggested demurely.

"Sweetie," said Sylvia, whose voice had turned slightly brassy, "how about passing the salt?"

On all fronts mental notes were promptly made. Yvonne reminded herself to have a little talk with Burt. He had led her to expect a gym teacher, hence these seating arrangements. But no gym teacher could afford those clothes. And Miss Hazen's swagger was not asexual. Far from it. Burt swore to himself that somebody else was going to have to handle Miss Hazen. His nerves weren't up to it. Charlie was asking himself what he had done to deserve this.

"One thing for certain," Yvonne resumed with a suggestive smile, "Fiord Haven is going to be a fun place. You know, we're going to have a rathskeller, for after-ski parties."

Dully, Burt recognized a cue. "You can drop in even if you don't ski, ha ha!"

"Ha ha!" said Miss Hazen.

Fortunately, they were interrupted. Eddie Quinlan stood over them.

After introductions, Sylvia Hazen looked him up and down. "You really put on a bash, don't you?"

Quinlan took her in stride. "Glad you could come," he replied easily. "We think you're going to like what we have to show you. Don't let me disturb you. I just want you to take over for me tonight, Burt. I've got to drive down to Boston."

"Sure Eddie," Burt was automatically cheerful. "Unless you want to, Yvonne?"

"Oh no," she said prettily. "I think public speaking is for you men."

Everybody but Sylvia laughed. She, in what was not an undertone, made a one-word comment.

Charlie hastily hurled his thoughts elsewhere. Could every Fiord Haven salesman deliver every sales pitch? Fiord Haven had gone beyond the hard sell into interchangeable parts.

After dinner, it became obvious that Burt O'Neil knew his piece. His remarks about the philosophy behind Fiord Haven were fairly well received.

"Although," said Jane Nicolls to her husband when they finally escaped, "I think I detected signs of restiveness. And Ken, did you know that the young Davidson couple was here when Steve Lester—"

To her mystification, Ken gestured for silence. Since they were alone in the privacy of their motel room, this struck her as odd until he bent down to whisper in her ear, "They may have bugged the room."

Jane went off into peals of laughter.

In an artificial voice, Ken said, "What about sitting out on the lawn for a while before we turn in?"

"Turn in?" she gurgled.

He saw that brute force would be necessary.

"C'mon," he said, grasping her by the elbow.

Outside, in the chill of an autumn night, Jane shivered in her light sweater and asked if he were serious.

"Sure I am," said Ken. "Some of these places do bug the rooms, to keep tabs on customer reaction."

"I'll bet they get a lot more than customer reaction," said Jane indignantly. "That's the most disgraceful thing I've ever heard of."

"That's why I didn't want you to mention Steve Lester's murder," he explained.

"Or the fact that I really am Amanda Lester and that you are impersonating Steve. All right, I'll be careful. But you, too. I don't want you to get clobbered."

Ken promised to do his best to avoid it.

For tomorrow would see a reenactment of the crime, although that was perhaps too ambitious a way to put it. The Nicollses were simply going to retrace the activities of Steve and Amanda Lester on the earlier fun weekend, the weekend that had ended in murder. Jane pulled her sweater closer. This was no more than a run-through, to check out some minor details. There was no real danger. Nevertheless, her shivering was not due solely to the cold. Ken put an arm around her.

Twenty-four hours later, Jane Nicolls was beginning to tire. Morning had been a tour of building sites; before lunch there had been a talk about property values; lunch had featured institutional jollity; after lunch there had been a slide showing followed by another lecture. And the evening, from the hour of sociability to the bitter end, had seemed far, far longer than their first night.

"What I'd like to do," she said, "is to knock one of them down and gag him."

"Mmph," said Ken.

"Your ankle still hurt?" she asked solicitously.

For Ken Nicolls, like Steve Lester before him, had bypassed the afternoon's organized activities, to take a long walk. He had, by prearrangement, bumped into Everett Gabler. He had doubled back to the motel, chatted with Jane. Then, he had gamely set out for the long hike to the lodge.

"And the whole upshot," he said, "was that I damn near sprained my ankle. Exactly what Thatcher thinks he's doing—"

"It's just until tomorrow night," Jane soothed him. She had perfect faith in John Thatcher, but had learned not to tell her husband so. "Do you know that the Willets, that nice doctor and his wife, are buying a lot?"

"Mmph," said Ken, even more grumpily.

"And," said Jane serenely, "I looked very interested. I said I was going to try to convince you—"

At this point, a contingency unforeseen by Thatcher obtruded—the stubborn intractability of the human spirit.

"Well, let me tell you one thing," Ken said ferociously. "I am not letting one of those zombies sell me a lot, not if it costs me my job at the Sloan!"

"Ken!"

"And that's that."

"But Mr. Thatcher said—"

Ken vented his feelings colorfully and at length. The relief this afforded him was short-lived.

"I know how you feel," said a glum voice. As both the Nicollses jumped, Charlie Trinkam appeared out of the darkness. "Although I'd watch where I said it. You don't want to blow our cover, do you, Ken?"

Ken remained tongue-tied, but Jane saw that currently Charlie was not functioning as a professional superior; he was a fellow afflicted spirit.

"How are things?" she asked carefully, having discovered that Sylvia Hazen had taken to calling Yvonne Little Miss Muffet.

"Things," said Charlie comprehensively, "are hell. I feel like a piece of meat."

Yvonne had last been heard deploring how New York hardens a woman.

"On top of everything else," Charlie grumbled aloud, "I'll be damned if I'll buy one of these rotten lots."

Surrounded by disaffection, Jane kept her head. "That settles it," she said cheerfully.

"Settles what?" her husband asked morosely.

"Mr. Thatcher said that somebody should buy a Fiord Haven lot. You won't. Charlie won't. That leaves . . ."

For the first time, Ken and Charlie felt slightly cheered.

Everett Gabler was not suffering as severely as his colleagues. He deemed Fiord Haven meretricious, but Everett was accustomed to institutions that did not win his approval, from the CIA to the Penn Central. Then, too, Everett enjoyed combat. He could not be pushed. Not for him the social lie or the larger capitulation that Fiord Haven extracted from most of its dazed guests. In his own way, Everett was a holy terror.

"No," he said to an importunate salesman, "with my stomach, another cocktail party and buffet supper would be fatal. I propose to take a cup of tea—if one is available—to my room, and retire early. Thank you very much. No, I have already looked at that literature. Very interesting indeed."

As a result, at sales meetings, Fiord Haven wrote Gabler off early in the game.

"How the hell did he get on the list, Eddie?" somebody asked very late Saturday night.

Quinlan ran a tanned hand through his hair. "This was . . . God, what the hell was it, Thelma?"

"They all have charge accounts at S.S. Pierce," said his secretary proudly. The idea, and the cousin this time, had been hers.

"Yeah, sure," said Quinlan. "We'll keep plugging with Gabler but don't waste time. Now, you know the Bremers and the Willets have already signed, thanks to Burt and Gerry—"

Ragged handclapping.

". . . and I think the Davidsons are just about ready."

"Do we want the Davidsons, Eddie?" somebody asked bluntly.

Eddie Quinlan was firm. "I don't know what you mean by that, Gus, but yes, we want the Davidsons—and anybody else we can sell. Let's concentrate on our best bets. How about the Nicollses?"

"She's hot," said a salesman, "and thank God, they don't go to church."

Devout churchgoers were one of Fiord Haven's banes. Religion had a way of eating up Sunday morning.

"Okay," said Quinlan, consulting a list. "Remember, everybody, work on the Nicollses and on the Davidsons. Then those two schoolteachers . . ."

In short, Fiord Haven was mounting the final assault.

This made Everett Gabler's announcement, when he finally delivered it, all the more stunning. At first he was not able to get a word in edgewise.

Eddie Quinlan was following his own instructions. At the breakfast table the next morning, he concentrated on better bets than Gabler.

"So you see, Sukey, Alan's right. You'll save all the money you spend on ski weekends now."

"You can't deny it, Sukey," Alan chimed in. "It's not investing in property. It's just spending money we'd spend anyway."

Sukey glowered from behind her grapefruit.

Quinlan inched away from a controversial area. "And you'll be able to get in more skiing. You won't have to wait in long lines for the tow."

"Ahem," said Everett.

It was not enough.

Alan was struck with a new line of reasoning.

"Think how good it will be for our health, too, Sukey. We'll get away from air pollution. Do you realize that we're breathing poison most of the time?"

If she did, Sukey gave no sign of caring.

"Ahem," said Everett again.

Both Alan and Quinlan were intent on Sukey.

"You'll have a place of your own whenever you feel like getting away," Quinlan said. "No reservations. No traffic jams. No—"

Everett abandoned his egg.

"I," he stated loudly, "have decided to purchase a lot."

All animation was suspended. Alan Davidson, marshaling arguments, had not heard him.

Eddie Quinlan had. After one moment of genuine human surprise, the Fiord Haven manner took over.

"Wonderful!" he exclaimed, his hand going to his breast pocket. "You'll never regret it. And I have here . . ."

While Alan Davidson looked on, contract number fifty-seven was handed to Everett Gabler.

"You see, Sukey," Alan said accusingly.

Everett, a man who spent much of his life reading every word of contracts, receipts, reports and even ticket stubs, took the document Quinlan proferred. He fixed his glasses firmly. Then, without further ado, he signed his name with a flourish.

He was the only person at the table who remained unmoved.

Eddie Quinlan ran through a small speech of congratulations and welcome, but he sounded almost confused.

"I hope you're going to be happy here at Fiord Haven," he said finally.

Everett had his small conceits. One was a fancy for literal truth. "I am sure," he said, "that this transaction is going to afford me considerable satisfaction."

But tension remained. And once again, Sukey Davidson responded to it.

She burst into tears.

Three genuinely astounded men, including her husband, gaped at her.

"Look!" she hiccuped helplessly. "Why are they here? Oh Alan, I want to go home."

They stared at Sukey, then they turned to stare at the doorway.

There stood Captain Frewen.

24 HIS LAST BOUGH

"I SEE your pal, Eddie Quinlan, pleaded guilty and was sentenced last week," said Charlie Trinkam. "I suppose you were at the trial."

"Call that a trial!" Henry Morland scoffed. "It was just a formality. As far as I'm concerned, the spice went out of those murders when Quinlan confessed."

It was two months since the great descent of the Sloan Guaranty Trust on Fiord Haven. Henry and Ruth Morland were spending the Thanksgiving season in New York. At the moment they were in the bar of the Algonquin with John Thatcher and Charlie Trinkam, waiting for the fifth member of their party.

"The spice may have gone for you, Henry, but I still want to know the facts," Ruth complained. "Why did Mr. Quinlan confess, anyway? I only met him during one lunch, but he looked like a last-ditch fighter to me. And he's a lawyer, too, for heaven's sake!"

"I think being a lawyer may have been a handicap in this case," Thatcher observed. "Quinlan realized the magnitude of the evidence we uncovered when Everett Gabler offered to buy that lot at Fiord Haven."

"You mean we actually accomplished something on that trip, John? I'm glad to hear it." Charlie's position was that he had braved serious peril in the cause of duty. "When you're stuck with Sylvia Hazen as Mrs. C. F. Trinkam at office parties for the rest of your life, will it be any consolation to know you got something for it?"

John Thatcher refused to be alarmed. Over the years, many potential Mrs. Trinkams had appeared on the horizon, only to vanish like mirages at the eleventh hour. Charlie had evaded graver threats to his domestic comfort. And if worse came to worst, Thatcher was prepared to derive pleasure from the spectacle of Miss Corsa offering a senior trust officer's wife a place to hang her crash helmet.

Now he replied to Trinkam's question, rather than his accusation.

"As usual, Everett managed to milk the situation of everything it had. First, he obtained a copy of the Fiord Haven prospectus which guaranteed a lake to its customers. Let's leave that aside for a moment. Far more important, he demonstrated that there's no nonsense about delay when a prospect has finally agreed to buy a lot."

"We should have spotted that," said a disgruntled Henry. "The first night that we saw the salesmen at work, they were all pushing contracts under people's noses."

Out of simple generosity, Thatcher did not reply that he, for one, had spotted it. He avoided particulars.

"Quinlan's story about the sale to Lester was always improbable. After all, the whole goal of Fiord Haven's frenzied sales effort is to make someone like Alan Davidson lose his head for one chaotic moment. And during that moment, the contract is signed."

Charlie reasoned otherwise. "Granted, Quinlan's story sounded implausible. But, what the hell, hundreds of murder suspects have stories like that. As long as no one can prove they're lying, they get away with it."

"Which brings us to Everett's final discovery," Thatcher riposted neatly. "The contract forms at Fiord Haven are numbered."

Charlie took the point instantly. Not so Henry Morland.

"Why are they numbered?" he asked, his old curiosity coming to the fore.

"Mostly to keep the salesmen honest. Each morning they're

issued a batch of forms. Each evening they have to account for them. A lot is either sold or unsold. That way, the salesmen don't succumb to the temptation to hold a lot for a promising prospect and ensure their own commission. And, of course, it simplifies keeping the master plan of the development up to date."

Charlie was moving effortlessly ahead of the argument. He whistled gently. "Now, don't tell me. Let me guess. There's a numbered form missing from the files of Fiord Haven. And there was nothing Quinlan could do about it once anyone got the idea of looking for it."

"Exactly."

"All right," Charlie continued. "That suggests Quinlan sold a lot to Lester and then destroyed the contract. I see that. But, for God's sake, why?"

"Because, like a good many other people, Quinlan tried unsuccessfully to compromise with Stephen Lester." Thatcher turned to Henry. "You remember how magnanimous Quinlan was with the people who had bought lots at Fiord Haven during the murder weekend? He immediately offered to let them off the hook. Obviously, that was a matter of policy with him. If there was anyone who had solid grounds for dissatisfaction about a sale, it was better business to release the malcontent than encourage him to foment trouble. The same policy operated just before the murder. When Stephen Lester pointed out a fatal flaw in the Fiord Haven setup, Quinlan theatrically tore up the contract and released Lester from his obligation to buy lot seventy-three. With nine out of ten people, that would have been the end of the matter. But not with Lester."

"Never mind the character analysis, John," Charlie directed sternly. "We all know Lester was a pain in the neck. I want to know about this fatal flaw. Can anyone put it into one word?"

This was Henry's great moment. From Olympian heights, he looked kindly at Trinkam.

"I can put it into two words," he offered. "The fatal flaw was the Appalachian Trail."

"I might have known we'd get back to that, sooner or later," Charlie grumbled. "What's so terrible about being next door to the Trail? Is it contagious or something?"

Ruth hastily thrust a bowl of nuts at Henry before he could vocalize his outrage, and Thatcher retrieved control of the conversation.

"Fiord Haven wasn't next door to the Trail. It straddled the Trail. Henry and I didn't realize this until we were back on our hiking trip. The original plans for the development called for roads across the Trail, leading to the lake. And a good deal of tow equipment right on the crest."

With a weather eye on her husband, Ruth asked a neutral question. "But, John, I don't see how Eddie Quinlan and Ralph Valenti could have gone so far with their plans, without realizing the location of the Trail."

"I suppose this case could be read as an inducement to employ local professionals," Thatcher mused. "Of course, if anybody in Gridleigh had been hired, he would have seen the problem instantly. But Quinlan did all the legal work himself, down in Boston. He bought four adjoining farms with a clear title. It never occurred to him that he couldn't treat the whole acreage as one unit, exploiting the terrain any way he wanted to."

Charlie Trinkam, as befitted a member of the Sloan, reserved his fire for incompetent performance of duty.

"For God's sake!" he exploded. "Didn't Quinlan examine the files at the Registry of Deeds?"

"Of course he did. It just didn't do him any good. The farms had been in the same families for generations. Examining title was largely a matter of reading wills."

"I know the sort of thing." Charlie nodded sagely. "Robert Jones, being of sane mind and sound body, leaves his real estate to his beloved son, Robert Jones, Junior. But if there was nothing recorded, was there a legal flaw?"

"It would certainly have been an interesting case." Thatcher's voice was tinged with muted relish. "For over thirty years, that section of the Trail had been openly and publicly used as a right of way. But as a matter of hard business, Quinlan couldn't afford to contest that right of way. He and Valenti had invested every penny they had in a development that had to sell quickly —or go under. At the very best, they would have been involved in extended litigation, with public pressure from every conservation group in the country."

"They were in a tough spot," Charlie conceded. "With every bird watcher in the country going up in smoke if you relocate a chickadee, I suppose you would have people mounting machine guns to protect this Appalachian Trail."

Charlie thought he was joking. But Thatcher, watching Henry's nod of sober approval, realized that Ruth would have had her hands full keeping Henry from the front line.

Ruth, happily unaware of perils averted, had a question of her own. "John, before you rushed off to New York, you said that it was Elvira Tilley who had given you the key to Eddie Quinlan's motive. What in the world did Elvira have to do with anything?"

"That's simple enough," Thatcher explained. "Long before Stephen Lester had appeared on the scene, Quinlan and Valenti learned about the existence and location of the Appalachian Trail. They realized their predicament instantly. They had issued a prospectus promising people a lake, but they didn't dare build roads to that lake. They had already sold lots on the basis of that prospectus. But they thought they saw a way to salvage the situation. There was nothing in the prospectus that identified the lake. If they came up with a sixteen-acre lake, they would satisfy their legal obligation. They owned a pond to the west, on the other side of the Trail, but it wasn't doing them any good. There was, however, a perfectly good pond to the east on Mrs. Tilley's adjoining property. So they bought an option on it. Then they launched a homeric campaign to sell lots, and raise enough money to exercise the option."

The Appalachian Trail left Charlie Trinkam cold. But talk

of options and frenetic attempts to raise money roused his banker's instincts.

"When," he asked with narrowed eyes, "did they acquire this option?"

Thatcher beamed. When it came to fundamentals, the men of the Sloan were never far behind.

"That's the point. When I was in New York, Miss Hazen had heard about the option. She assumed that it had been a shrewd business maneuver. That is, that Quinlan and Valenti had taken an option at the outset of their venture, when local farm prices were low. But when Ruth told me about Mrs. Tilley being a beneficiary of inflated land values, I realized that the option came much later. It could only have been inspired by desperation. No professional real estate operator launches a program which will skyrocket local values—without first acquiring all the land he needs. Then I remembered the very vague talk about their lake used by the Fiord Haven salesmen. No one was taken to see the lake. Whenever they had a feature on water sports, they used photographs of a development already in operation. They were planning to substitute one lake for the other, without any of their customers being the wiser."

"So," Charlie summarized, "until Lester came along, they were hoping to pull the whole thing off. They'd sell enough lots, buy Mrs. Tilley's place, and develop the second lake. Then, when Fiord Haven was a success, they could sell the original lake, on the other side of the mountains, at a nice fat price. Were they hoping to keep all this to themselves?"

Thatcher nodded vigorously. "They certainly were. I thought it was very significant that Elvira Tilley did not recognize Eddie Quinlan. She was punctiliously greeting everybody she knew in the Gridleigh Inn, but Quinlan was a stranger to her."

"You mean she didn't know she'd sold to Fiord Haven?"

Ruth bristled in defense of her friend. "How could she? The development was always called Fiord Haven locally. She was approached by something called Northern Land Development for an option. She never realized they were the same."

Henry had local loyalties too. "Maybe John and I wouldn't have been so fast on the draw ourselves, except that we were just back from Boston. Down there, the offices were labeled Northern Land."

"I expect, Charlie," Thatcher added, "that after they took out the option, Valenti and Quinlan were careful to keep their corporate name in the background up in New Hampshire."

As they paused to order more drinks, Ruth sighed gently. "Of course, all this information about real estate companies is very interesting," she lied politely, "but it doesn't really explain anything about Amanda, does it? I still don't understand why she acted the way she did."

Thatcher was old-fashioned enough to appreciate women who were more interested in people than in business firms. Or, exposure to Sylvia Hazen was rapidly making him so.

"The way Amanda acted is a good indication of the way Stephen Lester acted," he said. "We may never know for certain, but the police theory is quite clear. Stephen Lester bought a lot in good faith after lunch on Saturday. Then, as he was setting out for a walk, he told Eunice about the purchase. He almost surely expected to tell Amanda at the first opportunity. But during his walk, he came across the Appalachian Trail and he began to have suspicions about Fiord Haven's topography. By the time he returned from his walk, he was angry. Angry enough to snap at Amanda when she tried to question him about where he had gone and what he was planning to do. He had no intention of telling her that he had been gulled into buying land by a shady operation. What he wanted was more information. So he started off on a circuit of the critical area and ended up at Alec Prohack's trailer. There, you recall, he insisted on examining plans of the whole site and expressed interest, not in the buildings that were going to be erected, but in the development of the land—roads, trails, tows. By the time he finished with Prohack, his worst fears had been realized. So he waited until everybody had left the site. Except Quinlan whom he immediately taxed with his discoveries."

"From what we've heard about Lester, I can almost feel sorry for Quinlan," Henry growled. "You remember the attitude he took with Finley?"

"He was never as dangerous a threat to Finley as he was to Quinlan," Thatcher pointed out. "With Finley, Lester would have had to go to strangers, namely the Architectural Society, to create real trouble. But when Quinlan tore up the sales contract, Lester told him that wasn't enough. It was criminal for any businessman to sabotage one of the country's great wilderness trails. And he, Lester, would stop it. He trotted out his qualifications for the job. Remember, Lester had been a member of the conservation committee of the Sierra Club. He was on a committee of the Appalachian Mountain Club. He could organize enough pressure to ensure Fiord Haven's bankruptcy. And, on top of that, he was unbearably righteous about the whole thing."

Ruth contemplatively speared an olive. "Really, Sukey was quite right, wasn't she? For one terrible moment, it would be like being married to Stephen Lester."

Thatcher smiled wryly. "Even in his jail cell, Eddie Quinlan isn't likely to phrase a confession along those lines. He doesn't pretend to any remorse about Lester's death. As he sees it, the man was threatening his existence. He saw red and picked up a hammer. What bothers him is Valenti's death."

Henry perked up. Quinlan's trial for the murder of Stephen Lester, however abbreviated, had answered the major questions. There had been no mention of Ralph Valenti's death.

"Did Valenti begin to suspect him?"

"Valenti had suspected him for a long time. Quinlan never intended to leave the police with a murder case. You remember how Valenti told us he would have tumbled Lester's body down a hillside? Well, that was Quinlan's plan from the start. Sukey Davidson was right to sense something suspicious in the change of program for Saturday night. But she got it the wrong way round. The program said that Quinlan would speak that night. He asked Valenti to take his place. We should have realized that the change was likely to have been instituted by the man who was originally supposed to speak. And the murderer at that time wasn't thinking in terms of alibis. He was thinking about setting the stage for an unfortunate accident. But that part of the scheme was blown sky-high by Henry's premature discovery of the body."

"Then Mr. Valenti knew from the beginning?" Ruth asked.

"Not immediately. Like everybody else, he was sidetracked by Lester's wives. But only for a little while. Henry was broadcasting Lester's membership in the Appalachian Mountain Club. There was the change in speakers for Saturday night. And, after all, nobody was in better position than Valenti to realize that Quinlan's version of lot seventy-three was suspicious. I think that by the time we left Ralph Valenti in the lobby of the White Mountains Motel, he was already beginning to add two and two."

"And he didn't say anything?" Ruth was indignant.

"I think he said plenty to Quinlan. But, basically, Valenti was a very bewildered and confused man. He didn't know what to do. Quinlan, on the other hand, had absolutely no doubts at all. Quite apart from being the stronger character of the two. He told Valenti that he had done it for both of them. Nothing that Valenti did now was going to bring Lester back to life. But it could destroy Fiord Haven. Valenti was no sea-green incorruptible. He probably never came to a hard and fast decision. Instead, he put off any decision from day to day. That was enough for Quinlan. As time passed, it became harder and harder for Ralph Valenti to do anything on his own initiative. Then James Joel Finley emerged as a police suspect, and that was a real bombshell."

"But, John," Charlie protested, "Quinlan must have been grateful for anything that diverted suspicion from himself."

Thatcher was slightly impatient. "Oh, no, he wasn't. He wanted to keep the spotlight firmly on Eunice and Amanda.

That's why he tried to stir up trouble about Lester's son in-
heriting part of the estate."

"I knew Eunice was being victimized. I said so all along,"
Henry trumpeted.

"Eunice was a sore spot with Quinlan. He could have kicked
himself for corroborating her story about the sale of lot seventy-
three. Of course, at the time he did so, he assumed that
Amanda knew all about it. Then Amanda emerged from her
hysterics long enough to deny the sale. And Quinlan was left
in the position of having told a tale that was immediately fishy
to Valenti, at least, and in the long run to anyone who cared
to think about it. So he set about rectifying his errors. The last
thing he wanted was attention focusing on Finley. It was too
close to Fiord Haven, for one thing. And it threatened the
delicate balance of Valenti's loyalties."

"You mean Valenti was unquestioningly loyal to anybody
connected with Fiord Haven?" Charlie asked incredulously.
"Well, you met the guy and I didn't, but it doesn't sound likely."

Thatcher was becoming tolerant of Trinkam as devil's ad-
vocate.

"No, I don't mean that. I mean that Valenti could justify
remaining inactive as long as vague suspicion rested on the
wives. But he couldn't remain inactive when it came to Finley.
He was Finley's alibi. Inevitably he would be questioned further by the police. So would other people. Alan Davidson,
after all, told us that Valenti had gotten some house plans
changed for him between the Saturday afternoon tour and the
pre-dinner cocktail party. Valenti must have spent that time
with Finley. So, Quinlan wanted him to undermine Finley's
alibi."

Ruth was pleased to have virtue reappear. "And Valenti
refused?"

"According to Quinlan, Valenti didn't say anything that
positive. But it was obvious that he would cave in under
pressure. Quinlan took advantage of the movie showing that
night to stab Valenti. Quinlan knew better than anyone else
which movie feature would provide him with the most cover.

The only precaution he took was to call Sukey—as James Joel Finley. That gave him the Lester wives on the spot."

Henry preferred subjects where he was the expert. "You know, we saw Amanda when we were in Boston. She was outraged at Quinlan's confession. She's still convinced that the whole thing is some kind of conspiracy with Eunice as arch-villain. She wants to start a crusade."

"Amanda is merely passing the time." In some fields Ruth was the expert. "Before we know it, she'll get caught up in another marriage and forget this nonsense."

"Speaking of marriages," Thatcher said, "I understand you were in Boston for Eunice's."

"It was last week. Peter Vernon isn't good enough for her, of course." Henry's objections were now *pro forma.*

"They make a very nice couple," Ruth said firmly. "But what I want to know about is the future of Fiord Haven. In Gridleigh, they say it's going on."

"I think that's one of the reasons that Eddie Quinlan confessed," Thatcher ventured. "He decided he could spend his time in jail either organizing his defense, or ensuring Fiord Haven's survival, but not both. That's one thing to be said for single-minded people. It doesn't take them long to make up their minds when they have that kind of choice. Quinlan is determined to make some kind of restitution to his family and to Valenti's. He persuaded some local people and a New York realty firm to step into the breach and exercise the Tilley option."

"Don Cavers and Guy Villars have gone into it," Henry volunteered.

Charlie, for some reason, was disapproving as he made his contribution. "Sylvia Hazen's outfit is the New York partner."

The name touched a chord.

"That Miss Hazen seems like a nice young girl to me."

Henry and Sylvia had proven to be natural affinities. It took more than a crash helmet to shake Henry.

Ruth nodded approval. A long time ago she had told

Thatcher that, if Henry insisted on championing damsels in distress, it would be safer for him to concentrate on damsels without large husbands in residence. She had probably encouraged the shift from Eunice to Sylvia.

"Miss Hazen," she now said, placid as ever, "took Henry on a tour of New York, yesterday."

"But, Henry," Thatcher involuntarily protested, "you lived here for over fifteen years."

Henry was evasive. "It's all new, now."

"On her Vespa," Ruth continued serenely. "Henry rode pillion."

Thatcher and Charlie stared. Today Henry was resplendent in his city clothes—Saville Row tailoring, blazing white shirt, scarlet waistcoat. Before they could probe further, the fifth member of the party arrived.

"Hello, all," Sylvia Hazen caroled. She was dazzling in a short leather cape that she flaunted like a torero. Her final pivot before settling almost cleared the table.

"Well, Henry," she demanded, peeling off gauntlets. "What about the Pacific Crest Trail? Have you run it up the flagpole for them?"

Nothing loath, Henry straightened to this task. "Sylvia and I were talking, and I got to thinking, John. Maybe we're getting hidebound about the Appalachian Trail. After all, there are other trails. There are the Pennines in England. But maybe the West Coast would be the best bet. And Sylvia's interested, too."

"Splendid," Thatcher managed to say.

Miss Hazen looked at him piercingly. "No freaking out!" she said crisply, apparently to forestall lecherous suggestions. "We'll play it clean."

As Thatcher was beyond speech, Charlie Trinkam unwisely picked up the ball.

"How long is this one?" he asked, attempting a diversion.

"About twenty-three hundred miles," Sylvia shot back.

"It's too much to hope that the Lewis and Clark Trail will

be ready next year," Henry said dreamily. "Now that's going to be close to five thousand."

"Christ!" Charlie said with feeling.

Miss Hazen downed her martini militantly. "What's wrong with a foursome?" she challenged. Her eye passed coldly over Charlie Trinkam's unathletic contours. "It wouldn't do you any harm, you know."

Charlie goggled.

Henry Morland beamed.

And John Putnam Thatcher found himself reviewing a list of alternative pastimes.